PRAISE FOR THE SERIES

Book Sense Pick (*The Golden Hour*)

International Reading Association
Intermediate Fiction Award (*The Golden Hour*)

Southern California Booksellers' Association
Children's Book Prize (*The Golden Hour*)

"A trip well worth taking."
—*The New York Times*

"One of the few fantasies with any African
American characters . . ." —*Booklist*

"Action-packed and laden with good-natured
humor, Williams' tale is a journey worth
taking." —*Publishers Weekly*

"A good choice for reluctant readers."
—*School Library Journal*

ALSO BY MAIYA WILLIAMS

The Golden Hour
The Hour of the Outlaw

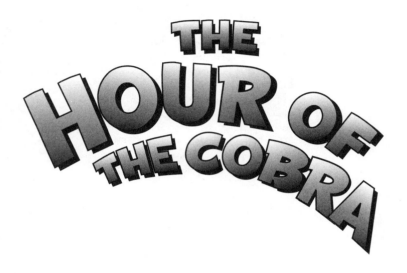

Maiya Williams

AMULET BOOKS

NEW YORK

The Library of Congress has cataloged the hardcover edition as follows:
Williams, Maiya.
Hour of the cobra / by Maiya Williams.
p. cm.
Sequel to: The golden hour.
Summary: When Rowan, Nina, Xanthe, and Xavier are reunited in a time travel mission to ancient Egypt in the time of Cleopatra, a jealous Xanthe makes decisions which put them all in jeopardy.
ISBN 10: 0-8109-5970-4 / ISBN 13: 978-0-8109-5970-5
[1. Time travel—Fiction. 2. Space and time—Fiction. 3. Adventure and adventurers—Fiction. 4. Brothers and sisters—Fiction. 5. Twins—Fiction. 6. Egypt—History—332 — 30 B.C.—Fiction. 7. Cleopatra, Queen of Egypt, d.30 B.C.—Fiction.] I. Title.
PZ7.W66687Hou 2006
[Fic]—dc22
2005015084
Paperback ISBN 13: 978-0-8109-9362-4
Paperback ISBN 10: 0-8109-9362-7

Originally published in hardcover by Amulet Books in 2006
Text copyright © 2006 Maiya Williams

Printed and bound in U.S.A.
10 9 8 7 6 5 4 3 2 1

HNA
harry n. abrams, inc.
a subsidiary of La Martinière Groupe
115 West 18th Street
New York, NY 10011
www.hnabooks.com

For my muses,
Patric, Marianne, and Teddy,
with love

CONTENTS

THE HOUR
OF THE COBRA

PROLOGUE

On any given day you could drive up the eastern seaboard to visit Owatannauk, Maine. Only the most determined tourist, however, would be able to find the dirt road that winds several miles through thick woods to a small sign that reads, "You are now entering Owatannauk, Maine. Population 104. Discover and Enjoy."

From there you would drive onto the only paved road in town, Main Street, and be rewarded with an array of charming shops: a cozy café, several boutiques, and a gallery showcasing beautiful crafts made by local artisans. The townspeople are friendly and helpful, and they all seem to know one another. You might stumble into Agatha and Gertrude's curio shop, a Victorian mansion filled with antiques and bric-a-brac. You'd probably have lunch at Hilda's Coffee Shop and Grocery, for a slice of the best homemade pie you'd ever eaten. Then, you could buy a handmade birdhouse from Annabelle Alexander, otherwise known as "Nana the Crazy Bird Lady." You might meet Mayor Silverstrini and Chief Morgan at Munson's Candies, buying sweets for their wives. If you're lucky, you might catch Miss O'Neill, the head librarian, who could give you a tour of the Owatannauk Library and tell you the history of the town, all the way from when it was still inhabited by Native Americans.

Around sunset, however, you would notice a change come over the townspeople. They would grow restless, glancing impatiently to the east. They would hurry you through your purchase and send you on your way. After you walked out the door, their shop would close. All the shops close before sunset. With nothing to do, you would leave town, feeling that you had truly been someplace special, even without having seen the Owatannauk Resort Hotel.

The rundown, abandoned Owatannauk sprawls over several acres on a hidden peninsula. Once a popular vacation spot, it has been all but forgotten, except by the locals. They know that every day at the golden hour, when day turns into night, and again at the silver hour, when night turns into day, the resort transforms back to the way it was at the turn of the twentieth century, becoming the spectacular luxury hotel whose whimsical design attracted an eclectic but impressive clientele. They know that the elevators won't take you anywhere in the building, but will transport you anywhere in history. They are, in fact, "alleviators," created to alleviate curiosity, and available to anyone who has a reservation, as part of the Owatannauk Twilight Tourist Program. They know that the Victorians who walk the halls aren't ghosts, but real people trapped in time. The locals also know the marvelous transformation lasts for only one magic hour, after which the resort returns to its dilapidated state.

The Owatannauk is a heavily guarded secret, but every once in a while new people are invited to discover its wonders. This happened to four children: Rowan and Nina Popplewell, and Xanthe and Xavier Alexander.

+ CHAPTER ONE +
CREATURE FROM THE DEEP

THUNK. THUNK. THUNK.

"Xanthe Alexander, stop banging your head on the table!"

Xanthe looked up. Her mother stood over her, arms crossed, the wooden spoon in her hand dripping spaghetti sauce onto the floor.

"Mom, you're dripping."

"Don't change the subject! You've been brooding all day. Snap out of it!" Helen Alexander flicked the spoon, spraying sauce across the back wall and the novelty sign, purchased from a roadside restaurant, that stated, "This Mess Is a Place." Xanthe stared at the red spatter, knowing it would forever be part of the kitchen decor.

She wished she could snap out of it, but she could not. Wallowing, brooding, obsessing, whatever you wanted to call it, was her way of punishing herself. And whether her mother understood it or not, Xanthe needed to be punished.

She did get up, however. Her mother needed all her powers of concentration to follow a recipe. Distracting her would result in a dinner undercooked and overly seasoned, so Xanthe dragged herself from the kitchen table into the living room and slumped on the sofa.

A number of things had put her in this dark state. First of all, Xavier was gone. She'd sensed the difference as soon as they dropped him off at the airport. Without her twin brother around she felt unbalanced and slightly confused. It was an awful feeling.

Most of their lives, Xanthe and Xavier had been inseparable. As twins they'd shared everything: clothes, bedrooms, toys, friends, teachers, even underwear if one of them ran out before laundry day, though neither one would admit it. They were so tuned in to each other, there were times it seemed as though they could read each other's thoughts. But even best friends need space. By the time they were ten, Xanthe had just about had it. Getting her own room helped, but not much. Four years later, she was still constantly tripping over her brother.

Until now. She didn't want to miss him, but she did. She'd hoped his absence would make her feel liberated, like a dark curse had been lifted. Unfortunately, she had come to rely on him for too many things: for companionship, for providing a quick answer to a problem, for getting a job done. She hated to admit it, but he was her right arm, and now her right arm was gone. She'd heard that foxes will chew off their own legs to escape from a trap; that was how she felt now. It was painful, but she was willing to sacrifice the right arm so that she could be free.

But she wasn't free. Xavier had left behind a reminder of the event that had set her to banging her head on the kitchen table to begin with. There, barely hidden by the towel she'd thrown over it, was a trophy. The grand prize for the Cicero Oration Contest.

That was the second thing that had put her in this funk. By all rights that trophy should've been hers. The contest pitted teenagers from all over Boston and its suburbs against each other, as they delivered speeches on a predetermined topic of a political nature. The point was to promote the art of public speaking, and if there was anything Xanthe was good at, it was speaking. Especially arguing. She could twist and turn a concept with skillful dexterity, like mental origami, and on more than one occasion she'd been praised as being "articulate, persuasive, and to the point." So how Xavier, who never showed any interest in politics or public speaking, could win, she had no idea, except that he could tell a joke or two, which always seemed to get him more credit than he really deserved.

The trophy was only part of the prize. There was also a check for seven hundred and fifty dollars, and a trip to Washington, D.C. That's where Xavier was right now. He had an itinerary jam-packed with sightseeing, behind-the-scenes tours, and introductions to dignitaries. Yes, she was jealous, but jealousy she could handle. There was something much more troubling at stake, and this third thing is what made her feel worst of all.

Xavier had won first prize. Okay, that was probably a fluke. But what about her? She hadn't come in second, she'd come in sixth. *Sixth.* That's what her bright-orange ribbon said. And by the way, *orange?* Who ever heard of an orange ribbon? A blue ribbon, a red ribbon—those were respectable colors. But bright, garish orange only signified one thing: that she wasn't nearly as smart as she had been led to believe.

But Xavier...Xavier *was.* All this time she'd been fooling herself. She was not the one with a chewed-off arm. She *was* the chewed off arm. *She* was being left behind. For all those reasons—for dropping the ball, for losing her sense of place in the cosmos, and for being utterly clueless about who she really was—she deserved to be smacked in the head, over and over again.

She started pounding her head against the sofa cushion, but it wasn't nearly as satisfying as the table.

"Xanthe." Helen touched her daughter's shoulder, startling her. Her mom's irritation had softened. Her large brown eyes, set in her light-brown, freckled face, looked deeply concerned. "I know how you feel. You're ambitious, and you've disappointed yourself. But you're not going to win all the time, sweetie, that's just life. Don't beat yourself up for being human, all right?"

Xanthe fumed. She didn't want the consolation speech. Consolation speeches were, by definition, for losers.

"Why don't you call Kendall? Or Emma?" Kendall and Emma were Xanthe's best friends, but she suspected both had been jealous of her at one time or another and probably wouldn't mind seeing her knocked down a peg.

"I don't think so."

"Then how about doing some schoolwork? It might take your mind off ... everything."

That sounded like a good idea. Because Xanthe and Xavier were home schooled, they had a lot of freedom in what they learned and how fast they learned it. They could take weeks off if they wanted to, but they usually did much more work than was asked of them. Algebra problems sounded like just the thing to distract her from her fall from grace.

Suddenly she smelled smoke.

"Mom! The meatballs are burning!"

Helen rushed back into the kitchen.

Xanthe went to sit on the deck with her math book and a yellow legal pad. She quickly solved five equations, then put her pencil down. Her gaze drifted to the pond in their back-yard. Home schooling had allowed the Alexanders to live wherever they wanted, regardless of proximity to good schools, and so Andrew and Helen had bought a small house on a large private pond in a Boston suburb. Two days a week, Andrew drove into the city to lecture at Boston University, then spent the rest of his time at home, in the seclusion of his study, writing about American History: the early American settlers, western expansion, and the Civil War.

Xanthe loved the pond. It was called Tyler's Pond, but she and Xavier called it the Loch Ness Lagoon because of the odd splashes and ripples that sometimes disturbed the water's surface. Helen, who had a degree in marine biology, assured them that it was probably a largemouth bass, a walleye pike, or perhaps even a snapping turtle. But it was more fun to think it was their own personal Loch Ness monster.

Xanthe saw one of these odd ripples in the water even now, caused by something as big as a seal, flapping and splashing. She jumped to her feet. This wasn't a fish or a turtle! It was a boy, struggling to get to shore!

She kicked off her shoes and dove into the water. As she swam, she searched for an overturned boat or sailboard . . . there was nothing. She grabbed the boy's sweater, flipped him onto his back to keep his face above water, and towed him in, dragging him onto the rocky beach. There she fell next to him, breathing heavily. The boy coughed up some water, then turned to her, smiling sheepishly. Xanthe gasped.

"Rowan!" she cried. "It's you!"

He slicked his hair back off his face. "Surprised?"

"Where were you . . . how did you . . . I can't believe you're here!"

It was like her secret wish had been granted. Rowan was her special friend. She and Xavier had first met him and his younger sister, Nina, last summer on the beach in Owatannauk, Maine, the small coastal town where her grandmother and Rowan's two great aunts, Gertrude Pembroke and Agatha Drake, lived. Her first impression of him was that he was cute but dumpy, like a sloppy puppy. Since then she'd come to see him quite differently.

They had all shared a most unusual adventure, exploring the mysterious abandoned Owatannauk Resort built by the equally mysterious Archibald Weber. The elevators in the building had turned out to be complicated time machines, and the children used them to take a dangerous trip to eighteenth-century France. There, Rowan's courage, perseverance, and leadership had saved them from literally losing their heads in the French Revolution. And so, despite his ordinary appearance, Xanthe knew Rowan to be a hero. Just being around him made her want to be a better person.

After they'd gone back to their regular lives—hers in Massachusetts and Rowan's in New York—they had written e-mails back and forth, but a month ago Rowan had stopped, without warning. Xanthe remembered now that she was angry with him, so she shoved him with her foot.

"Ouch!"

"That's for abandoning me. What happened? I thought you'd fallen off the planet."

"Sorry, computer problems. I thought of sending a letter by snail mail, but every time I started one, I got distracted."

Xanthe didn't bother asking why he hadn't used a phone. Rowan's mother had died recently and his father, in his grief, had neglected to pay the phone bill. Now Mr. Popplewell was having trouble getting any phone service to let him sign up. The family mainly used the phone in their bakery, but the line needed to be kept open for customers.

"Well, fix your computer. I miss having a pen pal."

"I can't. I mean, the computer isn't broken, I just keep getting shocked by it."

Rowan's face had turned a deep pink color. *What does he have to be embarrassed about?* Xanthe wondered. Then it dawned on her.

"You've been using the alleviators! You've gone back to the Owatannauk!" Xanthe remembered that when they'd first used the time machines they'd been given a list of rules and regulations which warned that one possible side effect of use of the alleviators is sensitivity to electricity and any electrical appliances.

"Where have you gone? I'm so jealous!"

"Hold on. I haven't been anywhere back in time. I'm just ... well, Aunt Agatha's got me in training. Nina, too." Rowan was grinning like the Cheshire Cat in *Alice's Adventures in Wonderland*.

"Come on, Rowan, tell me! Training for what?"

"To be her assistants! And she wants you and Xavier to join us! That's why I'm here!" Rowan squeezed some of Tyler's Pond out of his sweater. "Do you have anything dry I can borrow? I'm freezing."

"Sure. I'll be right back. But then you have to tell me everything—from the beginning." Xanthe dashed into the house and quickly changed into a pair of jeans and a sweatshirt. She grabbed one of Xavier's old sweat suits and raced back out.

"So let me guess." She was panting. "You took the alleviator here. Like a transporter."

"Bingo. The alleviators send you back in time to the same day of the year in which you're traveling, right? If you leave on January first, you'll arrive on January first of whatever year you've chosen. So, if you press the button for this year, you can be transported anywhere in the world, as long as it's the golden hour—or the silver hour, of course."

Of course. It was the golden hour right now. She'd been so caught up in her misery she hadn't noticed the entire pond, the surrounding firs, even the broken-down shed with its rusty hinges and peeling paint, were bathed in the golden glow of the late afternoon sun. Xanthe turned her back on Rowan as he slipped into the sweat suit. She noticed he wasn't quite as pudgy as he used to be. She also realized he'd gotten taller in the last few months.

"Why did you decide to land in the middle of Tyler's Pond?"

Rowan's face turned pink again. "Actually, I was trying to land on the deck and surprise you. Setting coordinates is harder than it looks."

They walked to the side of the house, out of view of the kitchen window and Xanthe's mother. Rowan filled Xanthe in on all that had happened since he'd stopped writing. At the end of August, his father had moved his business and his family from Brooklyn to Manhattan so that his sister could be closer to her piano teacher. Nina, an eleven-year-old music prodigy, had been deeply affected by her mother's death and had given up playing piano for a full year, but after their summer adventure she'd been eager to start up again.

"Since her music schedule was going to conflict with school, Dad enrolled us in this cool progressive school," Rowan continued. "Nina and I got full scholarships."

"'Progressive'? What does that mean?" Xanthe interrupted.

"It means, well, not traditional. There aren't any real grades.

You just work at your own level. And they don't hand out report cards, either. They use some other sort of evaluation system. But the best thing is that they don't mind if you take a week off here and there, as long as you write an essay about what you've done and make up the work you've missed. Which means..."

"You've got time for time travel."

Rowan beamed. "It all kind of works out perfectly, doesn't it?"

"Okay, but how did you end up back at the Owatannauk?"

"I'm getting to that. Aunt Agatha called Dad and asked if Nina and I could come up for Labor Day weekend to help out with the curio shop. At first I thought she finally wanted to sort through all that junk—you know what I'm talking about..."

"That would only take you a thousand years."

"Yes. Fortunately that's not what she wanted. She doesn't want us to help her organize it, she wants us to help her *collect* it." He paused, letting it sink in. "Xanthe, we're going to be frequent fliers!"

"Frequent fliers?" A slow smile spread across Xanthe's face. "Are you saying what I think you're saying?"

"Yeah! We're going to be hopping all over time! All over the world!"

"Oh, Rowan, this is fantastic! What does your dad say? Does he even know?"

"Are you kidding?" Rowan said, suddenly serious. "I haven't told anyone. First of all, I doubt anyone would believe me, and second, those alleviators are the best inventions since

...well, *ever*. If it got out, you know somebody would try to make money off of it and ruin it. Do *your* parents know?"

Xanthe shook her head. She and Xavier were the only ones in her family who knew about the time machines, except, of course, their grandmother, who lived in Owatannauk and used them herself.

Rowan peered over the treetops at the sinking sun. The golden hour was almost over; the sky was already showing the rosy orange hue of sunset. "I need to get back to the alleviator, and it's out *there*," he said, pointing to the middle of the pond. "Do you have a canoe or a rowboat or something?"

Xanthe led him to a shed, behind which lay a small purple sailboat. "My boat," she said proudly. "I bought it myself. It's called *Whisper*."

Rowan helped her drag it to the edge of the pond. After they both climbed in, Xanthe raised the sail. It immediately caught a breeze, carrying the boat toward the center of the pond.

Rowan trailed his hand in the water as Xanthe steered. Every once in a while, he would tell her to aim more to the right or left ("starboard" and "port," she informed him, were the correct nautical terms). She couldn't see the alleviator herself because she wasn't holding one of the golden alleviator keys, but Rowan could. When he held up his key, it shimmered brightly, indicating the strength of its magical power. The power lasted for seven days, the permitted length of an alleviator trip, after which the key disintegrated.

She didn't want him to leave.

"So, how am I going to explain all of this to my parents?"

"Don't worry about that. It's all taken care of." Rowan looked over the side of the boat. "Okay, stop," he said. "It's right below us. I'll give you back these clothes when I see you again." He dove into the water, disappearing into the blue-green ripples. Then he popped up again.

"Wow! This water is freezing!"

"Next time get your coordinates straight."

"Yeah, right." He treaded water in a circle. "I forgot to say 'bye.' So, bye."

"Wait, Rowan!" Xanthe called out before he could duck underwater. "Something doesn't make sense. The last time we used the alleviators we really screwed up. Why on earth does your aunt Agatha trust us to go anywhere else?"

"I don't know. I'm too cold to worry about it." Rowan swam to the boat and grabbed onto the side. "You're in, aren't you?" His teeth were starting to chatter. "I don't want to do it unless . . . I mean, it won't be as fun without . . ."

Xanthe laughed. "Of course, you idiot! Yes! You don't know how much I need this right now, Rowan. It's like you read my mind and showed up just in time to cheer me up."

Rowan smiled. "Yes," he chattered. "I think I did." He took a deep breath and dove under the water. A light flickered in the murky depths of the pond and she knew he was gone.

Xanthe had just dragged the boat behind the shed when Helen came out on the porch.

"You'll never guess who just called." Helen didn't give her

a chance to answer. "Nana is inviting you up to Owatannauk
for a week. She said a friend of hers is looking for some
helpers. And she mentioned that boy—Rowan Pumplewall—
he's going to be there with his sister. I think you should go."
Xanthe started to say something but Helen held up her hand.

"Xanthe, I know it's not as exciting as Washington, D.C.,
but at least it's something."

"Well, I guess..."

"You can't keep moping. It's not healthy."

"If that's what..."

"I don't want to argue about it. We're driving up tomorrow morning, and that's that. Now come in and set the table
for dinner. Your dad will be here soon. We're having scrambled eggs."

"What happened to the spaghetti and meatballs?"

"Don't ask."

Xanthe followed her mother inside and set the table, then
set about cleaning the bits of exploded meatball off the walls
and out of the light fixture on the ceiling. It was hard work
but she barely noticed, because inside she was singing.

+ CHAPTER TWO +
A MISSION IN TIME

OCTOBER IN MAINE SAW TREES IN FULL COLOR—GOLD, ORANGE, rust, and purple splashed like paintball hits against the dark evergreens. As Helen drove Xanthe up the driveway to Nana's house, the maples rustled with goldfinches, and flocks of chickadees filled the sky. Nana loved and nurtured her feathered friends. Homemade birdhouses and berry bushes attracted them to her garden. Their collective screeches, squawks, whistles, and twitters were deafening.

"I wish Nana had picked a quieter hobby!" Helen shouted. Xanthe only smiled. She wouldn't change anything about her Nana.

A firm hug awaited each of them. Nana seemed to have gotten younger since Xanthe had last seen her; her smooth, dark-brown face was wrinkle-free. Only her shockingly white hair betrayed her advanced years. She wore an orange-and-maroon head-wrap from her native Jamaica, and a matching skirt. Xanthe detected the familiar whiff of spice, which clung to Nana's clothes. It was a sharp, peppery smell that woke you up like a slap in the face.

"My goodness, how you're growin', gal!" Nana said, clucking her tongue. "You're taller than your old Nana now. Helen, what've you been feeding this child?"

Helen laughed uncomfortably. Xanthe knew that even after sixteen years of marriage, Helen still felt nervous around her mother-in-law, and for good reason. Nana was as changeable as the wind; sometimes laid back, other times as direct as a dagger. On one occasion Nana had claimed kinship to a famous voodoo priestess, making Helen leery of the unlabeled bottles in Nana's pantry. Xanthe's father had had a good long laugh about that, but the suspicion stayed.

"Oh, Xanthe eats what every teenager eats ... But of course she's got a healthy diet ... I see to that," Helen added hastily.

"Relax, Helen." Nana sucked her teeth. "Put your feet up. How 'bout some coffee, eh?"

"No, I really can't ..."

"You sure? I can drop something in it that'll get rid of that twitch in your eye."

"Oh, no, that won't be necessary. I need to ..."

"Let me tell you about the Canada geese I saw flying over the house yesterday."

"I really can't stay," Helen said, backing toward the door. "I've got all sorts of ... things ... that need my attention." She gave Xanthe a quick kiss on her forehead. "Have fun! Don't do anything you shouldn't do."

Xanthe nodded, not quite sure if whizzing through time and space was covered in that advice. In a matter of seconds, Helen was out the door and down the walkway. She waved as she peeled out of the gravel driveway, scattering rocks in a wide arc.

"Well, now!" Nana cried. "I thought she'd never leave. I want to hear everything you've been up to, but let's talk in the car. I promised the Sisters I'd bring you right over."

Nana drove a lime-green Chevy Bel Air, a model which had been manufactured in the 1950s, but hers looked brand-new. Xanthe had gotten used to the variety of cars, appliances, and clothing that one saw in the town of Owatannauk, spanning all eras and cultures. As far as she could tell, almost all of the townspeople used the time machines, and apparently took great pleasure in showing off their souvenirs.

Rowan's aunts' house was located behind the curio shop. It was, in fact, a renovated garage which now supported two extra stories as well as several chimneys and an outdoor staircase that looped around to the roof. As Xanthe and Nana got out of the car, a girl exploded out of the door of the house, her mass of curly black hair rolling behind her like a storm cloud.

"Yay! It's Xanthe!"

It took Xanthe a moment to recognize her. It was Nina, but she had changed. Her green eyes, once dulled by depression, sparkled impishly. Hugging her was like holding a humming-bird.

"Xanthe! Isn't this great?" Nina squealed. "What have you been doing? I only know what Rowan told me from your e-mails. Of course he didn't tell me the personal part. There was a personal part, right? 'Cause I know you guys like each other..." Rowan, who had come out of the house in time to hear this last comment, gave Nina a hard shove.

"She doesn't know what she's talking about...I mean..." He sighed. "She talks too much." He nodded to Xanthe's grandmother. "Hello, Mrs. Alexander...I mean, Nana."

"Howdy-do, Rowan, Nina." Nana started toward the house. "Don't mind me, I'm gonna rest my dogs," she said, indicating her feet. "You young folks go on and catch up with each other."

"Those are cute overalls," Nina said, circling Xanthe. "I wish I had long legs so I could wear overalls. I'm too short—they make me look like I'm in preschool. It's too bad Xave couldn't come. That's great he won that award though. Come on, Aunt Gertrude made chocolate hazelnut cookies!" Nina whirled around and flew back into the house.

"I'm getting exhausted just listening to her," Xanthe said.

"I know." Rowan grinned. "She's making up for the year she lost. You know, we should get in there before she eats all those cookies. She may look small, but she eats like a horse."

Xanthe entered the cozy dwelling and breathed in an odd mixture of smells: dark chocolate and nuts, furniture polish, plastic, vinyl, sandalwood incense, and dusty books. She was startled to see an enormous beach ball with legs bouncing toward her. It turned out to be Rowan and Nina's aunt Agatha, wearing one of her typically bright ensembles—this one orange with white stripes. Agatha's appearance was always something of a puzzlement. Though insightful and wise, she couldn't manage to button her blouse correctly or keep her hair from looking like a raccoon arranged it. And Xanthe was sure she bought her clothes at a circus outlet.

"Actually, I bought this in France," Agatha said, twirling like a pinwheel. "Though I must admit, it didn't look so beach-ballish on the mannequin."

"Oh, but I didn't mean . . . " Xanthe began, her ears turning hot. She'd forgotten about Agatha's ESP.

"But look at you!" Agatha turned Xanthe in a circle, appraising her. "You've grown, and it's only been a couple of months!"

"That's what I've been saying," Nana said, sitting in the living room and sucking on a long thin pipe. "She's gonna have to swat the boys away like flies."

"Give the poor girl some space, Sister," Gertrude boomed from the doorway to the kitchen. Rowan's other aunt, Gertrude, was a magnificent seven feet tall with her shoes off, and as humorless as the Statue of Liberty.

"I'm sorry, Sister." Agatha sighed. "I do have trouble keeping my hands to myself."

Agatha and Gertrude called each other "Sister" not because they were related but because they were Catholic nuns. That was their claim, anyway. If it was true, they were certainly the most intrepid and adventurous nuns Xanthe had ever met. They weren't really Rowan and Nina's aunts, either. They had been godparents to the children's dead mother, and the family called them "aunts" out of affection.

"It's a pleasure to see you again, Xanthe," Gertrude said. "Agatha will fill you in on why you're here. I'm afraid I've got to go. Somebody's lost himself in the Spanish-American War. I need to do some research before the next golden hour."

Xanthe twisted her overall strap and murmured, "That's okay." It was hard to feel comfortable around Gertrude. Something dark lay behind her fierce gaze. When Gertrude spoke to her, Xanthe always found herself looking away.

Gertrude turned to Agatha. "Don't wait up for me, Sister." She slipped on a dark gray poncho and strode out of the front door, her long straight braid bisecting her back, slick and motionless, like lacquered wood.

Nina came into the living room from the kitchen, her cheeks puffed out like a chipmunk's. Rowan's eyes widened. "How many cookies did you eat?!"

Nina's answer was lost in a muffled response that sent a spray of chocolate hazelnut crumbs from her lips. Xanthe and Rowan rushed past her, with Agatha and Nana not far behind.

After enjoying the cookies with fresh milk, they all followed Agatha into the living room where they took seats in front of an easel.

"Now, Xanthe, you may wonder what exactly you're doing here," Agatha said. "I don't know how much Rowan told you . . ."

"Not much," Xanthe said, breathlessly.

"Then I'll start from the beginning. As you know, Gertrude and I stock our curio shop with items we pick up during our travels through time. We have some walk-in customers, but over the years we have also collected a strong stable of clients—collectors of antiques and artifacts. Of course they don't know how we do it, but they're so appreciative they don't ask a lot of questions. They probably think we're a couple of high-class crooks. Anyway, as requests from these clients have increased, we've found it difficult to fill orders all by ourselves. So we decided to recruit some assistants. Rowan and Nina have already agreed, and I hope that you and Xavier will, too."

"Of course!" Xanthe spluttered. "I'd love to! But are you sure we can do it?" She bit her tongue. The last thing she wanted was to raise any doubts, but she also knew that they had barely gotten through the French Revolution with their heads intact.

"On the contrary. I thought you performed exceptionally well," Agatha said. Xanthe winced. Again Agatha had read her thoughts. "What I saw during your last trip was resourcefulness, clear thinking, and courage. And your youthfulness is a bonus, I think. You, Xavier, and Rowan are old enough to be considered adults in most historical situations, but too young to attract much attention. Gertrude and I have been mulling this over for a while. We think it's an ideal solution to our problem."

"I've helped Agatha a few times, and it's not as glamorous as it sounds," Nana warned. "Just a lot of poking around and cooling your heels. If anything, it'll teach you patience."

"Rowan said you had him in training," Xanthe said, ignoring Nana.

"Yes, if you plan on using the alleviators on a regular basis it's a good idea to be prepared for anything," Agatha answered. "You need to be physically fit. You need to expand your general knowledge about everything, from food, to manners, to games and other leisure activities..."

"I can ride a horse now," Nina said proudly. "English and Western!"

"I can waltz," Rowan added sheepishly.

"There are things you and Xavier will also need to learn," Agatha continued, "but I think you have the skills you'll need for this first trip. Speaking of which, it's getting late, so we should begin." She took a stack of large manila envelopes from the side table and handed them out. Her manner had become all business. Xanthe felt like a spy at a briefing.

"These envelopes contain information which I compiled with Miss O'Neill, the librarian. You can peruse them at your leisure, but we'll go over them quickly now, in case you have any questions. Please open them, remove the contents, and turn to the first page, marked 'A.'"

The three followed Agatha's instructions. Xanthe slid a binder from the envelope. "Alexandria, Egypt, 58 B.C.," was stenciled in gold on the burgundy cover, as well as her name, "Xanthe Alexander." She turned to the first page and saw a map. Meanwhile, Agatha placed a thick stack of poster-sized cards on the easel. The first card showed an enlarged version of the same map they had in their binders.

"Alexandria, Egypt, fifty-eight B.C., is our destination," Agatha began, pointing to the map with a knitting needle.

"This is North Africa, this is the Mediterranean Sea. This thick line here is the Nile River, the longest river in the world. You see how it spreads out as it reaches the sea into this delta. Here is Alexandria, to the west of the delta. Turn the page, to the photograph marked 'B.'" Agatha removed the first card, revealing the one behind it—a picture of a man on horseback.

"This is Alexander the Great, the founder of Alexandria. He envisioned that the city would become the most cosmopolitan in the world—" Nina raised her hand eagerly.

"Yes, Nina?"

"Are we going to meet Alexander the Great?"

"I'm afraid not. He'll be quite dead by the time we get there. Next page . . . " Agatha went to the next card—this one had a picture of a middle-aged man with a large nose. "This is Ptolemy. See how his name is spelled? But that is a silent 'P.' It was Ptolemy, Alexander's childhood friend and one of his finest generals, who inherited Egypt after Alexander died. He also foresaw Alexandria's importance as a city, turned it into the capital of Egypt, and set about filling it with monuments and buildings worthy of Alexander's vision . . . Yes, Nina?" Nina put her hand back down.

"Are we going to meet Ptolemy?"

"No, dear. He'll be dead also." Agatha turned back to the easel. "Now Ptolemy established a dynasty in Egypt which remained in power until the Romans took over from the Greeks. He built a palace, of course, but he was also responsible for constructing four very important structures." She removed the card. The next picture was of a white stone building.

"First, the Soma—a tomb for Alexander the Great. Ptolemy stole Alexander's corpse while it was being transported to Macedonia and placed it in a golden coffin in the Soma, to bring luck to the city."

The next picture was of a tall, three-tiered structure by the water. "He also built the Pharos, the first lighthouse, on an island directly in front of Alexandria. Four-hundred-and-fifty-feet high, it was one of the tallest buildings in the world at that time. Sailors could see its light from fifty miles away. It was considered one of the Seven Wonders of the Ancient World. The next two buildings, which are of the greatest interest to us, are the library and the museum."

"They had an art museum?" Rowan asked.

"No, 'museum' refers to the Muses, the ancient Greek Gods of the arts and literature. It was built as a research facility, to promote the study of the arts. Here it is..." She put up the next card. "Ptolemy invited scholars from all over the world to live, study, lecture, and conduct experiments there. His son, Ptolemy the Second, continued this tradition, and it was carried on down through the Ptolemaic Dynasty. That is how Alexandria became and remained the center of intellectual thought for centuries."

"So it's kind of like an ancient think tank," Xanthe said.

"Yes, exactly. An ancient think tank. Thank you, Xanthe. Now, right next to the museum is the library. Here's a better picture..."

The close-up picture took Xanthe's breath away. This was nothing like the dusty, crumbling structures she usually associated with Egypt. This was bright and lush with colors: blue, red, gold, and green. A forest of stone columns graced the courtyard, flaring slightly at the top like palm trees. They were decorated from top to bottom with hieroglyphs, a type of Egyptian writing using pictures and symbols to represent words or ideas. It occurred to Xanthe that it was a peculiar decoration for what was essentially a Greek building.

"The great library of Alexandria contained the largest collection of manuscripts in the world," Agatha continued. "This included treatises on philosophy, mathematics, astronomy, medicine, and literature, and original works by Euclid, Archimedes, Sophocles, Euripides, Aristarchus...Oh, my, I get faint just thinking about it."

Agatha sat and fanned herself with a book. Nana gave her a drink of water as Nina raised her hand again.

"I don't know who any of those people are, but are we going to—"

"No, sweetheart. They'll all be dead by the time we get there." Nina frowned and flipped through the pages of her binder.

Agatha resumed her presentation. "This is the library as it looked in fifty-eight B.C. Later, in about forty-eight B.C., Julius Caesar, in a battle against the then King Ptolemy the Thirteenth, accidentally set some of the warehouses that contained new books on fire. These warehouses." The next card showed several warehouses along the docks. "There were some very valuable manuscripts that disappeared in the flames. Our mission is to retrieve some of them *before* the fire." She turned to Nina. "And no, we won't be meeting Julius Caesar, either."

"I wasn't going to ask anything," Nina protested, lowering her half-raised hand.

"This is the plan," Agatha continued. "I will be posing as a honey merchant from Greece, with Nina as my assistant. Once we arrive, I'll get Rowan a job in the library so we'll have access to the warehouses. I've got some influence with the head librarian, you see. Xanthe, that's where you come in. You're going to be a bit of a free agent."

Xanthe straightened up. "So what do I have to do?"

"I'll tell Rowan which documents we need from the warehouse. He'll bring them to me, and I'll make counterfeit copies. Then Rowan will return the counterfeits to the warehouse and give the originals to you. You'll deliver them to the Owatannauk, where Gertrude will be waiting to take them from you."

"Okay!" Xanthe said eagerly.

"Now listen. This mission does have an element of danger to it, but if we all keep a low profile, we should accomplish it fairly easily... Why, Nina, whatever is the matter?"

Xanthe could see Nina's lip thrust out in a full pout.

"All I get to do is hang around you selling honey," she muttered. "How come I don't get to do anything exciting? I'm not a baby you know!"

"I'm sorry, Nina. You're right. I didn't give you anything particularly challenging to do. It's a precaution on my part. I want to make sure that we're allowed to go. You see, the Board sees you as a bit of a loose cannon because of your behavior during the last trip."

"You mean, you're not sure we're going?"

"No, I'm not certain at all. I guess I should've explained this. As you all know, one can only use the alleviators with a reservation. But to get a reservation, you must present a petition to the Owatannauk Board of Directors. They decide each case on its own merits. They also must approve all frequent-flier applications."

"I didn't know we were going to be judged," Rowan muttered.

"Everybody goes through it, my dear. We have to weed out the bad apples. There are many people who, if given the chance, might try to manipulate history for their own ends."

"I thought that changing history puts you in an alternate universe," Xanthe said, "and it doesn't have any effect on this universe." When they'd first used the alleviators, the children had been given an explanation for how time travel works. They were told that the easiest way to understand it was to picture a tree branch. If you changed something important in history, it would create another branch that you were bound to follow, so that if you tried to return to the present on your original branch, you would find yourself unable to do so. Meanwhile, the rest of the world continued on the original branch without you.

"Even so, there *is* an effect on this universe," Agatha said. "The time traveler is missing. It's hard to explain a sudden disappearance. That's what closed the hotel down in the first place, remember? The mysterious disappearances of the hotel guests—police get involved, families and friends ask questions, reporters start poking around . . . eventually somebody is bound to discover our little . . . local attraction."

"I bet somebody has slipped through," Rowan said. "You can't guard against everything."

"That's true," Agatha admitted. "One or two people have managed to elude our precautions . . . but that's a long story, and it's Gertrude's to tell. You'll have to ask her about it." From the looks on their faces it was obvious that nobody would do that anytime soon.

"Anyway, most people are satisfied with just one trip. Travel across the country is hard enough, let alone travel over the centuries. Only a very select group, carefully screened, are granted frequent-flier status and allowed to travel often. In my petition, I had to remove any fear that you would run off, Nina." She held up her hand against Nina's protests. "Now, now, I think you are very reliable, but it doesn't matter what I think. The Board is a little nervous. Even though children have used the alleviators before, they've never been granted frequent-flier status. If it happens, you four would be the first children to attain it. Tomorrow morning you have to meet with the Board in person to answer some questions."

She paused for a moment as if considering something, then, sensing their discomfort, managed a weak smile. "They can be a little intimidating. But if all goes well, we'll be on our way to Alexandria at the golden hour."

CHAPTER THREE

AN ODD QUESTIONNAIRE

Nana left her granddaughter to spend the night with the Sisters so that Xanthe could catch up with her friends. The children stayed up late, speculating on what was in store for them, but also talking about what they had done since they'd last seen each other over the summer. The Popplewells eagerly provided more details of their move and their new school, their new friends and activities. Rowan had joined the chess team. Nina was cutting a CD of Chopin's preludes. Rowan was into magic. Nina was into ice skating. When it was Xanthe's turn, she told them about writing short stories and taking a jazz dance class, and the teen environmental-activist group she had recently joined. After talking about herself, she gave them a cursory rundown of Xavier's activities, secretly gloating over her dry, factual version of his life. If Xavier had been there he would have embellished the stories beyond belief.

• • •

Early the next morning, when Agatha roused the three children from bed, it was still dark outside. Xanthe felt the bone-rattling chill that comes with being awakened prematurely—and putting on her wool sweater and windbreaker did nothing to relieve it. After a quick breakfast of oatmeal, homemade croissants, and jam, they all trundled into Agatha's Ford Model T convertible (which had the top up), and set out to reach the Owatannauk Resort before daybreak.

"Wouldn't it be easier to have a meeting during the day?" Rowan yawned.

"It's impossible for members of the Board to get together at any other time," Agatha said.

"Who is on the Board?" Nina asked. "Do we know them?"

"Some of them," Agatha answered. "I'm sorry, children. I need to concentrate or I'll miss my turn-off."

The Owatannauk Resort looked particularly foreboding against the early morning mist, its huge silhouette hunched like a desperate, dying thing. They approached the tall, locked gate that blocked the way.

Instead of stopping, Agatha took a sharp right off the road, heading straight into a large pile of boulders.

"Look out!" Xanthe squealed, but then one of the boulders flickered and disappeared, revealing an opening.

"We're entering the parking garage," Agatha said, driving between the rocks into a tunnel lit with lanterns that cast odd shadows on the walls. "All frequent fliers have indicators on our cars that reveal the holographic boulder. Just another precaution against intruders."

After several minutes, they entered the underground garage. A few other cars were already there, a collection which would rival that of an antique auto show, including a baby-blue pickup truck that Xanthe recognized as Gertrude's. Agatha parked next to an old-fashioned yellow race car with a large "5" painted on the side.

"Well!" Agatha said, turning off the motor. "We're here."

"Here" looked like the remnants of an underground dungeon, with crumbling stone walls that smelled of mildew and rot, and an uncomfortably low ceiling. Xanthe started to breathe heavily. Her hands shook.

"Are you all right?" Rowan asked.

"No!" Xanthe gulped. "Can we get out of here? I'm claustrophobic!"

Agatha gently took her by the arm. "There's a staircase over here."

Xanthe stumbled up the stairs, which emptied into the hotel's reception area. She stood for a moment, gasping for breath.

"I'm sorry, but I have this awful fear of being buried alive. I can't stand small, cramped places. It's not too bad if it's bright, but when it's dark..." She shuddered.

"Don't worry about it," Rowan said. "A lot of people are claustrophobic."

Xanthe nodded, but it was little comfort. She'd been claustrophobic ever since she was eight. During a game of hide-and-seek she'd gotten stuck in the window seat for two hours, until Xavier finally found her screaming her head off. He'd raced to find their father, who'd had to tear the seat apart to pull her out. That was one time when she was glad Xavier had been there.

They made their way to the reception desk which, like everything else in the room, was covered in a thick layer of dust. Stringy, ghostlike cobwebs floated from the wall sconces and the chandelier, which was tarnished and dull. The furniture, the wallpaper, and the carpets were dingy and colorless from decades of fading. The floorboards under the carpet creaked as they walked. The air smelled stale.

Then Xanthe felt the familiar tingle of the onset of the silver hour. Sure enough, the sensation intensified until she was entirely numb. Then came a sucking sound, a blinding flash, and an explosion of color.

A pattern of bright purple ivy twisted across the repaired wallpaper. Crystals sparkled as the chandelier candles blazed into life, and spots of light danced on the rich, violet carpet. Everything was clean, crisp, and vibrant like the air after a spring sun shower. The grand piano gleamed from the rotunda, its keys quiet but inviting.

In an instant, Nina was seated. She launched into a vigorous piece that sent her nimble fingers skittering up and down the keyboard. Xanthe watched over her shoulder, trying to follow them, but they were a blur. It was like some marvelous magic trick.

With the last staccato chord came enthusiastic applause.

Xanthe was startled to see a small crowd had formed. An elderly man in a dark-brown suit pushed forward.

"Bravo!" he called out in a raspy voice. "Stand up and take a bow, my dear. That was outstanding!" Nina modestly complied.

"Well, Nina, it looks like you've brought out some of the Board members!" Agatha said. "This is Mr. Joseph Silverstrini, our mayor; you've met Miss Jenny O'Neill, the head librarian; you may recognize Mrs. Hilda Bingham, owner of the coffee shop; you know Nana, of course; and this is Captain Dennis Morgan, our chief of police."

"Very impressive playing," Captain Morgan said, drawing himself up. "Quite a treat." The children politely shook everyone's hand. Xanthe flashed her most adult-pleasing smile, the one she'd perfected for internship interviews. It exuded confidence, intelligence, humor, eagerness, kindness, and modesty. It was a killer smile. Rowan, on the other hand, had a stricken look, like he'd just wet himself.

"Where's Aunt Gertrude?" Nina asked.

"I believe she's still in the Spanish-American War," Agatha said. She turned to Captain Morgan. "Is everybody here?"

"Not everybody, but they all should be here any minute."

"Good. We're just in time," Agatha said. "Let's go greet them." She turned to the children. "You three stay here. We'll get you when we're ready for you." She joined the others walking briskly down the hallway.

Xanthe, Rowan, and Nina sat on one of the sofas. They watched two young men in long stiff cloaks, mufflers, and top hats descend the staircase. They looked like they'd stepped out of a Victorian Christmas card. Xanthe wondered if she looked as strange to them as they looked to her. The young men didn't give them a second glance, but proceeded out the back door.

After a moment Nina nudged Rowan. "What do you think Aunt Agatha's really doing?"

"Greeting the rest of the Board. You heard her..."

"Then why did they go down the hallway? The front door is right there." Nina pointed. "And the door to the garage is back there." She pointed behind them.

"They went down the hallway that leads to the alleviators," Xanthe said slowly. "You don't think the rest of the Board is arriving by—" She had hardly gotten the words out before Nina darted toward the hallway.

"Nina!" Rowan shouted. "Come back here! Aunt Agatha said to wait!"

"I just want to peek!"

She skidded around the corner with Rowan on her heels. Xanthe jogged behind them, slowing when she turned the corner and saw the two of them peering around the next bend.

"What's going on?" she asked. Rowan put his fingers to his lips. Xanthe craned her head to see past him, just as the first of the alleviator doors slowly slid open.

From four different alleviators stepped four people: three men and a woman, all elderly, and definitely not of the twenty-first century. Their clothes looked like costumes Xanthe had seen in black-and-white movies, placing them, perhaps, in the nineteen-twenties and -thirties. One of the men looked very familiar. His sad-sack eyes and white, wild hair were known to just about anyone over the age of ten who had any interest in science.

"Wow!" Xanthe whispered gleefully. "Is that—"

She felt a light but determined tap on her shoulder and whirled around, finding herself face to face with Otto, the hotel concierge, his robust silver mustache twisted up at the tips. He smiled pleasantly, as was his way.

"Welcome," he said. "We've been expecting you."

The children exchanged looks. The last time they had faced Otto they had tried to determine if he was a sophisticated robot or just a confusing, persnickety resort employee. He had an annoying habit of being affably unhelpful.

Rowan cleared his throat. "We were just...looking for the bathroom."

"The alleviators are for the use of time travel only," Otto responded. "If you must relieve yourself, the proper facilities are down the East Hallway. Urinating in the machines is severely frowned upon, as it makes the entire ride quite unpleasant."

"I didn't mean...oh forget it," Rowan mumbled. "I don't have to go that badly."

Otto then produced three clipboards from behind his back. "If you would please follow me to the lobby, I have an application for each of you to fill out before your interviews."

He led them back to the sofas and handed them each a clipboard and a pen.

"Please answer each question fully and honestly, don't compare answers, and no talking." They started to move to different corners of the room. Nina already had her hand up.

"I don't understand what—"

"I'm sorry, there will be no questions. Just answer to the best of your ability. You should have no problem, the questions are easy and quite short. When you find a seat, you may begin."

Xanthe plunked herself down on a chair near the piano and looked at the application. The first page read, "Application for Twilight Tourist Frequent-Flier Club." She took a deep breath and turned the page. There were six questions, and they were about as short as they could be. This is what she saw:

WHO?

WHAT?

WHERE?

WHEN?

HOW?

WHY?

Xanthe glanced over at Nina, who was hunched over her clipboard, twisting her hair around her finger. Then she looked over at Rowan, who was scratching the back of his neck with his pen. A strange, sleepy smile settled across his face. Xanthe sighed and took the cap off her pen.

It was a beautiful writing implement, an old-fashioned silver fountain pen with black ink. It felt large and heavy in her hand, but warm to the touch, slippery, and silky. Just holding it made her feel relaxed, almost light-headed. Like swinging on the tire swing at home. You'd swing way far back, and then with a *whoosh* you'd rush past the ground, slowing, slowing until you were high over Tyler's Pond, then another whoosh brought you back, and another *whoosh* forward, and if you liked, you could let go, pausing in the air for a split second of flight before plummeting into the cold water below...

Clunk! Xanthe had dropped the pen—the sound on the clipboard snapped her back to reality. She looked down at her paper. To her surprise, she had already answered the first three questions. For "WHO," she'd written her full name, "Xanthe Christine Alexander," but for some reason she had decorated it with a border of stars and hearts. There was no way to erase it, so she cursed herself for daydreaming and looked at the next question, "WHAT?" There she had put, "time travel," and for "WHERE," she'd written "Alexandria, Egypt, 58 B.C."

Now that she had her wits about her, she quickly wrote, "as soon as possible" for "WHEN," and for "HOW," she figured the most obvious answer was the best and wrote the word "alleviators." Otto was right, the questions weren't hard at all. They hardly seemed worth asking. Then she got to the last question, "WHY?"

Here she knew she had to be careful. This was the only thing the Board really cared about. Rowan had told her that Aunt Agatha wanted them to be her assistants, but filling up a store with old junk did not seem quite a noble enough cause. Then WHY?

She tried to concentrate, but her brain yielded to the light-headed feeling again. She could say that Alexandria held some personal interest for her, but the truth was she didn't care where they went. She wanted to go for the thrill and excitement. She loved dressing up in costumes and experiencing the world the way people back in history experienced it. It was like being in a movie almost. She felt like Alice in Wonderland, but instead of being in a land of nonsense, she was visiting places she'd read about, meeting real people from the past.

"Pens down, please," Otto said, whisking her clipboard away. Xanthe blinked awake.

"Oh, wait. I didn't answer the last question!"

"I'm afraid you've run out of time," Otto said kindly, taking the pen from her hand. He had already collected the questionnaires from Rowan and Nina, both of whom looked equally flustered. Otto disappeared down the hallway.

"I think I fell asleep," grumbled Rowan. "I must be more tired than I thought."

"I drifted off, too," Xanthe admitted. "But surely they'll let us answer the questions once we get into the room . . . and by the way, you know those people who came out of the alleviators? Am I crazy or was that—"

"Rowan Popplewell, your presence is requested in the Constellation Room," Otto summoned from the hallway.

"Well, here goes nothing." Rowan sighed. He shuffled over to Otto, who escorted him away. Nina scooted next to Xanthe.

"I recognized him, too," Nina said quietly. "The man who came out of the alleviator, I mean. That was Albert Einstein."

"That's what I thought!"

"He must be a member of the Board," Nina said, her eyes big as pie plates.

"But doesn't that break every rule in the book? I mean, about messing around with history? And who are those other three people? Are they famous, too? What's wrong?"

Nina had cupped her head in her hands.

"I thought you wanted to meet somebody famous," Xanthe said. "Albert Einstein's a biggie."

"I thought I'd meet them while we were in disguise, not as myself," the younger girl groaned. "What can I say to Albert Einstein? I'm going to look so stupid."

"I really wouldn't worry about it, Nina. It's not like he's going to give us a physics test." Xanthe felt jittery, too, but consoling Nina boosted her own confidence. "Besides," she added, "he's supposed to be a nice guy."

"I have to throw up," Nina said.

"Really?" Xanthe asked. Nina did look quite pale.

"I've always had a nervous stomach. You know, I can't eat before a performance. I'm always afraid I'll barf in front of the audience."

"Well, Otto said the bathrooms are over there," Xanthe said, pointing to the hallway. Nina bolted, leaving Xanthe to try to figure out who the other Board members were by herself.

She ambled over to the reception desk, which was deserted, and leaned over the counter to see what was on the other side. The first thing she saw was Otto's big registration book—the book that contained the reservations for the alleviators. She touched it, wondering if it mentioned the Alexandria trip. She hesitated, then lifted the cover to take a peek.

"May I help you?" Otto asked.

Xanthe slammed the book shut. "Otto! I was looking for you—"

"It appears you have succeeded."

Her mind raced, trying to think of a good excuse. "Could you please answer some questions for me about the Board of Directors?" *It can't hurt to go into the room armed with some information,* she thought. Otto just looked at her, so she dove right in. "Who are they, and how are they elected?"

"The Owatannauk Board of Directors consists of nine people: four officers elected from the Platinum Level of the Frequent-Flier Club, and five overseers from the Founders Level. They meet the second Monday of every month to discuss operations of the facility—"

"But who are they exactly?" Xanthe interrupted. "What are their names?"

Just then, Rowan returned, his face dark.

"What happened?" Xanthe gasped.

"I don't want to talk about it."

"Well that's not going to be much help for me, is it?"

"Nothing's going to help you in there," Rowan muttered. He slumped down on the sofa.

"Xanthe Alexander," Otto said brightly. "Your presence is requested in the Constellation Room."

+ CHAPTER FOUR +
# THE BOARD OF DIRECTORS

THE ONLY WAY XANTHE COULD DESCRIBE STEPPING THROUGH THE door into the Constellation Room was that it felt like falling into infinity. As soon as she crossed the threshold, she was enveloped in the cosmos. Above her, below her, and on all sides stars twinkled, galaxies swirled, and meteors flashed by. The only stable and secure place was the floor beneath her, but it was just a small square, maybe seven feet on each side, a raft of polished wood floating through the universe. She felt disoriented, lost. She searched behind her for the doorknob, but the door had been closed, blending into the star field. She began to question the door's existence, wondering how exactly she'd come to be in the room to begin with.

The decor of the room, if it was indeed a room, was spare. There was a cushioned chair, which seemed to float in space. Opposite the chair was a long wooden table, also floating, illuminated by several gas lamps. Though seemingly unattached to solid ground, Xanthe was thankful for the pieces of furniture; if it weren't for them, she wasn't sure she would know which way was up. At the table sat the Board of Directors. Xanthe's eyes fell immediately upon Albert Einstein, who brought a handkerchief from his pocket and blew his nose into it, quite loudly. Captain Morgan, who sat in the center of the group, rose and motioned to the chair.

"Good morning, Miss Alexander," Captain Morgan said gruffly. "Please take a seat."

Xanthe lunged for it as though it were a life preserver, but after settling in and scooting around to face the Board, she had the sinking sensation that she was facing a firing squad. She flashed her killer smile, hoping it would draw attention away from her shaking hands.

"How do you like the Constellation Room?" Agatha asked brightly.

Xanthe jerked her head in the direction of her voice. As her eyes adjusted to the darkness she recognized the silhouettes of Agatha and Nana seated at a separate table off to the side. The table was not lit, and was therefore rendered practically invisible. For some reason Agatha and Nana were hidden. Then it dawned on Xanthe that Agatha must have sensed her apprehension and spoken to reveal her presence. She could also smell Nana's pipe smoke, which always helped put her at ease.

"Actually, it's kind of dark," Xanthe admitted.

"Oh, it doesn't have to be." Agatha laughed. "We like it this way. It's more dramatic, but we can set it for dawn if you prefer."

Xanthe heard Agatha fiddling with something. Immediately the star field disappeared, replaced by images of clouds at dawn. The brightest stars were still visible, as was the thin crescent moon, but the sky was tinted the color of creamy strawberry-and-tangerine sherbet. Now the floor raft seemed to glide along with the white flossy formations. It was equally disorienting, but at least it was lighter.

"It was Albert's idea," Agatha continued. "Uses the same technology as a planetarium, except the floor is mirrored, to complete the effect." Xanthe thought it was a good time for a compliment. She'd learned from experience that adults adore children who praise their appearance, good taste, and accomplishments. One well-timed comment could open all kinds of doors, so Xanthe turned her killer smile full force on Albert Einstein.

"Gosh, it's unbelievable how you come up with so many brilliant things, Mr. Einstein," she chirped. "Your brain must be turbo-powered. Wherever you are, your superior mind makes you a giant among dwarves."

"Thank you, my dear," Einstein said uncomfortably.

Captain Morgan cleared his throat. "Now that you've mentioned it, Miss Alexander, allow me introduce you to the so-called dwarves." Xanthe's killer smile drooped. How could she be such a dope? If she wouldn't have had to cross the clouds, she'd have run over and whacked her head on the long, wooden table a few times. Captain Morgan gestured to his left. "Next to Dr. Albert Einstein is Madame Marie Curie, then Mr. Thomas Edison, and Mr. Herbert George Wells. Everybody, meet Miss Xanthe Alexander."

"I'm sorry about the uh, dwarf remark ... I didn't mean ... " Nobody paid her any attention.

"Let's get down to business," the police captain said, resting a pair of reading glasses on his nose and flipping open the file in front of him. All the Board members had similar files.

"We've looked over your application, and we have a few questions for you," Captain Morgan continued. "I'll open up the meeting to general questions and discussion from the Board."

"I'm a bit confused," Madame Curie said, holding up a piece of paper. Xanthe was surprised. She thought Madame Curie was Polish, but she sounded American. Then she remembered that Jenny O'Neill, the head librarian, had at her disposal special translators that allowed time travelers to speak and understand any language to which the devices were set. Madame Curie was probably using one now.

"I thought your last name was Alexander," Madame Curie continued. "But on your application you've written 'Xanthe Christine Alexander Popplewell.' "

"I didn't write that!" Xanthe cried, jumping to her feet.

"You most certainly did!" Madame Curie turned the paper around for Xanthe to see. Xanthe leaned over and read what was on the paper. Sure enough, among the stars and hearts were the words "Xanthe Christine Alexander Popplewell."

"My last name is Alexander, I don't know how that ... that other name got there."

"Don't be alarmed, my dear," Mayor Silverstrini wheezed. "People write all kinds of things on their applications that they didn't expect to. It's the pens, you know. Verita-scripters.

They're made from a metal alloy infused with a chemical that bonds to the sweat on your fingertips—works as a truth serum of sorts."

"It taps into the unconscious mind," H. G. Wells added. "You see, most people aren't entirely truthful on their applications. They only write down what they think we want to see. But of course, what we want to see is the truth, something the applicant may not consciously know herself."

"Well, I still don't know how that other name got there," Xanthe mumbled.

"No need to be embarrassed, Miss Alexander. Let me assure you that what happens in this room stays in this room," Thomas Edison said kindly.

"Can we move on?" Xanthe sighed and sat back down.

"Yes, I agree. Let's move on." Captain Morgan harrumphed. "I'd like to address the issue that we're all concerned about with this young lady: her answer to the question of WHY?"

Xanthe froze. She hadn't answered that question. Or so she thought.

"Here you've written several things, Miss Alexander. You say you'd like to be of assistance to Ms. Drake. You write very eloquently about your desire for excitement and adventure in your life. Then there is something scribbled here about having fun dressing up, or some such trifle, but this is the part with which I take issue. You've written that you would like to finally, and you've underlined the word 'finally,' have something that Xavier does not."

"I wrote that?" Xanthe stammered. "I didn't mean to."

"You do understand that your brother is also being considered for frequent-flier status—just as you and Rowan and Nina Popplewell are?"

"Yes, of course..."

"Then what do you mean by this?"

Xanthe stole a glance at Nana, who said nothing but merely watched her curiously, dragging on her pipe. "I don't really know," Xanthe said finally. "Xavier and I do a lot of things together. I guess I'm looking forward to doing something without him."

There was some murmuring among the Board members. Xanthe noticed Edison intently studying people's faces as they spoke. When he turned to Hilda, she used sign language to communicate with him, and Xanthe realized he must be deaf. Finally, Albert Einstein stood and the room quieted.

"Miss Alexander," he started, folding his hands in front of him, "people have all sorts of reasons for using the time machines. We're not surprised by your answers to the questionnaire, but whether or not you have fun dressing up or enjoy an experience without your brother is not the point. Something very important is missing. Have you ever considered your role in the universe?"

Xanthe blinked stupidly. "Uh...yeah, sort of..."

"I don't think so," Einstein said gently. "At least not seriously. These alleviators, these time machines, have an awesome power, and those who use them have a tremendous responsibility. When we first built them I had my doubts, but—"

"I thought Archibald Weber built them," Xanthe interrupted. She cringed almost immediately. She was being rude but she couldn't help herself.

"We preferred to keep our participation secret, for obvious reasons," Thomas Edison responded.

"Yes, the entire project was secret!" added Madame Curie.

"So the three of you ... ?" Xanthe gasped.

"Albert, Thomas, and I had each stayed at this resort at one time or another, and became close friends with Archie. When he got the idea to create the alleviators, we combined our talents and the result is what we have here today. We are the founders."

"I just provided the inspiration." H. G. Wells laughed. "Archie and I have been best friends for ages, and we were both intrigued by the possibility of time travel. Perhaps you've read my book *The Time Machine*? No? Well, it's considered a science-fiction classic—"

"As I was saying," Einstein interrupted, "I had my doubts about the project. I know from experience that just because you *can* create something, doesn't mean you *should*."

Xanthe suspected he was referring to the atom bomb. Albert Einstein's research had been essential to developing and building the bomb, which the United States used against the Japanese in World War II. It effectively won the war for America in the Pacific, but a terrible cost was paid in innocent lives. It also ushered in the nuclear age, and the possibility that one day a weapon could be built capable of destroying the entire earth.

"At any rate," Einstein continued, "I agreed to lend my expertise, but only if we took a solemn oath that all who used the alleviators would use them for good, for the benefit of mankind. So far we have been successful. There are always variables which you can't control, but we are pleased with the results of our alleviators. But they are not toys, you see. And so I am disturbed when I see a candidate taking the opportunity to travel time so lightly."

"It is her age, Albert," Madame Curie remarked. "They are children. This is what I was talking about. They're more worried about the latest radio serials than the state of the universe."

"Actually, they don't listen to radio serials, they play video games and watch a lot of TV," Jenny, the librarian, corrected.

Madame Curie shrugged.

Xanthe could see this interview was sinking faster than the *Titanic*. She wondered why Agatha and Nana weren't supporting her more. Agatha was just sitting there, hands in her lap, and Nana had her eyes closed and her pipe clenched in her teeth, puffing away like a locomotive.

"I happen to think their youth is a distinct benefit," Wells countered. "They have a freshness, a willingness to learn, to try things unconventional."

"But they lack wisdom." Mayor Silverstrini coughed. "They're impulsive," he said. "They only think of themselves. All the applications have been the same in this respect."

"Let's not lose sight of the fact that they are a team, and a team is what we wanted," Hilda, the coffee shop owner, said.

"A weak team," Madame Curie corrected. "Liable to succumb to squabbling."

"Not weak!" Nana barked. Everyone turned, surprised at the outburst. "They have inner strength, more than most children. The strength to push past fear, to do what's right."

"I believe your opinion is somewhat biased," Captain Morgan retorted.

"I knew you'd say that!" Nana growled. "But my biased opinion is informed by years of watching two of them grow up, and knowing who they are and what they are capable of, maybe more than they know themselves. Agatha and Gertrude have watched the other two. They are much the same. None of us could've survived what they've survived. Not one of us."

"Annabelle, you and Agatha are not on the Board. You were only allowed to attend this meeting if you promised not to participate!" Mayor Silverstrini wheezed.

Nana curled her lip and gathered her wrap around her shoulders. "I'm not going to sit here and listen to a lot of horse hockey. You're not going to find a more ideal group. You know it, Agatha knows it, I know it."

"We're going over old ground," Captain Morgan said. "Bring in Nina Popplewell. Let's get this over with."

"You sound like you've already made up your mind!" Xanthe protested.

"Miss Popplewell is somewhat incapacitated," Otto said from the open doorway. "Nerves."

Marie Curie raised an eyebrow. "This is inner strength?"

"Excuse me," Xanthe snapped, rising to her feet. "Don't judge her. You don't know anything about her. Or any of us, for that matter. You can't tell anything from these ridiculously inadequate questions! Nina's brilliant. So what if she's a little nervous? She admires you people, and she wants you to like her. If you give her time, she'll be just like you. Maybe even better." Xanthe knew she should stop but her mouth wouldn't obey. Bitter words scattered from her lips like marbles on a waxed floor. "Maybe I haven't invented a lightbulb or made groundbreaking discoveries in radioactive elements or come up with a theory for the shape of the cosmos. And no, I don't know what my role in the universe is—not yet. Maybe I won't change the world, or maybe I will. Either way, I sure won't sit around judging other people afterward."

"This one will give you an honest response without the truth serum," Edison said.

"I think we're ready for the vote," Captain Morgan grumbled. "Nina Popplewell's application is no different from the other two."

In an instant, Otto reappeared with Rowan and Nina, who still looked pale but had regained a bit of her earlier swagger. She hesitated before coming into the room, momentarily thrown off by the floating clouds, but then girded herself and marched up to the table.

"I'm ready," Nina said, stoutly.

"That won't be necessary, my dear," Mayor Silverstrini rasped. "We don't want to tax you unduly. Just stand over by Miss Alexander. You, too, Mr. Popplewell."

"But I can answer questions! I'm okay!" Nina insisted.

"Forget it, Nina," Xanthe muttered. "It's over." She glanced at Rowan, who gave her a resigned shrug. Obviously, he had been raked over the coals during his interview as well.

"We've wasted enough time," Captain Morgan said. "The vote will be by ballot. If you think we should grant Rowan and Nina Popplewell and Xanthe and Xavier Alexander frequent-flier status, write 'yea.' If not, write 'nay.' Ballots go in the bowl."

The children watched silently. It was done quickly, and the bowl was handed back to Otto, who emptied the contents onto the table and counted. After he'd finished, he looked up, smiling.

"We have a tie. Four yeas, four nays."

"Wait," Xanthe said, recalling her conversation with Otto. "I thought there was supposed to be nine people. Where's the last Board member?"

Suddenly there was a loud *clunk*. They all turned their heads toward a corner of the room where a collection of long pipes stretched down from the ceiling, curving into a flat receiving basin. Xanthe hadn't noticed them before because they were clear. There were about twenty of them, and at the bottom of one sat a cylinder, about eight inches in length.

"What are they?" Nina whispered to Rowan.

"Pneumatic tubes. They use air compression to send cylinders up and down through a system of pipes," Rowan whispered back.

Otto retrieved the cylinder, opened it, and removed a note. After reading it, he looked up with a wide smile. "The vote has changed. It is now five to four, in favor of granting frequent-flier status."

Rowan, Xanthe, and Nina jumped up and down, cheering.

"I beg your pardon, but there is a condition, attached," Otto said loudly. The three children quickly quieted themselves.

"This trip is to be considered a test. Only if they pass the test will membership to the Frequent-Flier Club be granted." He passed the note to Captain Morgan, who read it and nodded.

"All right then, that's that. The silver hour's almost up, so this meeting's adjourned."

Einstein, Edison, Curie, and Wells left the room quickly, conversing among themselves. Xanthe hung back, her heart beating like she'd run a marathon. She felt such an incredible sense of relief that it took Rowan to remind her of the question on everybody's mind.

"Aunt Agatha, who sent that tube?" he asked. "Who put in the last vote?"

"Yeah," Nina added. "And why wasn't he—or she—at the meeting?"

"Oh, he was here," Agatha said. "He attends every meeting. He has to. He's one of the Founders, the president, and the chief executive officer. He's just very private, and a tad bit eccentric. The last vote was cast by Archibald Weber."

+ CHAPTER FIVE +
A TRANSFORMATION

"Archibald Weber is still alive?" Rowan blurted.

"Well, not really alive or dead," Agatha said. "I'll explain on the drive back. I don't want to be in here when all the dust and cobwebs show up. It plays havoc with my hay fever."

"Oh, yes, let's get out of here before the spiders come back," Nana agreed, pulling a knit cap onto her head. "And let's have breakfast at Hilda's. Arguing with that Curie woman always works up my appetite. I'll ride with you, Agatha, and pick up my car later."

When they descended into the garage, it didn't seem quite so oppressive in its refreshed, silver-hour mode. They all squeezed into the Model T, and drove out just as the garage resumed its dungeonlike state.

"Archibald Weber is one of the phantoms of the hotel," Agatha began as they passed the holographic boulder. "That's why the Board meetings are scheduled at the golden and silver hours. It's the only time he and Albert, Marie, Thomas, and Herbert can make the meetings."

"So what they said is all true?" Xanthe asked. "They helped build the alleviators?"

"Yes, indeed. It took them nine or ten years to get it right, and even then they were still testing and tinkering after the hotel closed down. At first, they were very possessive about their new invention, but Archie saw it as a tool for understanding the modern world, and as something that should be shared. They created a Board of Directors, made up of themselves and four officers from the present, to police its use. They installed safeguards; Gertrude is one. As you know, she is expert at tracking down people who have gotten lost in time—a Time Detective, so to speak."

"Why aren't you and Aunt Gertrude on the Board?" Nina asked.

"Unfortunately, we don't meet all the qualifications," Agatha answered. "But that's all right. The elected officers do an excellent job."

"How about you, Nana?" Xanthe asked.

"I served two years on the Board," Nana said. "And I'm sure I'll do it again, but I'm not looking forward to it. That Madame Curie rattles my cage. Thomas, on the other hand, is a real gentleman. We've traded many a story about experimenting. One day I'll have to get him over to my house and show him my pantry and see what he makes of it." Nana sat back with a smile on her lips, her mind now lost in this scenario.

As they entered the coffee shop, Hilda greeted them with a broad smile, and sat them at a table by the window. "I think congratulations are in order! How about celebrating with some banana pancakes, Canadian bacon, and orange juice—on the house!"

"That sounds lovely," Agatha said, and the children nodded their agreement. Hilda turned to head toward the kitchen when Xanthe stopped her.

"Mrs. Bingham, thanks for your support. We needed all the help we could get in there."

"You had more help than you knew," Hilda answered. "Mr. Weber likes you."

"Why?" Rowan said. "I mean, we're all right, but he's never met us."

"I don't know about that," Hilda said with a funny sort of smile. She hustled into the kitchen.

"I can't believe we're actually going," Rowan said. "I completely blew my interview. I felt like I was in the middle of that nightmare where you've got an important test and you suddenly realize you can't find the classroom, you didn't study, and you're naked."

"Hey, at least you got to *have* the interview," Nina said. "I was in the bathroom with my head in the toilet."

"Archibald Weber likes us. That's all we needed, right Nana?" Xanthe asked.

"Don't go off half-cocked, thinking you've got it made," Nana said. "Mr. Weber may be chief executive officer of the Board, but he's only got one vote."

"Yes, do remember this is a test," Agatha added. "While we're in Alexandria, I want all of you to be extra careful. Interact with as few people as possible. If you think you might be in the presence of somebody important, walk quickly in the other direction."

"But part of the fun is meeting famous people," Rowan protested.

"Oh, yes, it would be so much fun to meet somebody I've read about!" Nina pleaded.

Agatha shook her head. "I'm sorry, but the whole idea of being a Twilight Tourist is to drift through the past, observing events, but affecting them as little as possible. Don't get involved. It could make all the difference."

The threesome nodded reluctantly, but by the time breakfast arrived, their spirits were back up, and they chatted excitedly about what they might see in this capital of the ancient world.

After breakfast, Nana made her good-byes. She held Xanthe in a long hug.

"You take care now, you hear? Listen to what your heart tells you. And don't think so much. Sometimes you're too clever for your own good."

Xanthe nodded, not exactly sure what the old woman meant, gave her a kiss, and joined the others.

They drove back to the Sisters' house for a much needed nap. Xanthe was sure she was too excited to fall asleep, but discovered that the early morning anxiety had left her exhausted. She lay down and closed her eyes for only a minute, then was surprised when she woke up to Agatha's gentle prodding six hours later.

The Owatannauk Library was located in the center of the town. It was so enormous that it took up a whole block. It only made sense that the primary place people went to do research and prepare for time travel would be massive.

Jenny O'Neill, the librarian and youngest officer of the Board, was a strawberry blonde with a perky attitude. But she took her position seriously. She was responsible for providing travelers with the clothing, personal items, and knowledge to blend into whatever communities they were visiting. She found the children no less than fifty-three books about the ancient city of Alexandria and its people. The first book Xanthe opened was about the history of the Ptolemaic Dynasty. It described how the first three Ptolemies developed the city of Alexandria, but the ones who followed were self-serving, violent, greedy, and a little crazy. The book suggested that this was the result of inbreeding—the Ptolemaic kings married their sisters, in keeping with the tradition of Egyptian pharaohs. This effectively kept the power within the family, but at the risk of unhealthy offspring. Xanthe imagined what it would be like to be married to Xavier.

"Blechh," she said aloud.

"What's that you're reading?" Agatha asked, looking over Xanthe's shoulder. "Hmm, you're not really going to need to know politics, dear. How about this?" She handed Xanthe a book on Alexandrian social structure, whisking away the book on the Ptolemies, but not before Xanthe got a glimpse of the title of the next chapter: "Cleopatra, the last Pharaoh of Egypt."

"Wait!" Xanthe cried. "Cleopatra was related to the Ptolemies?"

"Uh, well, yes, she was," Agatha said, shoving the book under a stack of others.

"Cleopatra?" Rowan walked over with his book about Alexandrian sports and games. "She's supposed to be one of the most beautiful women of all time."

Nina looked up eagerly. "Are we going to meet—"

"No," Agatha interrupted. "Please don't get your hopes up. I told you we're not going to meet any famous people. I believe Jenny is ready for us in the wardrobe department."

"All right," Jenny began, looking them over and scratching her chin thoughtfully. "Agatha told me she wants to pose as a merchant. Rowan and Nina, you should be her assistants. The three of you can pass for Greek."

"You know what? Our mother was Greek," Nina piped up.

"Perfect. It'll be like going home, in a cosmic sort of way." She turned to Xanthe. "You should be an Egyptian. You're lucky—Egyptian women had a lot of freedom. But in Alexandria, Egyptians were second-class citizens. Actually, third-class citizens."

"Oh, come on! They're in *Egypt*, for heaven's sake!" Xanthe was tired of dark-skinned people getting the short end of the stick historically.

"Yes, well, I'm afraid the native Egyptians lost control of the country when the Persians took over in about five-twenty-five B.C. And then Alexander the Great defeated the Persians and brought in Greek rule. But it's not as bad as you think. The Ptolemies respected Egyptian traditions and religion. Alexandrian Egyptians had plenty of government jobs, especially as translators; it was the only way the Greek rulers could get information to the people they governed." She snapped her fingers. "Let's make you an upper-class Egyptian from Luxor. Educated, wealthy..."

"Now we're talking," said Xanthe, rubbing her hands together.

"And I'm going to set your translator for Greek, Latin, and Egyptian. And I'll throw in Hebrew while I'm at it. There was a large community of Jews living in Alexandria at that time." She turned to the other three. "For safety's sake, try to speak only Greek...It would be unusual for a Greek to take any interest in learning Egyptian."

Jenny handed a translator to each of them—an earpiece and a tiny microphone, smaller than an aspirin, that hung on the end of a long filament and clipped onto your back tooth. Xanthe's translator had three filaments attached to the microphone, and Jenny showed her that by biting down on the tooth clip she could control which language she spoke.

"And here's something else to make your lives easier," Jenny said, producing three small plastic cases. "These are the latest in translation. You're going to need to read Egyptian hieroglyphics and Greek—especially you, Rowan, if you're going to be a scribe in the library. That's a whole other alphabet than the one we're used to. You won't recognize the letters unless you use this."

She removed two small discs from one of the plastic cases.

"Contact lenses?" said Nina.

"They're a smidgen thicker. Try them."

After a lot of painful pokes in their eyes, they all stood blinking tearfully at Miss O'Neill.

"They're easier to put in once you get the hang of it," she said. "Now take a look at this book." She handed Rowan a large, ancient book, which he opened.

"'Speak to me of the man, oh muse, the man driven many times off course, once he had plundered the great heights of Troy...' Cool!" he said.

"That's the beginning of *The Odyssey*, written by Homer, in Greek." She handed Xanthe a scroll. "Now you give it a try. This is the *Egyptian Book of the Dead*, their bible of sorts."

Xanthe blinked her eyes a few times. The scroll was covered in hieroglyphs. She couldn't make heads or tails of them. Then, at the bottom of her field of vision, she noticed words forming in English, written in a thick, dark-blue type, as though she were reading subtitles on a foreign film.

"'Homage to thee, Osiris, Master of Eternity, Lord of the Gods, whose names are many...' Wow, I feel like a cyborg!"

"Try not to use them too much," Agatha warned. "I used them the last time I went to Alexandria, and they gave me a pounding headache for days."

"They're not perfect. By all means, take them out if they

start hurting...but try not to lose them." Miss O'Neill checked her watch, then clapped her hands brightly. "Well! I believe it is time to get dressed!"

The last time the children had used the alleviators they were in a hurry, so Miss O'Neill had given them their clothes in a garment bag. This time the experience was quite different. Jenny led them to the changing rooms. There they were each introduced to their own personal attendant. Xanthe's was a young man who looked to be in his mid-twenties, Sanjay. Sanjay was East Indian and quite handsome, Xanthe thought.

"This is going to be fun," Sanjay said, unzipping the garment bag. "Now go behind the screen and take off those tacky coveralls. We've got a lot of work to do."

"They're overalls, and I happen to like them," Xanthe grumbled, stepping behind the screen. "I think they make me look cute."

Sanjay snorted. "I guess...if you think plumbers are cute." He handed her a long, thin tunic of pleated white linen. "Now this is a *kalasiris*. It's going to be tight. The Egyptians thought the human form was beautiful, something to be shown off."

Xanthe squeezed into it. It was formfitting, all right. She felt almost naked, it was so light, and it stuck to her figure like paint.

"I'll put some sandals in your luggage," Sanjay continued, "but most people go barefoot. From the looks of your feet, you're used to that. This oil is for your hair." He held a ceramic bottle to her nose and she sniffed. It smelled of cinnamon and

other spices. Sanjay poured some on her head and lightly
rubbed it in. "It's scented to give you an aura of womanly
mystery," Sanjay said slyly.

"More like an aura of coffee cake."

"At least your hair already looks Egyptian. You don't have
to wear a wig. Wigs are no fun in hot weather. Now here's
your makeup kit. Guard it closely. It holds the secrets to your
allure."

"I'm not really into makeup. I like the natural look."

Sanjay raised an eyebrow. "Natural is overrated."

The kit was a bronze box containing several jars of different
colored pastes and powders. Sanjay showed her how to tint
her eyelids with kohl, an oily green eye shadow; how to use
the black eyeliner, drawing it out to the far corners of her lids;
how to color her lips and cheeks with red ochre powder; and
how to dye her fingernails orange with henna. There was also
an oil scented with flowers to rub into her skin. When she
was finished, Sanjay looked her over, tilting his head as
though appraising a piece of artwork.

"Something's missing," he said, tapping his chin. "Ah, I
know what it is." He produced another bronze box from a
drawer and opened it. Inside, gold and silver jewelry gleamed
against the black cloth lining: bracelets and amulets, rings,
earrings, and a wide collar inlaid with turquoise and other
semiprecious stones. "Go ahead, be my guest."

Xanthe gently picked out a collar with a falcon design
made of cobalt blue stones, arm bracelets of golden snakes, an
ankle bracelet, and a diadem, which was a thin sort of headband

with a coin-shaped circle of gold sitting between what looked like two horns. The jewelry felt cold and heavy, but it also made her feel substantial. She held her breath and turned slowly in front of the mirror. A sophisticated young Egyptian woman stared back.

"Who wants to be cute when you can look stunning?" Sanjay said quietly. He took her hand and led her to the main room.

"Oh, my goodness!" Agatha gasped. Nina and Rowan looked up.

"You look like a princess!" Nina squealed. "I want to be an Egyptian. All I get to wear is this plain ol' tunic."

"It's a *chiton*," Sanjay corrected, "and it's not plain, it's a delightful robin's-egg blue."

Rowan also wore a tunic, though a shorter one, dyed light green. Fastened to it with a large metal brooch was a short, dark-blue cloak of rough wool.

"Hey, you look like Hercules!" Xanthe said, looking him over.

"I don't know about that." Nina snickered. "Didn't Hercules have muscles?" Rowan threw her an annoyed look.

"You should go," Miss O'Neill said, checking her watch. "You each have one bag, so please try to keep track of its contents. And enjoy your trip! Alexandria, Egypt. If there was ever a more beautiful place on earth, I can't think of it."

By the time they reached the Owatannauk Resort, it had already gone through its evening transformation. The subterranean parking garage still gave Xanthe the chills, but Agatha quickly led them up a long ramp that was considerably wider than the staircase they'd used previously.

"This isn't the same way we went in the last time," Xanthe remarked.

"No, it's not," Agatha agreed. "This leads outside. We're going to use the service alleviator. I'm sure you've noticed that some of the things in this town have been brought back from other eras." The children nodded. "And many of them are quite big. Too big to fit in one of the twelve alleviators you've seen, and certainly too big to get out through the hotel hallway and doors. So there are two alleviators opening to the outside that handle bigger cargo—the service alleviators."

In no time, they were facing an alleviator with an entrance the size of a barn door. Otto was standing there, looking congenial as always.

"Hello, Otto," Agatha sang out. "We are ready to depart!"

"And right on time." Otto handed them each the shimmering golden key that would allow them to see and use the alleviators at the golden and silver hours. Xanthe put hers in a secret pocket sewn into her *kalasiris*. The key was the lifeline back to the twenty-first century. She patted it to make sure it was safe, and saw the others do the same thing.

Otto pressed the alleviator button, the doors opened, and they walked in. The service alleviator was as spacious as a barn. Though its internal hum was at a lower frequency than the indoor alleviators, it resembled them in every other way. Thousands of buttons lined the walls, each with a year engraved on it. Otto moved to the station in the corner where the keypad and screen were located, as well as the strange globe used for finding the coordinates of your destination.

Other than the actual travel, this was Xanthe's favorite part. She loved looking at the globe through the special handheld microscope which had a magnification so strong that you could see what seemed to be real people, buildings, and even actual events unfolding below. If you pressed a button on the wall and changed the date, the globe reflected the change. It was an exact replica of the world, showing everything that was happening or had ever happened, like a three-dimensional record of history. Normally Xanthe would have raced to be first to use it, but something else had captured her attention.

She slowly approached the long, sleek wooden boat that sat in the center of the alleviator. Its ends sloped elegantly to two points, and a railing ran along its side. The boat had a single mast with a sail that was rolled up and tied at the top of it. A gangplank led up to the deck.

"There's only one good way to get to Alexandria—especially if you're a merchant," Agatha said. "And that is by boat."

Nina was already scampering up the gangplank. "It's big!" she cried, climbing into the vessel. She disappeared for a moment and then popped her head up again. "There's a million jars of honey down here!"

"Those are my wares. I wouldn't be much of a honey merchant without honey." Agatha turned to Xanthe and Rowan.

"All right, you two set the coordinates. The more you practice using this equipment, the better you'll become."

Xanthe and Rowan charged over to Otto. Xanthe only beat Rowan by a split second. Apparently Rowan really *had* been getting in shape.

"Me first!" she said.

"Go ahead," he said, grinning. "I already know how to land in water."

Xanthe placed the microscope over the Mediterranean coastline of modern Egypt. As she focused it, apartment buildings came into view. They crowded the shore, extending inland. A few small boats floated in the water, anchored off several piers.

"Have you chosen the year you intend to visit?" Otto asked.

"Yes, indeed," Agatha said. "Rowan, press the button for the year fifty-eight B.C.!"

Rowan scanned the walls until he found the correct button and jabbed it. As he did, the image under the microscope wavered. Suddenly all the apartment buildings were gone, replaced by smaller buildings of Greek and Egyptian design, their white facades gleaming like pearls. Xanthe could see the famous Pharos lighthouse, its beacon already lit for the night.

"It's gorgeous," she murmured.

"Please read off the coordinates," Otto said.

Xanthe did. After Rowan typed them into the keypad, they both grabbed their bags and followed Agatha up the gangplank, joining Nina, who had already claimed the front seat.

Agatha grasped the tiller used for steering the ship. "Everyone insert your translators, and then hold on to something!" she called out. "We might hit the water with a splash. All right Otto, press the button!"

"In case of a water landing, there are flotation devices under the benches," Otto recited. "They're fairly crude, however. If the boat breaks up, your best bet is to climb onto some wood and refrain from kicking or bleeding. The Mediterranean Sea is a breeding ground for the great white shark." He smiled and pressed the button on the keypad. "Enjoy your trip."

"Aunt Agatha?" Nina gulped, eyes wide.

Xanthe was worried, too, but she didn't have time to think about it. She already felt the familiar ticklish vibration, as though thousands of moths were beating their wings against her. She clutched the side of the boat as the sensation swept over her. She closed her eyes as she catapulted through the whirling abyss of time.

+ CHAPTER SIX +
RETURN OF THE CHAMPION

The boat plunged into the sea, sending a great spray onto the deck. Agatha struggled with the wagging tiller as they spun around, but after a few minutes the boat righted itself and the waves slapped gently against the hull. Xanthe's arms hurt. She felt sticky with salt, and there was no land in sight.

"Are we lost?" she asked Agatha. "I'm sure I read the right coordinates, but those numbers are so small..."

"Don't worry about it," Agatha said, peering into the distance. "We're a little farther than I'd hoped, but I don't think we're too far off the mark."

Xanthe scanned the horizon. There was nothing there, except the deep orange sun, only half of it still visible. The moon was up and stars were beginning to dot the sky. To the south, Xanthe noticed a particularly bright star.

"Look!" she said, tugging on Agatha's sleeve. "There's a star over there. Does that help?"

Agatha smiled. "Yes. We'll head that way." She angled the tiller, and they moved forward.

"It's too low to be the North Star," Xanthe mused. "Maybe it's Venus."

"No, my dear. It's Pharos, the great lighthouse of Alexandria. And now you know why it is considered one of the Seven Wonders of the Ancient World."

As the boat drew closer to the light, the main harbor of Alexandria opened before them. Immediately Xanthe's eyes were drawn to a line of white buildings, the royal palaces, glowing from across the harbor. She had seen them before in the binder that Agatha had given them, but in the dim light of sunset, illuminated by flickering torch fire, they took on an air of romance and mystery.

"There's a ship graveyard beneath us," Agatha warned as she drew up the sail. "Those sharp rocks have sunk many a boat."

"What's that?" Xanthe asked, pointing at a small structure on an inlet near the lighthouse.

"That is a temple to the Egyptian Goddess Isis," Agatha said. "A very popular deity in Egypt right now. Legend has it she was born of the Earth and the Sky. She brought agriculture, law, and civilization to Egypt. She is the Goddess of powerful magic. And because she ruled Egypt with her brother Osiris at the beginning of time, she is also Queen of the Gods, and a favorite of Egyptian queens."

Xanthe remembered flipping through a book about Egyptian mythology at the Owatannauk Library. She'd learned that the Egyptians were a polytheistic culture. They worshiped many Gods that they believed were present in day-to-day life, directly influencing events and sometimes even taking the forms of people or animals to do so. In fact, many of them had animal heads, and each God was connected with some important function of Egyptian life. There was Anubis, the jackal-headed God of embalming and the dead; Bastet, the cat-headed Goddess of hunters and maternal protection; Thoth, the ibis-headed God of wisdom; Horus, the hawk-headed God of warriors and the protector of pharaohs; Sekhmet, the lion-headed Goddess of war; and Seth, the God of destruction. He had a strange, unidentifiable animal head with sharp ears and a long snout.

"Remember the location of that temple, Xanthe," Agatha went on. "When you take the documents back to the Owatannauk, you won't be able to use the service alleviator, since it's in the middle of the water. Gertrude and I have arranged for one of the regular alleviators to be stationed inside the temple. It's an ideal place, very quiet. Most worshipers of Isis use the larger temple on the mainland."

They reached a pier. Rowan climbed out of the boat and tied it down. The rest of them followed with their luggage.

"The first thing to do is get settled," Agatha said. "I found an inn when I was here last week that should do the trick.

Once we have rooms, we can talk about getting into the library."

Agatha hired a man with a mule and wagon to carry them. He started loading their bags, but when he saw Xanthe he gave her a strange look.

"You are all together?" he asked, suspiciously.

Xanthe froze. It must seem odd to him that a wealthy Egyptian woman was traveling with a Greek merchant. Maybe it would've been better if she had posed as a servant after all.

"My, uh, barge broke down," Xanthe said, clumsily. Where was Xavier when you needed him? He was the expert at lies. "I was stranded on those rocks. This merchant saved me from having to swim to shore."

"And you're staying at the same inn?"

"As a matter of fact, we are," Agatha huffed. "Interesting coincidence, isn't it? Now are you going to take us there or should I find somebody else who would rather have my drachmas?" She held out a handful of coins. The man grabbed the money and loaded their bags onto his cart.

As they rode through the city, they passed the warehouses that Julius Caesar would accidentally set on fire in the future. Close by was the marketplace, a series of low buildings, each with a roofed porch that faced a central courtyard. It was quiet in the evening twilight.

"It's like an outdoor mall," Xanthe whispered to Rowan and Nina. "All they need is a yogurt place ... Oh, wow, they *do* have a yogurt place!" She pointed at the sign over one of the cafés which advertised a variety of snacks and desserts.

"I wonder if they have M & M's mix-ins..." Rowan murmured, sending her into a fit of laughter.

They turned onto a large avenue lined with columns and divided by a wide strip of gardens and decorative pools, then turned down a smaller street and drew up to a large house on a corner with a wooden sign that read:

> **IF YOU ARE CLEAN AND NEAT THERE IS A BED INSIDE FOR YOU. IF YOU ARE NOT, I'M EMBARRASSED TO SAY, YOU ARE WELCOME, TOO.**

Nina giggled. "Whoever owns this place has a sense of humor."

"Very true," Agatha said. "It's cozy but comfortable, with lots of good company."

The driver took their bags from the wagon, and Agatha rang a bell that hung below the sign. After a moment, a short, pudgy man with a ruddy face and rust-colored hair answered. His eyes lit up as soon as he saw Agatha.

"My dear Agathina! Back again so soon! Come in, come in! We were all about to have some cake! Oh, I do hope you brought some more of that honey—it was divine."

"Dionysius, I'd like you to meet my assistants, Rowanus and Ninae. And I did bring more of the honey, but it's still in the boat."

"Ah, well." Dionysius sighed. "I suppose I can sweeten my beer with something else." He noticed Xanthe and held out his hand. "Good evening, my dear. Are you also here for a room?"

"Yes, yes I am," Xanthe said, drawing herself up. "I'm visiting from Luxor."

"Well, I must say, your Greek is excellent," Dionysius said. "I don't know if you know what you've gotten yourself into, coming to my little inn, but I have a few rules. First, you are free to use any of the public rooms: that is, the parlor, the courtyard, and the kitchen. My room is on the first floor— don't go in there. We all share the latrine, there are two, and the bath. There is a well in the courtyard for water. I also require that my guests join me in the evening for cake. I love hearing stories, and I love cake. It's the only reason I opened up this inn. My wife passed away, and my children have grown and scattered to the wind. This little business of mine is the only thing that stands between me and my tomb. And I can tell you, I'm not ready to go there. So if all of that is agreeable to you, come on in and meet the others."

Xanthe nodded and followed him inside, behind Agatha, Rowan, and Nina. Dionysius directed an Egyptian servant to take their bags to their rooms, then led them into the parlor. People reclined on the many sofas, eating cake and fruit, warmed by a fire in the hearth. No fewer than six cats waited alertly beneath them, poised to catch falling crumbs.

"Everybody! I'd like to introduce four more guests!" Dionysius cried. The conversation stopped as curious eyes turned toward them.

"This is my friend Agathina, a honey merchant from Greece. She brings with her two assistants, Rowanus and Ninae." The group murmured greetings as Dionysius turned to Xanthe.

"And this lovely vision is ... I'm sorry, dear, I don't believe you told me your name."

Xanthe's mind raced over the few Egyptian names she could remember. "I'm ... my name is Xanthetiti. Of Luxor." In the background she could hear Rowan and Nina snorting and coughing. Even Agatha seemed amused.

"Wonderful," Dionysius said. "And from your appearance I'd judge you are a descendant of the ancient queen of the Nile, Nefertiti herself."

"Yes," Xanthe said, cutting her friends a glare. "I believe that is true." More snorting and coughing from the back.

Some of the other guests sat up, making room on the sofas. Agatha, Nina, Rowan, and Xanthe spread out among them as Dionysius took a seat on the floor, grabbing a handful of purple grapes and tossing a few to the cats before he stuffed the rest in his mouth.

"This is Omar Ali, from Arabia," he said, gesturing to the slight man in the turban next to Rowan. "A perfume merchant, a doctor of mixology, creator of the most exotic and enticing scents you'll ever find." Omar raised his glass of wine as a sort of salute. Dionysius pointed at the woman next to Nina. "This is Isabella San Martin, from Spain. She's here with her husband, Diego, and their exquisite silver vases. You won't want to miss their shop."

"My husband will be here soon," Isabella said. "He was helping one last customer before locking up."

"Hopefully he hasn't run into that Alexandrian mob." Omar clucked. "They're on the prowl tonight. Would you believe I saw them beating a man for running his carriage over a cat?"

"Cats are sacred in Egypt," said a dark-skinned man wearing a red patterned waist cloth and vest, and a tribal design of scars on his cheek. "Even among the Greeks. Look at how Dionysius worships his! They run this place!"

The man made a sweeping gesture and Xanthe noticed that there were many more cats than the six clustered at Dionysius's feet. They lay on top of cabinets, crouched under furniture, and stretched themselves by the windows. A small cinnamon-colored cat played with the pleats at the bottom of Xanthe's dress. She reached for him but he scampered off, leaping into a large vase.

"Gosh, there must be a hundred!" squealed Nina, petting a particularly fat cat under the table. "Where do you keep all the litter boxes?"

"I'm sorry, the litter what?" Dionysius asked. Rowan glowered at his sister.

"Nothing," she said quickly.

Dionysius shrugged and picked up a silvery cat with black spots, scratching him behind the ears. "We Alexandrian Greeks are a strange hybrid. We've been here so long, we've adopted many Egyptian beliefs." He turned to Omar. "It's extremely bad luck to kill a cat, you know. That carriage driver should've been more careful. He's lucky he only got a beating. We Alexandrians can get a little emotional sometimes." Dionysius smiled suddenly, gesturing to the dark-skinned man. "Incidentally, this is my friend Kwame

Matungo, from North Africa, and his son, Jomo, hiding behind him."

A small dark-skinned boy of about nine years, wearing a dark-blue patterned wrap and vest, leaned out warily from behind Kwame.

"Kwame's responsible for stocking the zoo here, as well as providing animals for the games at the Coliseum in Rome. What have you brought with you this time, my friend?" Dionysius asked.

"Two baboons, a gorilla, and an elephant!" Kwame answered proudly. "And I've already sold three lions to the Romans. They're big ones, too."

"Oh, I love lions," Nina crooned. "They don't get hurt, do they?"

"Well, little Ninae, I love lions, too," Kwame said, leaning toward her. "But the Romans root for the gladiators. They don't revere cats as the Egyptians do. Even so, I'd be happy to show them to you. I've been selling animals to the Roman government for years, just as my father and my father's father did. I am passing my secrets along to my son. You see, you have to have a way with wild animals to be able to catch them and transport them without getting hurt."

Suddenly a dark, bearded man rushed in. "Sorry I'm late, but I've got incredible news!"

Isabella rose to her feet. "Diego! What is it?"

"Cleopatra Tryphaena has disappeared!" He took his wife's beer and drained the glass. "Her supporters are livid. They think her sister Berenice killed her so that she can be queen!"

"My goodness," Dionysius said. "So Berenice finally did it. I knew this would happen. They are a jealous bunch, those Ptolemies. They have a bad habit of killing each other off—"

"What do you mean?" Xanthe interrupted.

Dionysius took the cat from his shoulders. "I suppose you don't hear about Alexandrian politics way out there in Luxor," he said. "But you must have heard that Pharaoh Ptolemy the Twelfth has been ousted and is holed up on some distant island. And good riddance, I say. He's borrowed far too much money from the Romans to stay on the throne. And he had the gall to think he could repay them by raising taxes on us!"

"If that Ptolemy Auletes spent less time dancing and playing the flute, and more time with the affairs of state, he wouldn't be in this mess," Omar said, slicing himself a piece of cake.

"Oh, the flute playing was charming," Dionysius countered, "but the Romans always want their money. They'll get it back, one way or another. That's all we need, a bunch of Romans showing up and telling us what to do. They are such bores, you know. No fun at all. Everything good about them they stole from us Greeks. Their philosophy, their architecture, their art, their religion..."

"Ptolemy's daughters Cleopatra and Berenice have been fighting over who will rule in his place," Isabella said, refilling her goblet. "For a while, it was Cleopatra, but I, too, fear she's dead."

"Oh, I'm certain she is dead," Dionysius said. "It was only a matter of time. Have you met Berenice? She's an ambitious little creature. No doubt she poisoned her sister, or had her strangled. It is no use looking for Cleopatra, she is gone."

"But she can't be dead..." Rowan stopped himself.

"Why not?" Dionysius asked.

"Oh, nothing. It's just so sudden."

Kwame took a bite from a large fig. "And don't think this is the end of it. Oh, no. Pharaoh Ptolemy Auletes is nobody's fool. He'll be back to claim his throne from his wicked daughter Berenice, and you heard it from me first."

That night after Agatha went to sleep, Rowan and Nina snuck into Xanthe's room. The cinnamon-colored cat followed and hopped into Xanthe's makeup box. He curled up to sleep, paying no attention to the three agitated children.

"I can't believe Aunt Agatha would plan this trip so close to Cleopatra's death," Nina grumbled.

"I know," Xanthe agreed. "I understand that she doesn't want us to be around important people, but this is like rubbing it in our faces."

"But it doesn't make sense," Rowan said. "Even if you've never read anything about Cleopatra, what is the one thing everybody knows about her? The famous paintings of her... what do they show?"

"They usually show her..." Xanthe's eyes widened. "They show her with a poisonous snake, an Egyptian cobra, about to kill herself."

"Exactly. And she was a pretty important queen in her lifetime," Rowan continued. "Don't you think people would be more upset? What did you guys read about her?"

Nina shrugged. "I didn't get to read much. Agatha kept giving me books about Egyptian manners and daily life."

"You know, she kept grabbing books away from me, too," Xanthe said slowly. "Maybe there was something about this time she didn't want us to know."

None of them had any answers, but they resolved to talk about it more when they had a chance. Rowan and Nina returned to their room to go to sleep, but Xanthe remained awake. She lifted the cinnamon-colored cat out of her makeup box and put him in her lap, stroking his head and wondering what really happened to Cleopatra, and what Aunt Agatha was trying to hide.

The next morning, Dionysius made a breakfast of eggs, cheese, yogurt, and pastry. He chided them for rising so late, for the marketplace (the agora, as he called it) opened quite early. The other guests had already eaten and left to tend their shops.

Agatha and Nina finished first and decided to look at the statues in the garden. Dionysius fretted that the plants in the parlor were thirsty and went in search of his watering jug, leaving Xanthe and Rowan alone in the kitchen. Though several of the cats followed Dionysius out, just as many remained, slipping in and out of clay pots and lolling under the table. The cinnamon-colored cat leaped onto Xanthe's lap, causing her to knock over her juice. While Rowan fetched a cloth to mop up the spill, the cat hunkered down and nibbled on Xanthe's eggs.

"Well, I guess I'm finished." She sighed.

"I don't think having all these cats around can be very sanitary," Rowan said, shooing the animal off the table. Immediately the cat flattened his ears and hissed.

"Rowan, I wouldn't..." Xanthe started, but it was too late. Rowan received a quick swipe from the cat's claws. He yelped, pulling back his hand, which now had a long red scratch.

"Stupid cat!"

"I tried to warn you," Xanthe said. She got a cloth, soaked it in water in a basin, and wrapped it around Rowan's hand.

"I guess I'm more of a dog person," Rowan muttered. "Dog's aren't complicated. You feed them, play catch with them, let them slobber on your face, and you've got a pal for life."

"Cat's aren't so hard to understand," Xanthe said, looking at the cinnamon-colored cat. He had stopped eating and was now lying on his back, wiggling his belly to invite a stomach massage. Xanthe tickled him, and he batted playfully at her fingers. "If you give them respect, and space, they can be very loyal."

Xanthe opened the cloth and peered at Rowan's hand. The bleeding had stopped, but she ran her finger along his skin just to make sure.

"Anyway, they're mysterious creatures. It's why they're sacred to the Egyptians, I think."

"I think they're sacred because they keep mice out of the

food supply, but maybe I'm being too practical." Rowan laughed.

The bell at the door rang. A few seconds later, Dionysius could be heard talking to somebody in the entry. Then Xanthe heard a familiar laugh; a kind of loud, easy chuckle. She and Rowan left the kitchen and walked into the parlor, just as Dionysius ushered in a handsome young Egyptian, dressed in a white linen pleated kilt and vest. Around his neck hung a thick gold collar encrusted with a sunburst of colorful stones. The young man ran his fingers over his smooth, bald head.

"This is Xavankhaten," Dionysius announced. "A scribe from Luxor... Why that's your home, isn't it, Xanthetiti?"

"Sister!" cried Xavier, with a wide grin. "Father told me I could find you here!"

"What... You can't be... What are you doing here?" Xanthe squeaked. "Aren't you supposed to be somewhere else?"

"You didn't think you could have this little adventure without me, did you?" Xavier said, clapping his hand on her shoulder. It hit her like a ton of bricks.

+ CHAPTER SEVEN +
XAVIER'S TALE

As they all walked to the docks, Xavier talked nonstop about his trip to Washington, D.C. He told them about visiting the House of Representatives and the Senate, seeing the Supreme Court in session, and exploring the museums of the Smithsonian Institution.

"After that, we ate lunch at a little seafood place near the Washington Monument," he said, swatting at a fly with a palm frond that he was using as a fan. "Six of us had lobster bisque and six of us had crab salad. After about half an hour, everyone who had crab salad was rushing to the bathroom. Two people ended up in the hospital with food poisoning, so they canceled the rest of the trip and promised to reschedule it," Xavier finished.

"That's awful," Rowan said, pushing an empty cart they planned to use to carry the honey from the boat to the marketplace.

"Yes, I do hope those children are all right," Agatha added.

"But at least you get to come to Alexandria with us!" Nina said.

"I'd take ancient Egypt over Washington, D.C., any day!" Xavier laughed.

"You won't have to," Xanthe muttered. "You'll get to do both." Xavier gave her a weird look and ran his fingers over his smooth head, a new habit which Xanthe found irritating. "And what's with the bald head?" she sniped. "You look like your neck blew a bubble."

"Just trying to get into the spirit of things."

"I think it looks great," Nina said. "And it's got to be nice in this heat."

"And you'll save a lot on shampoo," Rowan added.

Xavier laughed.

Xanthe scowled, then tripped over the cinnamon-colored cat, who had been weaving in and out of her legs since they left the inn. He was becoming a nuisance.

"Go home!" Xanthe hissed. The cat stopped and tilted his head, as though not sure if she was talking to him. Xanthe wasn't so sure herself. "Go home," she muttered again. The cat took off.

On their way to the waterfront, they passed through the marketplace, which was in full swing. Customers bustled through the wide avenue as artisans and merchants hawked their merchandise, filling the air with their cries. The children stopped now and then to watch the action: metalworkers hammering sheets of silver around molds to make bowls, glassblowers adding color to molten glass, private bankers exchanging foreign currencies into Greek drachmas. An Indian man followed Agatha with a tray of precious gems. Agatha urged the children forward, finally arriving at a small kiosk set between a stand of ivory carvings and a cart overflowing with Chinese silks.

"This is our stand, Nina," Agatha said. "After you get the honey, bring it here and put the jars on the shelves while I set the boys up at the library. I shouldn't be long."

"You mean I don't get to see the library?" Nina whined.

Xanthe tugged on her sleeve. "I'll stay with you," she said. She wasn't interested in seeing the library anymore. When Xavier had announced at the inn that he'd come to Alexandria for a job as a scribe, Agatha immediately offered to help him get work in the library with Rowan. Logically, having Xavier at the library would be enormously helpful to Agatha, for now he could be the one to make the counterfeits that would replace the documents Rowan lifted from the warehouse. But deep down, Xanthe was disappointed. Now the library was just one more thing Xavier got to be a part of and she didn't.

After loading up the honey from the boat, and parting ways with Agatha and the boys, Xanthe and Nina walked back to the marketplace in silence. Nina kept glancing at her.

"You feel left out," Nina said, matter-of-factly.

"I . . . Well, yes, I do," Xanthe stammered. She'd forgotten how direct Nina could be.

"So do I. 'Assistant honey merchant.' Give me a break. Aunt Agatha thinks I'm useless!"

"I'm sure she doesn't think that, Nina. She's just being careful. You know, for the test."

Nina shook her head, unconvinced. "You're the luckiest, Xanthe. We all have jobs here. But you're pretending to be on vacation. You can do anything you want!"

Nina was right. Xanthe had gotten so knotted up about Xavier she'd forgotten that she was in one of the most exciting cities of the ancient world and had the freedom to go almost anywhere. How stupid of her! *She* was the lucky one, not Xavier.

"Thanks," Xanthe said, giving Nina a squeeze. "For reminding me."

"Of what?"

"Everything." She saw Agatha in the distance, making her way back to them through the crowd. "Aunt Agatha's coming to help you," she said. "I'll see you at dinner. I've got some exploring to do."

That day, Xanthe roamed through the Jewish quarter in the northeastern part of the city, where she noticed the houses were slightly smaller and humbler than the ones in the Greek quarter. She had to sneak into the gymnasium, which was for men only, and was amazed by how similar it was to a modern-day gym. She found a weight room, an open room for wrestling and gymnastics, a massage room, several pools, and a steam room before she was chased out by an attendant and warned never to return.

After eating lunch in the agora and checking in on Aunt Agatha and Nina, Xanthe spent the rest of the afternoon sitting on a bench in the zoo, people-watching. Wealthy matrons, Greek students, foreign scholars, Egyptian servants on errands, and many, many tourists crisscrossed the paths in front of her. The only people who gave her any notice were the Egyptians, especially the young men. She was both thrilled and embarrassed, and very thankful that her wealthy appearance discouraged them from approaching her.

When the group met back at the inn for dinner, Xanthe was bursting to report the chronicle of her day. Unfortunately, she never had a chance. Xavier and Rowan hogged the conversation. Between their descriptions of the library ("Thousands of scrolls tucked away in thousands of bins!" Xavier crowed) and the inside jokes about the snooty head librarian, Theodictes, that she didn't understand ("Sorry, Xanthe, I guess you had to be there," Rowan remarked), she couldn't get a word in edgewise.

As the other guests finished dinner, Xanthe was drawn to the parlor where Kwame the animal trainer plucked a sultry tune on a lyre, a small harp. Nina was already there listening attentively, but she wasn't the only one. The cats had stopped playing and sat, still as stone, transfixed by the music.

"Teach me to play like that!" Nina pleaded.

"No, child," Kwame chided. "It's a special technique, a Matungo family secret, you know." He leaned forward. "You should see what it does to the lions."

He continued to play, but through it all, Xavier's annoying voice kept buzzing in from the dining room like a persistent mosquito. When he entered the parlor blathering his opinions, it broke the spell. The cats returned to their slinking, stretching, and chasing.

"The thing about Julius Caesar..." Xavier started, "is that he's an amazing tactician. He wins every battle, even if the numbers are against him."

Oh, shut up, you big dummy! thought Xanthe. *You're supposed to be an Egyptian, and Egyptians don't like the Romans. You're supposed to be afraid they're going to take over, remember?* But now Dionysius and Agatha had joined the group, carrying in platters of cake, cheese, and fruit, and Kwame stopped playing the lyre to grab an after-dinner snack.

"And he's an amazing leader," Xavier continued. "His men will follow him to the end of the earth. He makes them feel like he is one of them. He eats what they eat, asks what they think, and leads them into battle."

"Effective leader he may be," Diego the Spanish silver merchant said, cutting himself a chunk of cheese, "but I've heard the Roman senators are nervous about his popularity and his tendency to ignore them and do whatever he pleases."

"I don't like him," Diego's wife, Isabella, added. "He is hungry for power."

"That he is," Dionysius said, licking honey off his fingers. "Did you know he was once captured by pirates and held for quite a large ransom? But he was fearless. In fact, he joked with them! He ordered them around like servants and told

them that when he was released he would have them all exe-
cuted. Now *that* is nerve!"

"You've left out the best part of the story," Kwame broke
in. "After the ransom came through, he left the island,
immediately gathered some local soldiers, and returned to
capture those pirates. Then he crucified them. Every one."
The cinnamon-colored cat uttered a plaintive yowl as if in
response to this, and the group laughed.

As the conversation continued, Agatha slid up to Xanthe
and motioned to her to follow her out. Xanthe nodded, then
touched Rowan's hand lightly to get his attention.

"I'm going to the alleviator now," she whispered. "You
want to come?"

Rowan hesitated. "I want to hear this conversation. You'll
be okay, won't you?"

"Yeah," Xanthe muttered. "I'll be just fine."

In the hallway, Agatha handed her a satchel. "Go directly
to the Temple of Isis. You don't want to be caught with these
scrolls."

Xanthe grabbed the satchel and bolted out the door. She
couldn't wait to leave. She was so angry she was almost in
tears. It was happening again: Xavier was stealing her friends.

He'd done it before in third grade, when they still attended
public school. Her friend Melanie had come over to play and
Xavier would not leave them alone, pestering the girls to be in
a movie he wanted to film. Melanie sparked to the idea. She
and Xavier wrote a script. Xavier was the director and
Melanie was the star. Xanthe had three lines. After that,

Melanie made several more movies with Xavier, some of which were shown in class. Xanthe wasn't in any of them.

Now he had his sights on Rowan, and she couldn't bear it. First he won her trophy, then he invaded her adventure, and now he was stealing Rowan. It was really too much.

By the time she got to the temple, she was sobbing out loud. She leaped up the steps, taking them two at a time, and ran through the colonnade to the center. There sat Isis on her throne—a stunning statue, three times the size of a normal human being.

I wish I could be that wise and powerful, Xanthe thought. *Then I would look serene, too.*

Xanthe felt for her alleviator key to make sure she still had it. She found it safe in a hidden pocket of her *kalasiris.* Agatha said Gertrude had arranged for an alleviator to meet her here. She wondered if Gertrude had pressed the button, then jumped out before the doors closed. That cheered her up, imagining Gertrude springing through the alleviator doors like a grasshopper.

Xanthe detected a shimmer in the air, and in the next moment the alleviator appeared. She stepped inside, pressed the return button, and disappeared from the temple.

+ CHAPTER EIGHT +
ISIS INCARNATE

Xanthe came out of the dizzying vortex sprawled on the floor of the alleviator. The doors opened, and her eyes fastened on a pair of boots, then dark brown corduroy pants, then a black turtleneck, and finally met Gertrude's fierce gaze.

"Are you all right?"

"Sure," Xanthe said quickly. "I just lost my balance." She scrambled to her feet.

"You look upset."

"I'm fine." Xanthe put her hurt feelings aside for the moment. They suddenly seemed foolish. Gertrude's manner had that effect, snapping you into shape as if she were a school principal.

The old woman turned without a word and strode down the hallway. Xanthe shuffled after her as quickly as her dress would allow, but stopped when they reached the lobby of the

Owatannauk Hotel. It had been newly decorated for a party, what looked like an autumn festival.

A steady stream of people flowed in from a side door, past sumptuous bouquets and columns lined with gold, orange, and maroon streamers. Ladies decked out in silk gowns, looking like frothy ice cream desserts, swished by with their escorts. Otto directed them down the hall, where strains of a waltz could be heard. Nobody gave Xanthe a second glance, as though seeing a person in Egyptian dress was as normal as seeing a glass of water. Curious, she started to follow them.

"Xanthe."

"Aunt Gertrude, is it a wedding? Can I please take a look—just for a second?"

"I'm afraid not. Some areas of the Owatannauk are off-limits to all except the overnight guests." By "overnight guests," Xanthe figured she meant the hotel phantoms. "Come, we don't have much time. I expected you a little earlier."

Xanthe followed Gertrude behind the reception desk. The old woman produced a set of keys from her pocket that resembled the alleviator keys, except that they were silver instead of gold.

"There is a good chance I won't be here when you make your deliveries," Gertrude said. "So you need to know how to get into the vault." Gertrude took a step toward the mailboxes and suddenly disappeared. Xanthe blinked, startled, and rushed forward, running headlong into a wall. With a thud, she fell to the floor. In an instant, Gertrude reappeared.

"I'm sorry about that, Xanthe," she said, helping her up. "As you know, Archibald Weber built a lot of...shall we say, 'puzzles' into the hotel. This wall isn't a wall, it's a mirror. Two mirrors, actually, angled to reflect that corner." Gertrude pointed.

Xanthe nodded, rubbing her forehead. "A wall that isn't a wall." She sighed. "Figures." She timidly put one hand on the wall-mirror, half expecting the floor to fall out from under her.

"The room I'm going to take you to is a secret," Gertrude said. "There are reasons it is kept hidden."

Her interest piqued, Xanthe followed Gertrude behind the mirror and found herself in a maze of reflections. She and Gertrude had been multiplied a hundredfold.

"The way you get through this mirror maze is to keep your eyes on the floor so you're not distracted by the reflections," Gertrude said. "Put your hand on the left wall and move counterclockwise. Archie's favorite pattern is a spiral. You go first, so you get a feel for it."

This was not as easy as it sounded. Xanthe started out looking at the floor but soon yielded to temptation and started glancing up at her image, admiring her lean figure from twenty different angles, then aimlessly wandered around to find new views of herself, forgetting what it was she was supposed to be doing. She turned one corner and saw Gertrude scowling from fifty different angles, and she quickly went back to scanning the floor, but it was too late. She'd lost the path. Gertrude found her and brought her back to the beginning. After three more attempts, Xanthe finally mustered enough self-control to make it to the thick, rough-hewn door at the end of the maze.

"Sorry." Xanthe blushed. "I can't pick up a spoon without looking at myself in it."

"Vanity is a common vice," Gertrude said. "People are so focused on themselves they lose their sense of direction. Archie understood human nature, you see. That's why I'm certain this room is safe."

The room behind the door was pitch-black, except for a bank of bright lights on the opposite wall. As Xanthe's eyes adjusted, she realized that the lights were, in fact, hundreds of small television monitors. As she drew closer to them, she realized that each monitor showed a different room in the hotel or on the grounds. Every few seconds the screens flickered, revealing new angles. There was the boathouse, the tennis courts, the cabanas by the pool. Below that were the kitchen, the laundry room, the alleviators. Another group of monitors showed what seemed to be the bedrooms. Now Xanthe found the lobby, where the party guests moved through the hallway right into the next monitor, which showed the ballroom. There the party guests waltzed on the dance floor, moving in patterns like a human kaleidoscope.

"This is where I work," Gertrude said quietly.

Xanthe jerked out of her reverie. "Is this the security room?" The low hum of the monitors made her feel as if she was in the brain of the building, and she was looking through its eyes.

"Yes. Perhaps you're wondering why there are so many cameras stationed around the hotel. There are over a thousand, you know."

"As a matter of fact, there are one thousand three hundred and fifty cameras positioned around the resort," announced a familiar voice with a gentle country twang. The chair in front of the monitors twirled around. Xanthe jumped.

It was Otto. She glanced up at the monitor that showed the partygoers. There he was on the screen, still showing guests into the ballroom. Now she was more certain than ever that he was a robot. The question was, how many Ottos were there?

"Xanthe, this is the hotel safe," Gertrude said, leading her to a large, heavy-looking silver door with a wheel in the center. "Otto? If you please..." Otto joined her and they each produced a set of silver keys. When they inserted their keys into the locks and turned them together, the entire wall groaned, and a low rumble shook the floor. The noise stopped, and Gertrude turned the wheel until she heard a loud click. Then she pulled the door open, releasing a hiss of air.

The contents of the safe looked like booty from a pirate's cave. Thrones of gold encrusted with gems were shoved next to chests of jewelry, crowns, gleaming platters, and goblets, all carved from precious metals. There was all manner of weaponry with intricately decorated blades, and these were piled next to racks and racks of fancy robes, capes, and silk carpets. Paintings were stacked against a far wall. And then there were large glass jars of what seemed to be medicine or spices that recalled Nana's mysterious pantry.

"Wow, look at all this stuff," Xanthe said, picking up a large silver goblet covered in ancient runes, which, for all she knew, could be the Holy Grail. "Is everything in this safe yours?"

"Yes and no," said Gertrude. "Otto...?"

"The hotel safe consists of a series of vaults on a conveyor belt behind an indestructible door," Otto said. "My key starts the belt; the member's key tells the mechanism which vault to place before the doors. That way, each member has access to his or her vault alone. Only frequent fliers at the Platinum Level qualify for a vault."

"But why do you need all of this protection?" Xanthe asked. "You have tons of stuff just like this sitting in your curio shop, and all that's protecting it is a layer of dust."

Gertrude folded her arms.

Xanthe spoke quickly, hoping to cover the fact that she had probably offended her. "If somebody wanted to steal something, they wouldn't have to come here."

"We're not worried about trespassers, Xanthe. The security measures are for the phantoms."

"The phantoms?"

"Yes. The hotel guests that you've seen during the golden and silver hours. Not all of them are honest. Or friendly, for that matter. Still, this is the best place to keep our...shall we call them treasures? As long as they are in the hotel, they are immune from the effects of aging. Time works differently here, you know. It's like keeping a toy in its original packaging to retain its value. We like to keep items as close to their original condition as we can before delivering them to our clients." Gertrude unlocked a leather chest, pushed open the lid, and pulled out a metal cylinder. "You can put the manuscripts here. Put each scroll in its own tube. They seal up airtight for protection."

Xanthe removed the three manuscripts from the satchel, placed each in a tube, and shut the lid of the chest.

"It's *that* easy," Gertrude said, leading her back into the main room. She handed her the silver key to the vault, as well as the key to the chest. "Keep these safe. I'm trusting you."

Xanthe took the keys.

As Otto shut the door and turned the wheel, she noticed an area off to the side of the monitors that was even darker than the rest of the room. She craned her neck, trying to get a better look.

"That is my personal workstation." Gertrude said. "It's where I go to find clues for tracking down time travelers who have gotten in trouble." Gertrude hesitated. "Would you like to see it?"

"Yes, please."

Gertrude cocked her head for a moment, gave a slight nod, then motioned for Xanthe to follow her. Xanthe was only a few feet behind her, but when the old woman disappeared into the darkness she felt immediately lost. Xanthe stumbled forward, listening for footsteps, but they were muted by the carpeting. She whirled around in a panic, searching for the light of Otto's security monitors, but they, too, had disappeared, no doubt behind another wall that wasn't a wall.

Xanthe wasn't sure if she should stay put, lest she trip over something, or charge forward until she crashed—at least then she might have some clue that would help her identify her surroundings. She decided to yell instead.

"Aunt Gertrude! Where are you?!"

"I'm right next to you." Indeed the voice was so close Xanthe could've been sitting in Gertrude's lap.

"Is there any light in here?"

"Light is distracting."

"How can anyone do anything worthwhile in the dark?" Xanthe sputtered. She was getting tired of constantly being thrown into disorienting circumstances.

"I'll show you how." Xanthe felt Gertrude's firm hand on her shoulder, pressing her forward, then stopping her. An object was placed before her, a swivel chair, and she took a seat. She felt herself being wheeled several feet, then after a left-hand turn, she came to a stop.

"Put your hands down and tell me what you feel," Gertrude said.

"I feel...stupid."

"Xanthe."

"Why can't we just turn on the lights? Using your eyes is so much easier."

"Reach out and tell me what's in front of you."

Xanthe stretched her hands in front of her, fingers spread wide. They hit a flat surface, which felt smooth, like polished wood. Soon they found a knob, which she turned. It clicked six times before it stopped. A dial. Then she found another dial, and another. Fourteen in all. In front of each dial was a push-button. She described all of this to Gertrude in detail.

"Why don't you try pushing one of those buttons?" Gertrude suggested.

Xanthe did. Suddenly voices surrounded her on all sides. She was so startled she nearly fell off the chair.

"Where are we?" Xanthe cried. "Aunt Gertrude! Are you still there?"

"Don't worry, Xanthe." Gertrude said, apparently standing right behind her. "Just listen."

She did. It became clear to her that the room was not, in fact, filled with people. The voices sounded amplified, as though coming through a speaker. One voice sounded louder than the others—a woman, speaking Italian. Xanthe turned the dial, and now the woman's voice became fainter, though still audible. Then a man spoke, also faintly, also in Italian, and then the woman again, and now the loudest voice was a second man, who seemed to ask something of the first man. There were background noises as well, clinking glasses, footsteps, and the low rumble of conversations sprinkled now and then with laughter. Xanthe turned the dial again, and discovered the first click amplified the woman's voice, the second click the man's, and the last four clicks had no sound at all.

She became so absorbed in what she was doing, she forgot about Gertrude. In the darkness, her mind's eye formed an image. In a few seconds, a full-blown scene unfolded in her head.

"We're in a restaurant in Italy!" Xanthe exclaimed gleefully.

"There's a man and a woman at a table, ordering food from a waiter!"

Before Gertrude could say anything, Xanthe jabbed the button under the next dial.

The sound of grass rustling. Low conversation in a language Xanthe couldn't recognize. More footfalls, swishing grass, and then the loudest voice, a man saying something, ordering people around. Then giggles of children and a lot of laughing and shrieking and running. Water in the background. A river.

"Let me guess. We're in a jungle and the man is in a village with a bunch of kids who are bothering him."

"Very good, Xanthe. It seems you've got a knack for this."

"So this is how you figure out where people are? You listen to them?"

"Well, I start with their drop-off point, of course. That information in the alleviator log is kept on a need-to-know basis, but it's always available to me. But after that, this is all I have. There are fourteen dials, one for each alleviator, including the freight alleviators. Each dial has six stops, one for each person, six being the maximum number of people allowed on any one trip. The alleviator keys are 'bugged' so to speak. They broadcast back to this room, and through the speakers that surround us."

"So your job is to eavesdrop on everybody?"

"Good lord, no. After all, everyone has a right to their privacy. Remember, people travel back in time for any number of reasons, some of which can be quite...delicate. If I misinterpret something, and bumble in at the wrong moment, it could be disastrous. But if somebody does need help, I come here and listen for clues. That's why there's no light; I can't be distracted. I need to hear everything—any sound could be helpful. I have headphones here that work like the translators from the library, but oddly enough I get the most useful information listening to the background noise. Once I've narrowed down my field here, I can usually find the person I'm looking for visually by using the globe. I have one that's a bit larger than the one you've used in the alleviator, but it's identical in every other way."

"But how do you know if somebody's in trouble if you aren't listening?" Xanthe asked.

"I *am* listening. Just not to their voices." Gertrude did something to adjust the sound, turning down the volume on the man's voice and the shrieking children. As she did, another sound emerged. The thumping of a dull drum. It took Xanthe only a moment to realize that it was the sound of a heartbeat.

"The key picks up any sudden change in vital functions," Gertrude said. "Like a lie detector. If there is a change in heartbeat, breathing, sweat production, or body temperature, a signal is sent that registers here, at my station, which Otto can also pick up at his station. He calls me, and I start to investigate. Or, as you say, 'eavesdrop.' It's a judgment call. I have a feel for when to jump in, and when to stay out." She pressed the button, turning off the heartbeat. "We're running out of time," she said. "Take my hand. I'll lead you out."

Gertrude brought Xanthe back into the main part of the

security room. "The quickest way to the alleviators is through that passage. It'll drop you at the other end of the hallway." She pointed at an ordinary-looking door. "There's another mirror maze on the other side of it, but just remember to walk in a spiral, only this time, move clockwise."

"Why is there a puzzle to leave?"

"Because my dear, sometimes it is easier to get into something than to get out."

As soon as Xanthe left, Gertrude hurried back to her station and turned on the lights, illuminating the room, the console which Xanthe had explored, and the huge, elephant-sized globe which she had completely missed, as well as the eight people sitting behind it.

"Oh, my!"

"You've blinded us!"

"Give us some warning, Gertrude!"

The members of the Board rubbed their eyes and blinked until their eyes grew accustomed to the light.

"I'm sorry," Gertrude said. "But the golden hour is almost over. Some of you will want to be getting back."

"I have to admit, she's good," Albert Einstein said, getting to his feet. "Quite perceptive."

"Perceptive?" Madame Curie scoffed. "She couldn't tell we were in the room, even though the mayor's sinuses were whistling like a teakettle!"

"I'm sorry," Mayor Silverstrini wheezed. "I'm nearly eighty-four years old. I'm happy to be breathing at all."

"You all overheard her when she was still in Alexandria," Captain Morgan said, rubbing his whiskers. "When her brother showed up, she shut down. They're children, Gertrude. They act like children."

"I *need* children, Captain Morgan. *These* children," Gertrude said.

"I need more information," Thomas Edison said. "Let's not make up our minds quite yet."

Finally in agreement, four of the directors quickly left the room through a trapdoor to a passageway that led directly to the alleviators.

Xanthe landed back in the Temple of Isis in a daze. Her head ached a little from too much information, like guzzling an ice-cold Slurpee on a hot day. Brain freeze.

She strolled through the large hall, past the statue of Isis. Fire from the recently lit torches illuminated the walls with a flickering light that made the pictures seem to move. There was Isis, married to her brother, Osiris, ruling all of Egypt. Farther along the wall, jealous Seth, their brother, locking Osiris in a chest, setting it adrift on the Nile. Now Isis finds him, brings him back to Egypt, and Seth flies into a rage. He tears Osiris's body into fourteen pieces and throws them into the river for the crocodiles to eat. Farther down, a distraught Isis searches for the pieces, finds all but one, and puts her brother back together. Into his body she breathes life, but with one piece missing, Osiris is consigned to the underworld, to forever be known as Lord of the Dead.

Xanthe heard a sharp cry. She spun around and locked eyes with a girl, not twenty feet away, who quickly dropped to one knee, bowing her head.

"I honor you, Goddess, and thank you for coming in my hour of need."

Xanthe groaned quietly. This was bad. Obviously this girl had seen her walk out of the alleviator. It must have looked as if she appeared magically out of nowhere. And now the girl had mistaken her for Isis. Xanthe drew herself up, not sure what else to do but play the part.

"You are most welcome," Xanthe said haughtily, trying to sound goddess-like.

The girl kept her head lowered, but peered curiously at Xanthe just the same. "I did not expect you to be so...young. You look not much older than me."

"I appear in many forms," Xanthe said. "This form pleases me for now." The girl nodded slowly, and Xanthe plowed forward. "And who may I ask has summoned me from the heavens?"

The girl lifted her head, her large brown eyes gazing beseechingly at Xanthe. "I am Princess Cleopatra," she said. "I need your help desperately."

CHAPTER NINE

NOT DEAD YET

"I THOUGHT YOU WERE DEAD!" XANTHE SQUEALED, in a distinctly un-goddess-like manner.

Cleopatra jumped to her feet. "What do you mean? Do you see my future? Will my sister murder me?"

Xanthe paused, choosing her words carefully. "I received news that Princess Cleopatra had disappeared. Is that not true?"

The girl gave a sad sort of laugh. "Ah, yes. Cleopatra Tryphaena, the sixth Cleopatra, was my older sister. She's gone, and nobody can find her."

Cleopatra the Sixth? thought Xanthe. *So this must be Cleopatra the Seventh. Those Ptolemies sure weren't very creative about coming up with names for their kids.* But her heart lifted, for Cleopatra, the historically important Cleopatra, was very much alive and standing right in front of her.

"She's dead, though. I know she is." Cleopatra sighed.

"Berenice isn't even trying to find her. She just smirks and watches me like a cat watching a locust. I'm next. That's why I've come to you, oh, exalted one."

The young Cleopatra threw herself prostrate in front of Xanthe. Instinctively, Xanthe reached down to comfort her, but Agatha's warning rang in the back of her head and she pulled her hand back.

Don't interact with famous people. Agatha had said it more than once. Did being worshiped as a God by a future queen break that rule? Most certainly. But at this moment, when she looked at Cleopatra she didn't see a queen, she saw a scared little kid who needed help.

Xanthe gently placed her hand on Cleopatra's shoulder, bidding her to rise. As she did, Xanthe could see in the princess's eyes a strength and intelligence that was electrifying. Berenice had every reason to feel threatened by her.

"Don't worry," Xanthe said. "You have nothing to fear from your sister." She thought she could say that much.

"But I can't eat without worrying my food is poisoned! I can't walk without thinking I'll be pulled into a dark corner and strangled! Every night I check my bed for snakes!" Cleopatra's jaw tightened as she looked away. "I wish my father was here. The sound of his voice and his flute are a great comfort to me. He is the only one who truly understands me."

"And he has been banished," Xanthe said, recalling Dionysius's criticism of the troubled flute-playing ruler, Ptolemy Auletes.

"He'll be back."

"Yes, he will," Xanthe murmured, almost unconsciously. "And you will be queen."

"You see this?" Cleopatra's eyes widened.

"I see it." Now the alarm blaring in Xanthe's head had been joined by wailing sirens and a voice through a bullhorn urging, *Step away from the princess! Step away from the princess!* She ignored them all, mentally pulling the plug on her early warning system. Later on, she would come to realize that this was the turning point, the fork in the road where she'd taken a wrong turn. But for now, her head was quiet, and she relaxed.

After all, what was the big deal? Cleopatra really was going to be queen—it didn't matter if Xanthe told her or not. "I see it, but you must still take care," Xanthe added. "Do not challenge your sister. Do not anger her. You are not truly safe until your father returns."

"I will do as you say," Cleopatra said. "And I thank you." Cleopatra bowed and started to leave, then turned suddenly. Her large dark eyes were like tractor beams, drawing Xanthe in; she was ensnared.

"Will I see you again?" Cleopatra said.

Xanthe took a deep breath and prayed for guidance.

By the time Xanthe returned to the inn, the beer-and-cake party was just breaking up. She tried to slip upstairs without being noticed, but Agatha caught her midway up the flight.

"I was beginning to worry about you."

"Sorry. I took my time coming back. I visited the lighthouse," Xanthe said, not untruthfully.

"I don't blame you. This city grows on you after a while. The longer you're here, the longer you want to stay. I believe you are under its spell."

Xanthe laughed nervously and faked a yawn. "Well, time for bed," she said quickly. She shuffled up the rest of the staircase, then, once out of sight, flew to her room. She didn't know if Agatha could truly read minds or not, but now was not the time to find out. Rowan came up a few moments later.

"How'd it go, Slim?" he growled like a mobster. "Did you make the drop?"

"Mission accomplished," Xanthe growled back. Then she laughed. "Gertrude was right there, and she took me into the coolest room."

"The security room?"

"Yes," Xanthe said, a little disappointed that she hadn't been the first one back there. But Rowan hadn't seen the vault or visited Gertrude's station, so she told him all about them and showed him the silver key Gertrude had given her.

"Cool," Rowan said, rolling it in his hand. "It's weird. Every time you turn a corner at the Owatannauk, something new pops out at you."

"Yeah, either that or you run into it."

"I wish I had time to explore it more."

"I know. Me, too." Talking to Rowan again felt good. An idea twinkled in the corner of her mind. She could tell Rowan about her big discovery—that Cleopatra was alive. It could be their secret, binding them together and leaving Xavier in the dark. She might even tell him about her brilliant plan.

But the idea dimmed almost immediately. Rowan was a good friend, but not a good receptacle for a secret. For one thing, he was too honest. He'd want to tell Xavier and Nina, and if he did, they'd want to follow her, or worse, try to talk her out of it.

So she couldn't tell Rowan. Which meant that now, as much as she hated to do it, she had to get him out of her room before he figured out she was hiding something. She faked another yawn and rubbed her eyes.

"Boy, I am wiped out," she said. "I think I'm going to go to sleep. If you see Xave, tell him not to make a lot of noise when he comes in here."

"Oh. Okay." Rowan seemed surprised that she was kicking him out. She was surprised herself, but she did need to get some rest. She had an appointment to keep at the silver hour.

But after Rowan left, she couldn't relax. So she waited. And watched. She washed her face and slipped into the linen nightdress that Miss O'Neill had packed in her bag. When Xavier came in a half hour later, she closed her eyes just enough to peer at him through the slits. She breathed heavily, snorting a few times for a truly convincing effect. Soon Xavier's own measured breathing joined hers and she stopped.

She leaned on the window ledge and her gaze followed the moon as it crept across the sky. She wouldn't have thought it possible, but it was surprising how patient you could be if you had to. Finally, the color of night softened and she quickly dressed and reapplied her makeup. Walking lightly on the floorboards, she slipped down the stairs and out onto the street.

It was unbelievable, really, how prayers could be answered. Almost as soon as Cleopatra asked the question, *Will I see you again?*, an idea had flown into Xanthe's head. No, it didn't fly in exactly. It had been silently growing there, germinating, waiting for just the right moment to spring forth in all of its genius. It was not a good idea, she knew that much, but it was a very good *bad* idea.

Cleopatra needed a friend. Xanthe, or rather, Isis, could be that friend. After all, historically Cleopatra had always felt close to the Goddess Isis. Xanthe wouldn't be hurting that relationship at all; if anything, she was strengthening it. She *had* agreed not to interact with famous people, but that was before she knew that she and Cleopatra were soulmates. She could feel it; a special energy radiating between them. They had discovered each other through two millennia, against all reasonable odds. It would be a cosmic injustice to keep them apart.

Will I see you again?

You will see me in four years and a day, Xanthe had answered, looking ahead to 54 B.C. At that time, Cleopatra would be fourteen, Xanthe's age. *Meet me here at the hour of silver, just before Ra, the sun God, awakens the world.*

With that, Xanthe had stepped into the alleviator and shut the door. It would seem to Cleopatra that she had vanished into thin air. She didn't press any of the buttons, she just waited and crossed her fingers, hoping the golden hour wouldn't end before Cleopatra left the temple.

A minute passed. Then two, then five. The alleviator's hum grew fainter, the walls faded, and Xanthe found herself in the now-empty temple. She hurried down the steps in time to see the sky glowing a dark, burnished orange.

Xanthe couldn't bring herself to be among the others quite yet. She needed to think.

As she wandered the coastline of the island, she was drawn to the lighthouse. As she went inside, the smell of mule dung pinched her nose, but she was barely aware of it. She drifted up the ramp that wound around the walls, passing an observation deck on the second level. Tourists anxious to see the view of the sunset crowded the area, but Xanthe sought solitude, so upward she went.

She reached the less popular second observation deck and grasped the railing. On one side of her lay the darkening sea, the roar of its waves filling her ears. On the other burned the fire in the pergola, the dome holding the large curved mirror that reflected the flame, focusing it into a ray of salvation to sailors. The intense heat scorched her, but she barely felt it. She was hardly connected to reality anymore—she'd been lifted to another level.

The golden and silver hours held the answer. An hour wasn't much time, but it was enough for a visit. At the silver hour, she could sneak out while everyone else was asleep. At the golden hour, she could quickly make her manuscript drop at the Owatannauk. Then she could use both magic hours to travel ahead in time and visit Cleopatra. In that way, she would see the princess during different stages of her life, each a few years apart, watch her grow up and become queen, and be her adviser, her confidante, her friend.

Of course she would be careful and only reveal harmless information to Cleopatra, just enough to maintain her disguise as a Goddess. Gertrude wouldn't catch her because she wouldn't have any reason to tune in and listen. Xanthe's vital functions wouldn't be affected by a few harmless conversations.

The waters were getting darker and Xanthe strained to see beyond the ray of the lighthouse beacon, the wind whistling to her like a master to a dog.

That had happened only twelve hours ago, though it felt longer. Now, as Xanthe arrived at the temple at the silver hour, the alleviator shimmered before the statue.

The trip was almost instantaneous—just a bright flash, but no swirling, no dizziness, no vertigo. She wondered if she'd even gone anywhere until she stepped through the doors and was immediately greeted by the fourteen-year-old princess.

"Oh, great Goddess, I am most pleased to see you again," Cleopatra said, dropping to one knee. Xanthe tapped her on the shoulder.

"Rise, Cleopatra, for we are friends."

Cleopatra rose to her full height. She was slightly taller than Xanthe, but gangly. Her nose had lost its pertness, and now sloped in a noble curve. It occurred to Xanthe that Cleopatra's reputation for being a great beauty was based not so much on her physical appearance, but on her mesmerizing personality.

"I have but an hour. Tell me of your life. Your father has returned?"

"Yes, he is back! With help from the Romans and their General Pompey, he has returned. We celebrated for days, with a most amazing feast!" She started to say something, but stopped, her lips pulled into a tight grin.

"There is something else you want to tell me? Speak freely, Princess. I judge you not," Xanthe said, trying not to sound too eager.

Cleopatra lowered her eyes as a rush of blood came to her cheeks. "A young man caught my attention. He commanded a force under General Gabinius of the Roman army. He is . . . very handsome."

"Really? What was he like?" Xanthe said. Even if she didn't know any of these people, she couldn't resist hearing some good gossip.

"Dark hair, dark eyes, a well-balanced face," Cleopatra said wistfully. "A broad smile and a hearty laugh. But he caught my eye not for his looks, but for what he did at the feast."

"And what was that?"

"It's difficult to explain. We served the Romans many courses, with sweetened wine and many varieties of pastry for dessert. They all took their fill, but this man . . . he smelled the food before he put it in his mouth, and afterward, licked his fingers. Then, as the music began, he lay back on the couch and closed his eyes. First he tapped his finger, then his foot. Soon his whole body was moving. My father picked up his flute and began to play, dancing around our guest like the God Pan himself. I nearly cried, it lifted my heart so! Most of the Romans looked at my father as though he were mad, but not this man. Truly, I think if it weren't for the other soldiers, he would've joined my father's dance. He is a man who knows how to enjoy life. I asked about him. His name is Marcus Antonius."

Xanthe raised her eyebrows. Marcus Antonius, also known as Mark Antony, would figure prominently in Cleopatra's future; a man with whom she was destined to fall in love and bear children. His death would leave her unprotected against Roman imperialism, spurring her decision to kill herself. Xanthe hoped Cleopatra wasn't looking for advice; she couldn't risk saying anything about this man. He was too important.

Fortunately, Cleopatra provided her own answer. "He is not for me," she continued. "I am next in line for the throne. My marriage is already decided."

"And Berenice?" Xanthe said. "What happened to her?"

"She's been rewarded for her treasonous behavior. My father relieved her of the throne, as well as her head."

Xanthe shuddered. *Those Ptolemies sure hand down some harsh punishments. And I thought being grounded for a week was bad.*

Suddenly Cleopatra's eyes brightened. "It is early yet. Can you leave the temple?"

Xanthe nodded. "But I must return within the hour."

"Come with me. There is something I must show you!"

Cleopatra skipped down the stairs and ran along the shore, turning every now and then to make sure Xanthe was following. Xanthe's dignified stride turned into a light jog, and soon she was gathering up her dress and running after the princess, kicking up sand in her wake.

At the farthest point of Pharos Island, a small wooden skiff rocked in the water. Though compact, it was built with exquisite craftsmanship, decorated with bright colors, and fitted with soft, burgundy cushions.

"This is my boat," Cleopatra said, motioning for Xanthe to step inside. The princess loosened the rope and the boat drifted into the bay. "I love boats. They're never still. You're always going somewhere."

"I know what you mean," Xanthe murmured. The water rippled away from the bow as they glided across the dark, velvety bay.

"Do you?" Cleopatra laughed. "Then you're the first. Nobody understands me, except perhaps my father. Certainly none of the girls my age. 'Why do you always have your nose in a scroll?' they say. 'Why are you forever studying? Can't you relax and have fun?'"

"Studying is fun," Xanthe scoffed. She'd heard these same comments from her classmates before she left school. She couldn't understand why anyone would consider learning to be a chore. To her it was what made life worth living. She could spend hours in a library—and often did, going from one section to the next, picking out books on subjects she'd never even heard of and devouring them like a starving man with a steak dinner.

After sailing under the Heptastadion causeway, they headed into a canal that flowed south through Alexandria. Torches cast pools of light against the stone buildings. Once in a while they would see an early riser with a task or a journey to start, but no one noticed them. The houses they passed were much different from those around Dionysius's inn. They were smaller, with no windows. From the few people she saw, Xanthe realized that they were in an Egyptian neighborhood. *Just like a modern city,* she thought. *Everybody split up into different ghettos. The Greeks, the Egyptians, the Jews . . . Some things never change.*

"Where are you taking me?" Xanthe asked. It didn't really matter. She'd go anywhere Cleopatra wanted to go.

"We are in Rhakotis, where the Egyptians live," Cleopatra confirmed. "It was here before the Great Alexander conquered the city for the Greeks." She pointed at a modest home made of earth and stone. "There. That is what I wanted to show you. My tutor lives there. He has taught me more than all the palace tutors put together." Cleopatra's voice changed slightly, and the words came out with a harder edge. It took a moment for Xanthe to realize that Cleopatra had switched languages, from Greek to Egyptian.

"Tryphaena and Berenice didn't understand, but these are the people who give them power. Not the Greeks, not Alexander's cold corpse. It is your people, Goddess, the people of the ages. People of the earth. People who built mountains where before there were none. I love these people. They did not."

Xanthe bit hard on her back teeth to switch her translator to Egyptian. "I know," she said. "And that is why I am here with you now."

Cleopatra smiled and turned the boat around, and they headed back toward the temple.

+ CHAPTER TEN +
A NARROW ESCAPE

X ANTHE SLEPT THROUGH BREAKFAST, AND IN THAT way avoided seeing the others so soon after her clandestine operation. Her sudden gleeful mood was bound to raise suspicions. And yet it was all she could do not to click her heels and turn ten cartwheels. She and Cleopatra were friends. Friends! And she would see her again, today, at the golden hour!

Or so she thought. She hadn't counted on the holiday. Berenice, feeling generous, had declared a citywide holiday to celebrate her rise to the throne. Subsequently, the library and the marketplace were closed. Rowan couldn't get into the warehouses, so Xanthe had nothing to deliver to the Owatannauk vault. That was her only excuse for using the alleviator, so if she wanted to sneak a visit to Cleopatra at the golden hour, she needed to come up with a new one.

Meanwhile, a chariot race to mark Berenice's coronation

was being held at the hippodrome, the stadium just outside the city walls. Everyone was invited to attend. A small, select group from the inn decided to go together. Xanthe found herself trudging to the stadium with Dionysius, Kwame, Jomo, and, of course, Agatha, Rowan, Nina, and Xavier.

The lively sounding hippodrome turned out to be just a dirt track. Xanthe was disappointed to see that there were no seats—people merely stood on the mounds of soil lining the perimeter. A crowd had already gathered, so they squeezed among them to get a view.

"Well, there she is, the fool," Dionysius said, wagging a finger at the tent erected for Berenice at the far end of the track. "Take a good look. I suspect she won't be there for long."

"Why not?" Nina asked, munching on some peanuts she'd bought from a vendor.

Dionysius shrugged and cuddled the cat he'd tucked into his toga. "She's doing everything wrong. If she really cared about gaining the support of the people, she would marry her brother, Ptolemy the Thirteenth." He took one of Nina's peanuts and waved it over the cat. "Here puss-puss! Have a peanut!"

"Ptolemy the Thirteenth is only four years old," Kwame said. "He still sucks his thumb. Not much of a king for a queen of such obvious distinction."

"So? At least it would give her legitimacy. And besides, her taste in men is atrocious. That clod next to her is her boyfriend, Archilaus. A boob if I've ever seen one."

Xanthe strained to catch a glimplse of Berenice, who sat

under an awning with the rest of the royal family, the ten-year-old Cleopatra among them. Directly in front of them on the track stood a line of six chariots, each with four horses and a driver.

"Keep your eyes on the chariot driven by the youth in the green tunic," Dionysius said. "Those horses belong to my friend, Eugenia, and they never lose. Anyone care to place a bet?"

Berenice held up a white handkerchief, and a hush fell over the crowd. The only sound was the stamping of hooves and the snorting and whinnying of horses. She opened her fingers, and the cloth fluttered to the ground. The horses surged forward, a roar went up, and almost immediately Xanthe lost her view of the track as people pushed in front of her.

Xanthe squeezed back through the crowd, finally reaching an open area off the dirt mound. She plunked herself down on a large rock. She didn't care who won the race; she needed to figure out how she was going to sneak off to see Cleopatra. She couldn't wait out the festivities—this was only the first of twelve races. After that, a series of wrestling matches was scheduled in the gymnasium, and then a feast in the palace courtyard that was bound to go on all night. She needed an excuse to leave early.

But what would she say to Cleopatra once she got there? The princess would be roughly eighteen years old, not a distraught ten-year-old kid or a love-struck teen. Xanthe would have to fool one of the sharpest women in history if she was to continue the ruse of being a Goddess, and that wouldn't be easy. She rested her chin in her hands and concentrated on what her opening line would be.

Hello, Cleopatra. So we meet again. No, that sounded like something from a bad spy movie. *Cleopatra, I'm glad you could make it.* Too eager. *Yo, whassup, Queenie?* Huh? That one was terrible. She really must be tired.

Suddenly, Rowan emerged from the crowd. Xanthe waved to him and he jogged down the slope to join her. The others trailed behind him. Dionysius was collecting drachmas from both Kwame and Agatha.

"You missed a great race!"

"I just got tired of standing." She nodded at Dionysius. "I guess the guy in the green won?"

"He bumped one of the other guys. Horses flipped over each other. It wasn't pretty."

"I'm glad I missed it," Xanthe said. "I can't stand blood."

"Neither can I," said Nina, her face screwed up in disgust. "Are all the races going to be that violent?"

Dionysius laughed, dropping the drachmas into his pouch. "You think *that's* violent? You should see the Roman games. Those folks really go for the blood sport. Isn't that right, Kwame?"

"Yes, it's true." Kwame said. "Most of the animals I sell are taken to the Roman Colosseum to fight slaves. Attack slaves, really. It always ends in death. The Romans think it's very entertaining."

"That's awful," Nina said, wrinkling her nose.

Kwame shrugged. "Sometimes they just have the slaves

fight each other. If the magistrate allows it, the victor can spare the life of the loser. But if the crowd is in a bloodthirsty mood, the winner must kill the loser or die himself."

"Ugh. That's just ... just—"

"Barbaric? Yes." Dionysius said. "But those are the Romans."

"Well, I don't think you could call it barbarism, exactly..." Xavier protested. "It's a contest, that's all. A noble contest of strength and will, skill and agility."

"You've never seen one of these gladiator bouts, have you, my friend?" Dionysius said, putting his hand on Xavier's shoulder. Xavier shook his head. "There is nothing noble about it. It's just two people forced to beat and stab at each other until one cannot. We Greeks use sport to celebrate the human body. This 'entertainment' is a desecration. An abomination."

Xanthe pulled Agatha aside. "Do you mind if I go to the Owatannauk at the golden hour?" she whispered. "I have a wicked headache. I could use a couple of aspirin."

"You aren't coming down with something, are you?" Agatha said.

"No!" Xanthe assured her. One of the rules for riding the alleviators was that you had to be in good health. If you were sick, you had to terminate your trip immediately. One couldn't risk passing diseases to people who weren't immunized for them. "I'm just, you know, out of sorts," she added vaguely.

"You poor thing. Why don't you go back to the inn and take a nap? Then, if you're still feeling badly, go ahead and pick up some medicine. I hope it puts you back in the swing of things. You seem very distracted."

"I know," Xanthe said. "I've got a lot on my mind."

Xanthe really did have a lot on her mind, and it really was giving her a splitting headache. Pretending she wasn't livid over Xavier's arrival, pretending she didn't have a crush on Rowan, pretending she was a tourist for the Alexandrians, pretending she was a Goddess to Cleopatra, pretending that she wasn't the sneakiest, most underhanded person on earth to just about everybody—those were a lot of things to juggle. No wonder she was exhausted. She watched the next two races then headed back to the inn.

Xanthe tried to take a nap but couldn't get comfortable; she was too nervous about seeing Cleopatra. Also Dionysius's cats had taken over her room, sprawling on her bed, chasing lizards across the floor, curling up on the windowsill.

"Ow!" Something was yanking on her braids. One of the cats had been batting at the beads and gotten a claw caught in her hair. She scooped him up with one hand and untangled him with the other. It was the cinnamon-colored cat of course.

"You must like me," Xanthe said aloud, as he rubbed himself against her. "Well, I like you, too." She placed him in her lap, where he settled, purring like a small engine.

Xanthe was definitely a cat person. She figured that this was the reason she felt a kinship with the Egyptians and Cleopatra; fellow worshipers of feline mystery. In her mind, cat people shared an appreciation for balance—after all, cats embodied balance. Their skill in running across fence tops and landing on their feet after a fall was legendary. But there were other kinds of balance: philosophical balance, mental balance, cosmic balance.

When she'd read about the Egyptian Gods in the Owatannauk Library, she'd been utterly fascinated by the two feline Gods, Bastet and Sehkmet. The cat and the lion. One the Goddess of domesticity, family, protector of women, and the other her sister Goddess of war and pestilence. Both sides were important. Both sides had use. Cat people understood this.

Cats also possess an intelligence far superior to most animals, in Xanthe's view. That's why some people were so intimidated by them. Cats have minds of their own; they don't live to please others but only to satisfy themselves. They have independent souls and calculating minds. They watch, they analyze . . . and then they strike.

By the time Xanthe arrived in 50 b.c., she had figured out what she was going to say to the eighteen-year-old Cleopatra. It was a pretty good speech, if she did say so herself, but when the alleviator doors opened, she forgot every word.

Cleopatra wore an elaborate headdress with a golden cobra head curling from its center. Two thick plates etched to resemble vulture's wings sloped toward her ears, pressing against the hundreds of dark, beaded braids in her wig. Her golden collar, decorated with blue and red glass, lay heavily against her gauzy, white *kalasiris*. Wrapped around her like a silken cocoon was a light blue robe, which shimmered from the silver thread woven into the fabric. Bracelets circled her arms like thin snakes, and on her feet were golden sandals. There was no sign of her former awkwardness; this was an Egyptian queen.

Egyptian queen. Cleopatra was dressed in Egyptian attire, not to intimidate Xanthe, but to appease Isis. This was a good sign. Xanthe stepped out of the alleviator.

"Oh, mighty Goddess, I am overjoyed at your arrival," Cleopatra announced.

"Queen Cleopatra," Xanthe said, trying to keep her voice even. "You honor me with your devotion. I am much pleased." *Well! Thank goodness I came up with something decent to say!* Xanthe thought. She noticed that Cleopatra had the same needy look in her eye as she'd had when she was ten. Something was wrong.

"You look troubled, Cleopatra."

"The Nile did not rise this year as it should have," Cleopatra answered. "We had a disappointing harvest. The people blame me, for to them, I am the Goddess on earth. I don't know what to do to increase our food supply, except appeal to you."

"I will do what I can," Xanthe said. "But I sense there is something else bothering you."

Cleopatra sighed. "When my father died, I became queen and married my brother, Ptolemy the Thirteenth. But he is a twelve-year-old brat, with no sense for governing. What's worse, he's guided by his Regency Council, three cunning and ambitious men who would just as soon see me dead as have me as their ruler. They are always spying on me ."

Xanthe nodded solemnly, but was barely listening. She was

marveling at Cleopatra's confidence. She hoped she could be that together when she was eighteen.

"Ptolemy is so irritating!" Cleopatra continued. "He makes no effort at all to learn politics, geography, rhetoric, literature, or mathematics. Truly I think his only interest is athletics. We couldn't be more different. I speak Greek, Latin, Ethiopian, Hebrew, Aramaic, Syriac, Median, and Parthian. He speaks only Greek, and that he speaks badly. And yet I'm supposed to consult him on matters of finance and law? It's absurd! Do you know what it is like to have to share everything with an imbecile?"

"I sure do," Xanthe said. She immediately regretted it.

"But your brother is Osiris," Cleopatra protested. "You have the perfect relationship of brother and sister, husband and wife. It is what we rulers of Egypt have strived for in our marriages. And your love for him is legendary. Surely you are not referring to the great God Osiris."

"The legends don't always tell the whole story," Xanthe muttered. Just then, she heard the echo of footsteps on the stone tile. She quickly backed into the alleviator.

"I do not wish to be seen by others," Xanthe said, pressing the button. Just before the alleviator door slid shut, she caught a glimpse of the gaunt figure who had just entered the hall. His red robe hung loosely over his stooped back. Greasy black ringlets slithered down his neck and his face bore makeup spread as thick as peanut butter.

"Who was that you were talking to, my Queen?" Xanthe heard him ask from behind the closed door.

"No one," Cleopatra spat back.

"Really?" His voice was thin and high, like an old woman's. "You are awfully dressed up for 'no one.'"

"What are you doing here, Photinus? Shouldn't you be tutoring the king? He knows as much as a flea!"

"Don't belittle my skills, Cleopatra," Photinus hissed. "And as for why I'm here, part of my job is knowing what the enemies of the king are up to, at all times. Even if the enemy is his sister."

"Does that include interrupting my prayers? Can I not even have a private moment with the Gods?"

Xanthe heard some muttering which she couldn't make out. Then she heard Cleopatra again, but her tone had sweetened.

"Please. A few more minutes, Photinus. Perhaps we judge each other too harshly. But it was my father's will, and the will of the people, that Ptolemy and I work together. I ask only for a few more minutes alone for prayer. I must honor those who are greater than we. They are watching, you know."

There was a long pause, and more muttering. Then Photinus growled, "Do as you wish. These Egyptian temples leave me cold, but if you like babbling nonsense to their Gods, so be it."

Xanthe could hear the sound of his footsteps get fainter as he departed from the temple. As soon as she was pretty sure he was gone, she emerged from the alleviator. She could see through the pillars that the sky was darkening outside. The golden hour was almost over.

"Well done, Cleopatra," Xanthe said.

"That was Photinus, the head of the Regency Council. Now you see what I'm up against."

Xanthe wanted to stay longer, but time was growing short. "I must depart," she said, stepping back into the alleviator and reaching for the button.

"Wait! Don't leave me, I need you!" Cleopatra cried. Xanthe hesitated, then stepped back out.

"Too much time passes between your visits," Cleopatra said, almost whispering. "Why must you be gone so long?"

"I wish I could be here all the time, I really do." Xanthe sighed. "But I can't. My life is . . . complicated." She saw a deep disappointment in Cleopatra's eyes. It made Xanthe feel like a traitor, like she was abandoning her best friend. She put a firm hand on Cleopatra's shoulder, trying to convey her love and solidarity, then stepped back into the alleviator. "I must go."

"Then tell me," Cleopatra pleaded. "How can I rule effectively with my idiot brother and his Council holding me back?"

Xanthe thought for a moment, then remembered the typical Ptolemaic method for solving problems. "Don't kill anybody," she answered. "Your brother will not be in your way for long. I will send you help. I cannot tell you the form it will take, but just know I am watching, and I am with you. Meet me again in . . . two years and a day, at the hour of gold. Farewell, Queen Cleopatra."

Xanthe pressed the button and the doors closed, whisking her back to the others, unaware of the damage she had done.

CHAPTER ELEVEN

CAUGHT IN THE ACT

By the time Xanthe returned to 58 b.c., the festivities had moved from the streets to the palace. Those not invited to the feast wandered back to their homes, leaving behind torn decorations and half-eaten snacks.

As soon as she stepped through the door of the inn, Nina rushed up to her.

"Xanthetiti! You missed it! It was so much fun!"

"We just came back from water jousting in the harbor," Rowan explained. "Anybody could compete, so we entered a boat. Jomo and I were rowers, Kwame and Xavankhaten were the stick men."

"We beat *two* boats!" Xavier bragged. "But then we were toppled over by a bunch of Greek athletes."

Xanthe nodded but barely listened. Her mind dwelled instead on Cleopatra's struggles in the future with her brother and his Regency Council. "I'm sorry, I'm a little tired, and my head still hurts. I think I'll just go right to bed." She ran up the stairs before anyone could stop her.

After about twenty minutes, she heard footsteps approaching the door. Xavier edged in sideways, like a crab, trying to appear casual. He sauntered over to the window and drummed his fingers nonchalantly on the window ledge.

"So. How's your headache?" From his tone, Xanthe knew very well he had no interest in her headache. She and Xavier knew each other inside and out. Reading each other's minds had been a private joke on their parents, but there was some truth to it. They were so tuned in to each other that at times they fell into speaking a strange sort of code, where ordinary words took on hidden meaning. So when Xavier asked about her headache, what he really meant was, *What are you up to?*

"Not so good," she answered with a smile. "The aspirin hasn't kicked in yet." Which was her way of saying, *None of your business.*

"You know, there are leaves that you can chew here that get rid of a headaches," Xavier offered. *You don't have a headache, and you didn't get aspirin. What did you do?*

"Thanks. I'll remember that the next time." *That's for me to know and you to find out.*

"After the water jousting, Rowan and I went to the wrestling match, and then to the baths. It was fun, but a little too much 'letting it all hang out,' if you know what I mean. No women allowed, of course." *Me and Rowan are friends and we can do things together that you can never do.*

That stung. But Xanthe saw it for what it was, a desperate, last-ditch attempt to make her feel bad. Which meant she was winning. She played her trump card.

"Sounds like fun. I'm tired. I'm going to sleep." *I don't care.*

Xavier winced.

Xanthe smiled sweetly and pulled up the covers as Xavier shambled out the door and down the stairs.

As she lay on the straw mattress, Xanthe wondered how Xavier had figured out that she was up to anything at all. He seemed so full of himself lately. At what point did he notice she was missing? Then it dawned on her that most of his obnoxious behavior was for her benefit. He *wanted* her to comment on his bald head. He *wanted* her to be irritated by his long-winded lectures on Caesar. When she wasn't there scowling, it probably took all the fun out of it for him. So now he wanted to know why she went to the Owatannauk. Well good, he could just sit and wonder. It was all part of the game—the game they'd been playing for as long as she could remember. This was the game: Whoever loses their cool, loses. Now it was his move.

Fifteen minutes later, there came a knock on the door. Xanthe rose to answer it, prepared to stonewall Xavier some more. She was shocked to see Rowan.

"Hey, how are you feeling?" he said.

"A little better. Aunt Agatha gave me permission to get some medicine."

"Yeah, I know." Rowan twisted the belt on his tunic. He

looked at her with his big puppy-dog eyes, and for the second time Xanthe considered telling him everything. It seemed like the perfect moment. Maybe too perfect. They were alone, it was nighttime—just the right scenario for sharing secrets. But where was Nina? Where was Xavier? It had setup written all over it. *Oh, you are good, Xave. I have to give you credit for that.*

"Xanthe," Rowan began hesitantly. He scratched his head and looked at his sandals. "It feels like you aren't really here with the rest of us. Like you're always thinking about something else. I don't mean to pry, but..." His ears were bright red. *This isn't easy for him,* Xanthe thought. *He's only doing it because Xave asked him to.* She decided to let him off the hook.

"You're right, Rowan," she said. "My mind has been on something else."

"Is something wrong?"

"No. Well, yes. Kind of, but not really. I've got a secret. I'll tell you, but you can't tell anybody else."

"I feel really weird about keeping stuff from the others," Rowan said, his whole face now a bright pink.

"Okay, you can tell Nina and Xave, but not Aunt Agatha," Xanthe said. "It's really important, Rowan. If she finds out, she'll cut our trip short."

He sat on the bed. "All right. What's the big secret?"

"Cleopatra is alive. I've met her. She's a ten-year-old princess living under Berenice's thumb. Cleopatra Tryphaena is the one who disappeared, but the famous Cleopatra is here. In fact, she was at the races."

Rowan's eyes grew wide. "What do you mean when you say you 'met' her?"

"I bumped into her at the zoological garden," Xanthe lied. "We got into a conversation and I figured out who she was pretty quickly. I just can't stop thinking about her."

"Well you absolutely can't see her again," Rowan said seriously. "If Aunt Agatha found out, we'd flunk this frequent-flier test for sure. It's not worth it."

"Yeah, I guess so." She had been right about Rowan. She'd told him enough.

"You know, I was thinking," Rowan said. "You must be lonely, being by yourself all the time. Xave and I get to work together, Aunt Agatha and Nina get to work together, but you're on your own. That must not seem very fair."

No it doesn't, Xanthe thought, but she just shrugged.

"Why don't we have lunch every day, until we leave," Rowan suggested. "Xavier likes going through the library scrolls during lunch, but I get sick of being indoors. We can try out different restaurants in the marketplace and pick up some souvenirs."

"I'd really like that," Xanthe said. She meant it. She wondered if this idea was also Xavier's, but then could tell by the color of Rowan's ears that it was all his. In fact, his frightened grin made her wonder if this was the first time he'd ever asked a girl out.

"Okay! Well that's settled. Good night!" He bumbled his way through the door, as though trying to escape before she changed her mind.

Xanthe crept quietly to the door and listened. Sure enough, she heard hushed whispers; Xavier's voice, then Rowan's, then a squeal from Nina, followed by a barrage of shushing. *Good ol' predictable Rowan*, she thought.

She climbed into bed, not sure who was winning the game anymore. She had the upper hand because she had a secret, and secrets give you power. But putting Rowan in the middle of it...that was truly a brilliant move on Xave's part, though he might not know how brilliant.

Rowan's goodness and honesty were irresistible to Xanthe. It was disarming. How could she be devious when faced with that? It would kill her to disappoint him. So even though she still had a most amazing and wondrous secret, after talking to Rowan she knew her visits with Cleopatra had to come to an end. Rowan was right, the stakes were too high.

There was only one problem: Cleopatra was expecting to see her. Xanthe couldn't break off the friendship without warning; it might affect Cleopatra's opinion of Isis, which in turn might sour her opinion of all Egyptians. That could spell disaster. Cleopatra's affinity with the Egyptians was too much a part of her personality. No, Xanthe would have to see her one last time, at the golden hour, as planned. During her next manuscript drop at the Owatannauk, she would make a detour to 48 B.C. There she would say good-bye, leaving the queen with hope and confidence for the future of her reign.

The next day, Xanthe was in a sullen mood. She knew she had to stop her visits with Cleopatra, she knew she had to say good-bye to her new friend, but she was not looking forward to it. She felt like a wad of gum being pulled away from a shoe; some part of her would be left behind.

When Rowan showed up for lunch, Xanthe was a little disappointed that he brought Nina with him; she had been hoping it would be just the two of them. But Nina had such a broad smile on her face that Xanthe's curiosity was piqued.

"You'll never guess what I have!" Nina teased. "I just bought it in the marketplace." Before Xanthe could answer, Nina produced a small lyre from behind her back, which she tucked in the crook of her arm, slowly drawing her finger across the strings. The rising tones hung in the air like invisible steps. She closed her eyes and began plucking something delicate and sweet. The crowd had grown quiet, and when Nina finally stopped playing, they groaned, as though pulled prematurely from a wonderful dream.

"That was really beautiful, Nina," Xanthe said.

"Oh, I don't know, I played too fast," Nina said, laughing nervously. "And I guess you didn't hear those clinkers."

"You're nuts, you know that?" Xanthe laughed. "Whatever that was it sure sounded perfect to me. And you only picked up a lyre for the first time a couple of days ago!"

"Well, a piano is nothing but a big harp lying on its side, and a lyre is nothing but a little harp, so all I needed was for my fingers to make the connection." Nina gave a modest shrug. "Well, I told Aunt Agatha I'd only be gone for a minute. I'd better get back. I'm drawing people to the honey cart with music." She ran down the street, her hair flying behind her.

"She's been waiting all day to show you that," Rowan said. "She got it yesterday at the festival and was practicing all night."

"Why? She doesn't need me to tell her she's good; she's cut three CDs for heaven's sake."

"She cares what you think," Rowan said simply. "She used to do the same thing to our mom. It didn't matter to her if she got a standing ovation, she wasn't satisfied until Mom gave her a thumbs-up."

"Geez, I'm not ready to be a mom, Rowan, not even a mother substitute."

He shrugged. "I'm just saying that your opinion is important to her. Hey, I've got about half an hour. Let's take a look at Alexander the Great's body in the Soma. Have you seen it yet?"

"No, not yet." Xanthe hadn't gone inside the Soma because it gave her the creeps, but if Rowan wanted to go, she was willing to join him.

They ordered a couple of sausages with bread at one of the taverns, and ate as they walked. The Soma was open for visitors, but quite empty. They descended into a large chamber painted with hieroglyphs depicting scenes from Alexander's life. In the center of the room was a golden casket with a transparent cover. They crept toward it. Xanthe was holding her breath.

"He looks smaller than I thought he would," Rowan said after a moment. "And skinnier."

"Rowan, he's a mummy, just without all the wrapping paper. Now can we get out of here, please? I really don't like dead bodies."

"Here's a news flash: Nobody likes dead bodies."

"That's not true," Xanthe said. "Any real Egyptian wouldn't think twice about seeing a mummy. To them, death is just a natural passage of the soul from one place to another, like going on a long trip. That's why Egyptians buried mummies with so much stuff. The tomb was like...I don't know, the moving van."

Xanthe had seen photographs of some of the treasures found when King Tut's tomb had been opened in the twenties. Along with the jewelry and statues, there were mundane items, such as weapons, toys, boats, chairs, clothing, and even food, so that the boy king would have his favorite things when he reached his final destination.

"I get it. It's just that the trip is to the Underworld instead of Disney World," Rowan said.

Xanthe laughed. Rowan had a way of putting her at ease.

"Okay, let's get out of here," he continued. "I've got to go back to work, and you're right, it's kind of creepy." Rowan started to go, hesitated, and turned back. "By the way, I told Xavier and Nina about Cleopatra being alive."

"I know. And it's okay. We really shouldn't keep secrets from each other."

"Then maybe you can tell me what's going on between you and Xave."

"What do you mean?" Xanthe murmured, knowing exactly what he meant.

"I'm picking up a weird vibe from you guys. Did you know you barely look at each other? And I haven't heard you say anything to him except that joke about his head."

"There's nothing going on," Xanthe said. She was too ashamed to try to explain.

Rowan shrugged. "Okay, if you say so. I'll see you when you get back." Rowan gave her a little wave and darted up the stairs.

Yes you will, thought Xanthe. *And I'll be through with all of this sneaking around. I can be the person you think I am, Rowan Popplewell. I can be worthy.* She took one last look at the shriveled body of the great conqueror under the glass lid. *Why was it that dead bodies always seemed to have leering, accusatory expressions on their faces?*

"Oh, shut up," she said to the corpse. "Nobody asked you." She dashed up the steps and out into the crowds.

As she strolled back to the inn, Xanthe realized that Rowan was right. She hadn't said a civil thing to Xavier in the last two days. Now that she thought about it, Xavier had been very quiet lately. "The game," for what it was worth, was taking its toll on him, too. It was time to call a truce, at least for the duration of the trip.

By the time Xanthe set out to the temple with the new batch of manuscripts, the sun was resting on the tops of the buildings. The alleviator was already there, shimmering, and so she jumped in and pressed the button to take her back to the Owatannauk. Arriving in her usual disoriented sprawl, she picked herself up and tore through the lobby, ignoring the four people in Shakespearean attire, the couple dressed in kimonos, and a short, smelly pirate. She buzzed through the mirror maze and was happy to see Otto waiting for her by the vault.

Together they opened the steel door. Xanthe slipped the manuscripts into the cylinders, locked the chest, and raced back to the alleviators. She wanted her last visit with Cleopatra to be as long as possible. She brought with her a gift: a cobra bracelet. She would present it to the queen, assuring her that she needn't ever feel alone again, for Isis lived inside her; she only needed to look deep within if she ever needed assistance. Xanthe thought it was the perfect profound, yet mystical advice that you would expect from a Goddess.

Xanthe was so pleased with herself that she failed to notice the cloaked figure huddled in the corner of the alleviator; a figure who had followed her from 58 B.C. She closed the door, then punched in the year 48 B.C. When she leaned against the back of the alleviator for support the cloaked figure rose and grabbed her arm.

Xanthe screamed and disappeared in a flash of white.

+ CHAPTER TWELVE +
A GRAND ENTRANCE

"Xavier, what are you doing here?!" Xanthe screamed. She picked herself up off the floor and walloped him in the arm. "Get out!" She took another swing, which he dodged.

"Oh, man, you should've seen yourself! You jumped like you'd seen a rat!"

"I *did* see a rat! You!" She looked around, breathing hard. Something brushed by her leg and she leaped back. There at her feet was the cinnamon-colored cat. "Oh, Xave, you brought a stowaway! What were you thinking?"

"He didn't come in with me. Maybe he followed *you.*"

Xanthe sighed and picked him up, scratching his ears. "Well we can't leave him here." She had to stop herself from explaining why. Xavier didn't know what year they were in, but she knew that if the cat from 58 b.c. found his future self, he would explode in a flash of light.

The alleviator door slid open and she stepped out, her mind racing to come up with an explanation for who the beautiful queen in the temple was—but there was no beautiful queen in the temple. Cleopatra was not there waiting for her as they had planned.

"Wait. Something's wrong." Xanthe paced around the temple, looking behind the large statue of Isis, searching the shadows in the corners.

"What? What's wrong?" Xavier asked, following her. "C'mon, we better hurry. Dionysius is going to get his toga in a knot if we aren't back in time for his cake." He started to walk away but Xanthe grabbed his arm.

"Wait. Don't go out there."

"Why not?"

She bit her lip.

"All right, Xanthe, what are you up to?"

"I'm not up to anything! What makes you think I'm up to something? That's ridiculous!" She gave a fairly weak and unconvincing laugh.

"First Rowan tells me that you met Princess Cleopatra, the future queen of Egypt. And I already noticed that every time you make a drop-off you take your time coming back. Put two and two together, and I figured you've been swinging by the palace to see Cleopatra, so today I left work early to follow you. But when you didn't see me in the alleviator, it was too tempting so I changed my mind and decided to scare you."

"Yeah, well, you did."

"But you *have* been meeting Cleopatra, haven't you? That's why you're always creeping around like a criminal? You may as well admit it, kiddo. You are stone-cold busted." He turned and strutted out of the temple. Xanthe girded herself and rushed after him.

Xavier stood frozen on the temple steps, staring speech-lessly at the bay which was filled with military ships, some nearly two hundred feet long, with oars that stuck out from their sides, making them look like huge water bugs. There were also smaller, angular ships painted in fierce, bright colors, cutting swiftly through the water. Soldiers stood on the decks, their helmets gleaming in the rays of the golden hour sun.

"What the heck's going on here?" Xavier yelled, finally finding his voice.

"I'll only tell you if you promise not to tell."

"Okay, whatever. I promise."

"I need your solemn word," said Xanthe. "If you tell any-one you have to admit that you are the biggest liar and the worst stinking skunk in all of the universe."

"You know what? Instead of doing that, why don't I just find out for myself?" Xavier said, and he took off toward the Heptastadion. Xanthe chased after him, the cinnamon-colored cat wriggling in her arms. They raced through the marketplace to the stairs that led down to the water. A large crowd blocked them from moving farther.

"Xave, you didn't have to ditch me like that!" Xanthe hissed.

"Shh," Xavier whispered. "Look!"

Seated at the top of the stairs, on a small, portable throne, was a boy about their age. He wore the double crown of the pharaohs—a white bulbous headpiece, sitting like an egg within a cuplike red headpiece that sloped up in the back. In one hand, he held a hooked staff, and in the other a flail—a rod with long strands of hair flowing from the top. He had the olive skin of a Greek, the prominent nose of a Ptolemy, and the bored expression of a spoiled brat.

"That must be Ptolemy the Thirteenth," Xanthe whispered. "Cleopatra's little brother."

"That can't be him. He's only supposed to be, like, four years old."

"No, it's him. I'm sure of it."

Xavier turned to look at her. His eyes widened in realization. "Wait a minute. You're not saying that we're..."

"You're totally right about my visiting Cleopatra," Xanthe confessed. "I have been seeing her. But I couldn't risk seeing her too many times within such a short period, or I'd influence her too much..."

"And somebody might find out," Xavier added.

"Yes. Somebody might find out. So I started visiting her in her future. I saw her when she was fourteen, then again when she became queen at eighteen. There, now you have it. That's the big secret."

Xavier stared at her for a full minute. "I am impressed," he said finally.

"Ha ha, very funny."

"No, truly, I am in awe of you. I have never known you to do something this bad and this brilliant. I wish I had thought of it first."

"Oh, stop messing around. It's wrong, and we both know it. I don't know what possessed me to do it in the first place, but at least I've come to my senses. This was going to be my last trip, to tell her I couldn't see her anymore. But something's happened because she's not here."

"Maybe now that she's queen, she's too important to meet with some rich kid from Luxor."

"Actually...she reveres me. She thinks I'm Isis. The Goddess."

"What?!" Xavier smacked his hand against his head. "What are you saying?!"

"She saw me coming from the alleviator in the temple. It was the easiest explanation."

"Oh, man, Xanthe." Xavier laughed. "This gets better and better! You are incredible! A Goddess! That takes some guts. I tip my shiny bald head to you. Even I wouldn't try to pass off a whopper like that one."

"Guess what, dummy—now that you're here, you have to. If I'm a Goddess, you're a God. You've got to be my brother, Osiris." Xanthe proceeded to tell Xavier about the significance of the two Gods in Egyptian religion, and how the Ptolemies, particularly Cleopatra, had adopted these beliefs as their own. She explained that she was Cleopatra's confidante, and had been giving her advice. When she was finished, Xavier just stared at her with his mouth open.

"You're serious aren't you? Did you wake up one day and intentionally set out to break every single rule in the Twilight Tourist book?"

"I'm being careful, you know, I'm not telling her anything that's going to change history. I just drop a few prophecies here and there to give the impression that I know the future, which, of course, I do."

"And I'm supposed to play along with this."

"You've got to do it, Xave."

"Well, maybe not. I don't see her here. If this is an important royal event, which it seems to be, then where is she? Maybe she's dead after all."

"No, I don't think that's it. But I do wonder where she is."

Just then, a murmur rose in the crowd. From a small but impressive boat came a man, flanked by twelve armed guards. Instead of a helmet, he wore a laurel wreath, and his armor was draped with a white toga that had a wide purple stripe around the hem. He ascended the stairs quickly, purposefully. Xavier grabbed Xanthe's hand.

"It's Caesar," he whispered excitedly. "It's Julius Caesar! This is the Roman Legion!"

Xavier's deduction was confirmed when Photinus, the leader of the Regency Council who had interrupted Xanthe's last meeting with Cleopatra, scuttled up and bowed his already hunched body even lower so that his chin almost scraped the ground.

"Hail, mighty Caesar of Rome. Welcome to the fair city of

Alexandria. The king of Egypt offers you his hospitality and . . . a gift."

Photinus motioned to two Egyptian servants. They approached Caesar with a large basket and placed it on the steps in front of him. One of them opened it while the other lifted out a platter. On the platter sat a human head.

"Oh, gross!" groaned Xanthe, covering her eyes.

"Pompey was your greatest rival, is that not so?" Photinus continued. "He came here expecting to receive provisions and build up his army. He thought he could count on us for support, but we see which way the wind blows. We're casting our lots with the great Caesar."

Caesar said nothing, but his eyes narrowed. His expression was grave.

"We have done you a favor," Photinus said uneasily, sensing Caesar's mood. "With Pompey gone, Rome is now yours and yours alone."

"Pompey did not deserve this ignominious death," Caesar answered, measuring his words with quiet intensity. "At one time, we were family. He was husband to my daughter. I respected him. He was a great man." He dismissed the gift with a wave of his hand. "Remove that from my sight. It offends me." He walked up the remaining stairs and stood before Ptolemy, who shrank back in his throne.

"King Ptolemy, I've come to collect on your father's debt. As you are well aware, he owed a great deal to the financiers of Rome for his protection when regaining his throne. Until it is paid, I will need accommodations for myself and my men."

"You can stay in my palace," Ptolemy said, his voice cracking. "But your men must stay on the ships."

"I don't think so," Caesar said. "We will all stay in the palace, thank you. And where is your sister, Queen Cleopatra?"

"She's gone," Ptolemy said curtly. "Any business you have with Egypt, you can conduct with me."

"Your father's will states that you and your sister should rule together. For the sake of peace, I intend to see that happen. Wherever she is, I am summoning her back. Make sure she gets the message." Caesar's stern eyes emphasized his meaning. He was issuing a warning.

As Caesar and his cadre of guards swept by the cowed king, Photinus hurried after him.

"Wait! What shall we do with the . . . gift?"

Caesar cut him a cold glance, then turned to a general by his side. "See if you can find the body so that we can give him an honorable burial at home. I myself will place the coins on his eyes for his safe passage through the Underworld." He glanced at Ptolemy and his retinue. "They know nothing of honor here."

With that, the Roman general marched upon the palace with his soldiers, who flicked their cloaks at the young king as they passed.

Once they were out of sight, Ptolemy rose from the throne and whacked Photinus with the flail. "You said killing Pompey would make Caesar grateful! Now he hates me! You idiot!"

"Sire, I still believe this was the best way to ensure that he would leave Egypt alone. He has no reason to stay here since he won't be fighting Pompey, and that is the point, after all. To keep Egypt independent—free of Roman rule. Fear not. He will get over his sorrow. After all, Pompey was his enemy. Julius Caesar grieves not for the man, but for the lost glory of killing the man himself." Photinus snapped his fingers. The slaves lifted Ptolemy's throne and marched in a procession toward the palace. The crowd dispersed, a palpable anger brewing among them.

"Who does Caesar think he is, coming here with all of these soldiers?" Xanthe overheard someone griping.

"He's probably going to take over, like he has everyplace else he's been. Greedy pig!"

"And now we have dirty Romans tramping through our beautiful streets!"

Xavier turned to Xanthe. "Let's get out of here. I don't like where all this is going."

"Oh, no!" Xanthe cried, a little too loudly.

Hearing the exclamation, Photinus's eyes landed on Xanthe. He gave her a curious look so she backed into the crowd, drawing Xavier with her.

"What's wrong?"

"Look!" She pointed to the sky. "The stars are out. The golden hour is over. We're stuck here for the night!"

"Uh-oh. What is Aunt Agatha going to say?"

Xanthe thought for a moment. "I'll tell her I spent the night with Aunt Gertrude. Hopefully she won't double-check that. And you?"

"I'll think of something." Xavier shrugged. "I always do."

"Where are we really going to spend the night?"

"I don't know. But I'm hungry. I've got some money. Let's get something to eat."

They found a tavern in the marketplace and ordered a couple of grilled boar sausages, cheese, and cups of *henket*—a light beer sweetened with juice, which neither one of them cared for. Xanthe kept the cinnamon-colored cat safely tucked in the satchel she carried the manuscripts in and fed him crusts of bread.

"If you're not having anything else, that's two drachmas for the sausages," the waiter said. Xavier fumbled for his pouch, spilling the coins onto the counter.

"There you go, count out what you need."

"I can't. That's only a handful of obols."

"Uhh, that's all I have," Xavier said. "I thought they were drachmas."

"Sure you did." The waiter pulled out a sharp knife. "And I think this is a gold ring, ready to slip on your finger." His hand shot out, snatching Xavier's wrist.

"Whoa! I've got jewelry!" Xanthe cried. "How about an earring? A bracelet? Here's a big golden cockroach—"

"Scarab, Xanthetiti, it's a scarab!" hissed Xavier.

"Right, scarab, that's what I meant. It's got to be worth something!"

"Leave them be, Hathtet," an Egyptian at the end of the counter said, standing. "Why dirty a good knife with the blood of imbeciles? Here, this should cover it." He threw some coins on the counter.

"You always ruin my fun, Apollonius," the waiter said, scooping up the money.

"No, that won't be necessary," Xanthe insisted. Something about this stranger seemed suspicious. He was tall with broad shoulders and a low, quiet voice, but his eyes kept scanning the room. "We can pay for ourselves." She slipped off one of her bracelets and pushed it toward the waiter. Apollonius pushed it back.

"Keep your jewelry, miss. It's worth a lot more than pig intestines and beer."

Apollonius started to leave, but just then the cinnamon-colored cat sprung from the satchel and careened between the Egyptian's legs. The large man tried to avoid him, but his foot came down on the cat's tail. The cat howled, sinking its claws into the Egyptian, who also howled, and down he went with a loud thud, raising a cloud of dust.

"I'm sorry! Are you all right?" Xanthe said, jumping off her stool. Out of the corner of her eye she saw the cat scamper out the doorway.

"Oh, my back!" Apollonius groaned. He struggled to sit up, but his arm gave way beneath him and he fell back down.

Xavier took a look at it. "I think your shoulder's out of its socket. I can try to push it back in for you." He grabbed Apollonius's shoulder and pushed hard. The bellow that followed drew curious stares from people in the tavern, as well as passersby on the street.

"Sorry," Xavier said. "Maybe . . . I guess I don't really know what I'm doing."

"Curse you!" Apollonius moaned, grasping his shoulder. "What am I going to do? I have to deliver an important package tonight, to the Roman! I can barely lift my arm!"

"We'll deliver it for you!" Xavier offered. Xanthe stared at him, disbelievingly.

"You've done enough damage," Apollonius muttered, but he sounded as though he could be convinced, so Xavier charged on, despite Xanthe's glares and mouthing the word "No!"

"My sister's cat caused your fall. He must have meant for this to happen. Fate has brought us together in this manner," Xavier reasoned, his silver tongue working its charm.

Apollonius thought this over and nodded. "Perhaps you are right," he said. "The package I speak of is a rug. Meet me at the docks when the moon sits on top of the lighthouse. Don't be late. I don't think I have to describe what will happen to you if you don't show up." Apollonius nodded to the waiter, who smiled, rolling the handle of the knife between his palms. With that, the large Egyptian limped into the marketplace, cradling his injured arm.

Xanthe pulled Xavier from the tavern. "All right. What do you think you're doing?"

"Xanthe, we have to help him."

"Well, yeah, *now* we do! Unless we want to be turned into hamburger! Have you forgotten that we're not supposed to get involved in anything? The only reason you wanted to help him was so that you could meet Julius Caesar!"

"That's not true!"

"Oh, give me a break, Xave, it's obvious. We should be hiding in the temple until the silver hour so we can get the heck out of here. Maybe you didn't see the bloody head on the silver platter. *Hello!* Danger alert!"

"Xanthe, you're not listening to me. Yes, maybe I do want to meet Julius Caesar, but that's not why I volunteered. Apollonius said it was an important package. If Julius Caesar doesn't get an important package because of something we did..."

"The cat did it."

"All right, something the cat did. A cat that *you* brought into the tavern. Anyway, it could affect the future in ways we can't imagine. We have to do it."

It made sense, but Xanthe wasn't going to admit it. "You should've asked me," she said.

"Why?" Xavier grumbled. "You didn't ask me when you decided to meet Cleopatra, oh, high-and-mighty Isis."

Xanthe grimaced. "Okay, fair is fair. I met Cleopatra, you can meet Caesar. But then we go right to the temple and sit there until the silver hour. All right?"

"Okay, deal." They spit into their palms and shook hands. It wasn't a Greek or Egyptian tradition, but something much more sacred and binding: the schoolyard code.

• • •

The moon crested on the statue of Zeus, which stood on the tip of the lighthouse. Apollonius was waiting for them at the end of the pier, with a rolled-up rug of Persian design.

"Pick up both ends at the same time and follow me," Apollonius said. "But be careful. It's very valuable. If you drop it, I'll cut off your finger."

They hoisted the rug onto their shoulders. "This is heavier than it looks." Xavier grunted.

"So? It'll help make you look nice and beefy for Mr. Julius Caesar," Xanthe said.

"Stop making me laugh—you'll make me drop it!" Xavier chuckled.

"Shh!" said Apollonius. They stopped talking.

When they arrived at the palace, Apollonius explained to the guard that they were delivering a rug to Caesar as an appeasement for Pompey's murder. Xanthe doubted this was true, Apollonius's story seemed slick and well-rehearsed. She said nothing, but merely shifted the rug to her other shoulder and entered the palace.

On their way to Caesar's room, they passed through an opulent hallway with black onyx floors. Xanthe noticed many of the young female servants were practically naked, dressed only in undergarments and jewelry. Then she noticed Xavier noticing the same thing and gave him a reproachful glare.

"It's the culture, Xanthetiti," Xavier murmured. "I'm just here as an observer."

"Keep going to the end of the hall," Apollonius instructed, "then take a right."

"You know your way around here pretty well," Xanthe remarked. Apollonius ignored her.

At the end of the second hall, they came to a set of massive doors inlaid with tortoiseshell and precious stones. Apollonius knocked. A guard appeared.

"Yes?" he said brusquely. "State your business."

"I've come with a gift for the great Julius Caesar."

"He's busy," the guard growled. "Leave it here and I'll see that he gets it."

"I was instructed to give it to him personally," Apollonius said. "It comes with a message from Cleopatra, queen of Egypt." Xanthe's ears pricked up at the mention of Cleopatra. The guard scrutinized Apollonius for a moment, then shifted his gaze to Xavier and Xanthe, who flashed him her killer smile. The guard frowned. She dropped the smile.

"Wait here," the guard said, and disappeared behind the door.

A moment later, the door opened wide, and the guard gestured for them to enter what appeared to be a grand sitting area. In one corner, several couches surrounded a table laden with fruit and cheese, while in the opposite corner, a large fountain with spurting dolphins and dancing cherubs added an exotic, picturesque touch. Handsome sculptures of Greek Gods and exquisite vases were tucked between palm trees and flowering plants. It was a room of hidden delights.

Julius Caesar sat stiffly at a desk, looking as out of place in this pleasure chamber as a pickle in an ice-cream sundae. Not far from him, on one of the sofas, lay a slender teenage boy with short, blond hair. His legs were curled under him and he looked pale. A servant fanned him with an ostrich feather. A second guard stood by the door. Caesar rose as Apollonius, Xanthe, and Xavier laid the rug on the floor.

"Forgive me if I keep my guards here," Caesar said. "I've come to mistrust Alexandrian gifts." He adjusted his toga. "You may thank the young queen for the rug, but I am much more interested in the message. Tell me quickly, her brother is expecting me for dinner."

"The gift and the message are one and the same," Apollonius said, grabbing the ends of the rug. Then many things happened quickly: In a smooth motion, Apollonius flicked the carpet. Caesar and the guard grabbed their swords. Xavier pulled Xanthe behind a palm. A woman spun out of the rug and lay on the floor, then everything seemed to slow down as she rose to her feet. She pulled her sheer, turquoise robe around her shoulders and adjusted the golden diadem encircling her copper hair, and then Queen Cleopatra raised her head.

"Hail, great Caesar," she said.

+ CHAPTER THIRTEEN +
CAESAR AND CLEOPATRA

Caesar sheathed his sword. "Your Highness has given me quite a valuable gift," he said, the corners of his mouth hinting a smile. "Am I to believe that I now own the rug and the woman?"

"Nobody owns me," Cleopatra retorted. "What I have given you is my attention. That in itself has great value, if you know how to take advantage of it."

Caesar laughed. "I see. Well then, I have a challenge." He stroked his chin, scrutinizing her like a puzzle. "I assume your brother does not know you're here. You took a great risk."

"For which I expect a great reward," she countered. A slight smile twitched at her lips.

Xanthe felt a strange energy in the air. Caesar and Cleopatra were like a proton and electron circling each other, connected in an irresistible dance.

At first she hadn't been able to follow their conversation;

they were speaking neither Greek nor Egyptian. Then she realized they were speaking Latin.

Caesar turned to his guards. "Leave us. We have matters of state to discuss." The guards nodded and departed. Caesar tapped the boy who was lying on the sofa. "Octavian, I am foregoing dinner. Give my regrets to the young king. Do not tell him about this 'gift.' I'll see you in the morning."

"Do I have to go?" Octavian whined. "My stomach is tied up in knots."

"Sometimes a gesture of good will is more important than personal comfort, nephew."

Octavian dragged himself from the sofa and plodded after the guard, followed by the servant with the ostrich feather. Xanthe, feeling it was a good time to make her presence known, emerged from the palms, and Xavier followed.

Cleopatra's eyes widened but Xanthe rushed up to her before she could speak, knelt down, and took her hand.

"Say nothing of me," Xanthe whispered in Egyptian. "I must leave at daybreak. Meet me at the temple then, if you wish." With that, she backed out of the room with Xavier in tow. Apollonius stayed in the room to receive instructions from Cleopatra, for he was, in fact, her most loyal servant.

As soon as the twins were out of the room, they rushed down the main hall and then ducked into an alcove.

"Caesar and Cleopatra aren't going to discuss matters of state!" snickered Xavier. "They're going to make out!"

"Oh, grow up, Xave," Xanthe said. But he was probably right. Despite the almost thirty-year age difference between them, Cleopatra and Julius Caesar were undeniably attracted to each other.

And yet it all seemed so calculated. Cleopatra had been banished by her brother and his Regency Council. She needed an ally to get her back on the throne. Who better than the most powerful man in Rome, who had tens of thousands of soldiers at his beck and call? Cleopatra's grand entrance was tailored to entice him, and it worked. Caesar was clearly intrigued.

But he was not fooled. Caesar was just as calculating as she was. Rome wanted Egypt. It wanted the treasures, the resources. Egypt was the last independent region in the Mediterranean to elude Rome's grasp. Caesar had a lot to gain from a union with the Egyptian queen.

And yet despite all of the political maneuvering, Xanthe sensed that they really did have an instant affection for one another. They were in many ways the same; both charming, intelligent, and ambitious. *They're the true soulmates*, Xanthe mused. It occurred to her that she'd used that same word to describe her own relationship with Cleopatra, and she wondered if the queen had the same magnetic effect on everybody.

"Do you still want to spend the night in the temple?" Xavier asked, interrupting her thoughts. "Because it looks to me like nobody's kicking us out of the palace. The guards must think we belong here."

"Well..." Xanthe sighed. The deed was done, they'd missed the golden hour window of opportunity to travel, and their next chance wouldn't be until dawn. "Okay, let's explore. But we have to stay together, and we can't fall asleep or we might miss the silver hour."

"Oh, I don't plan on sleeping." Xavier laughed. "I'm in Cleopatra's palace! With Julius Caesar! This is a dream come true!"

"We should try to look like we belong here," Xanthe said. "Let's take off the jewelry. If we look like servants we'll blend into the background. Right now we look like dignitaries." She started to remove her magnificent collar and a few of the bracelets. "Lose the vest, Xave. The men servants are topless."

Xavier complied and handed the garment to Xanthe, who stuffed it, along with most of her jewelry, into the satchel she'd used to carry the manuscripts. She hid everything behind a statue of Poseidon, the Greek God of the sea. Then she took a pillow from one of the sofas, arranging her jeweled collar on top.

"Xave, pick up that bowl of fruit over there," she said, pointing. Xavier grabbed the bowl. "Okay, now let's look like we know where we're going."

"Where *are* we going?"

Xanthe looked down the hall at the door which separated them from Caesar and Cleopatra. "This way," she said, heading in the opposite direction. "Those two are busy making history."

Carrying the fruit and the pillow, they walked through the palace virtually unnoticed. It was a complex of several palaces, set up like dominoes, one stacked against the next. Marble statues lined every hallway, each one a remarkably beautiful rendering of the human form.

Xanthe and Xavier whispered excitedly as they went. It reminded Xanthe of the time when the two of them had been in their Greek mythology phase, gobbling up the ancient tales as fast as they could read them. They spent hours pretending that they had exceptional powers and lived among the Gods of Mount Olympus. She had dubbed Xavier the God of Cheesy Jokes, and he had dubbed her the Goddess of Good Penmanship. And now here they were, surrounded by ancient Greek culture.

When they reached the last palace in the complex, they followed the sound of a hornpipe into a sitting room. There, eight dancing girls swayed and twirled, flicking long silk scarves into rainbows of color. Ptolemy lay on a sofa in front of a table crowded with platters, gorging himself with food. Lined up at the ready stood several servants holding even more roasted meats, breads, and stewed vegetables. On a different sofa, Photinus hunched over a table, chewing slowly on a piece of bread. Octavian was curled up on a third sofa, not at all interested in eating.

"You're missing out on a great meal." Ptolemy sucked on a bone. Xanthe noticed that he didn't even try to speak Latin. *He really is a poor politician compared to his sister,* she thought.

"Our cooks make a savory roasted peacock brain," Ptolemy continued. "And don't miss out on this delicacy," he added, picking up a small pinkish item with his two fingers and thumb. "Flamingo tongue. It's very rare."

Octavian groaned. "It sounds delightful," he said. He tried to sit up, took one look at the food, and slumped back down.

"It's a shame the great Caesar was unable to join us,"

Photinus said. "We were hoping to make up for the earlier, ah, misunderstanding. The young king is anxious to show his willingness to work with Rome. Caesar can trust his highness will pay his father's debt; there is no need for occupation of Egypt."

"Yes, I'm good for it," Ptolemy drawled, his mouth full of stewed rabbit. He searched the table, agitated, then turned to the head servant. "Where's the grilled nightingale?" he whined. "I told you I want it on every menu!"

The servant pointed to a dish at the far end of the table. Ptolemy glared at him. "What are you trying to do, hide it from me over there?" He reached out and snatched the small bird carcass, then tore off a tiny drumstick and gnawed at it hungrily. "Want some?" he asked, waving the ripped flesh at his guest.

"Maybe if I just had some fruit it would settle my stomach," Octavian responded weakly.

"You heard him, get some fruit!" Ptolemy barked at the head servant. The servant looked around and caught sight of Xavier, who was still holding the bowl.

"You! Fruit!" he called, waving him over.

"I guess I'd better get over there," Xavier murmured. He hurried over to Octavian and knelt, offering the bowl. Octavian took one grape and nibbled on it reluctantly.

Suddenly, Xanthe noticed Photinus staring at her, just as he had at the harbor. Thinking quickly, she snatched a pair of silks as the dancers twirled by. Winding one around her face and waving the other, she joined the wild, whirling group. Her attempt to match their moves soon gave way to hip-hop gyrations, which was more her style. She managed to shimmy her way to the other side of the room. Photinus threw down his bread and rose from the couch.

Xanthe followed the dancing girls around Octavian, then spun over to Xavier, waving the scarves feverishly.

"Call that a dance? You look like someone dropped an ice cube down your dress."

"Shut up, Xave!" Xanthe whispered. "I've been spotted! I've got to get out of here!" Photinus was edging along the walls, coming closer.

"You mean that creepy-looking guy?"

"Yeah, him. Look, I'll explain later, but I think he knows I'm not a servant, so I'll meet you at the temple at the silver hour. Don't be late!"

"Xanthe, if you're in trouble I'm going with you!" Xavier said, suddenly serious.

"Don't! I can handle it!"

She wiggled her hips, then ducked into a cluster of palm trees. From there she snuck behind some curtains near an open window. Through a gap, she saw Photinus pick up the scarves she'd dropped and peer out the window for what seemed an eternity. Finally he threw them down and stalked out of her range of vision.

"Your Highness, I'm going to be ill if I don't get some rest," Xanthe heard Octavian say.

"You! With the fruit bowl. Take him back to his room." Ptolemy snapped.

"Yes, your Majesty," Xavier said. Xanthe heard some shuffling around, furniture creaking, and a few groans which she supposed came from Octavian. Finally, footsteps headed toward the door.

Now the room was quiet. Xanthe wondered how long she would have to stand there without moving. She was just about to poke her head out from behind the curtains when she heard Photinus speak.

"Cleopatra's back, I'm sure of it."

"That's impossible. She'd never be able to get by the soldiers," Ptolemy drawled.

"She has friends, and she is a clever girl, not to be underestimated."

"Did you see her?"

"No, not her. But a friend of hers...a spirit of sorts. I saw it once at the Temple of Isis, then again at the harbor, and now here. It is a sign, I'm sure of it. The queen is back."

Xanthe bit her lip. Photinus had recognized her, and he suspected Cleopatra was in the palace. She needed to get out of the room and warn her.

"If my sister is here, why doesn't she show herself?"

"I don't know. But we must prepare ourselves for the worst. I have an idea. It's risky, my King, but necessary, I think."

Xanthe heard Ptolemy rise from the sofa. He and Photinus spoke in whispers in the far corner of the room. She poked her head out, saw they had their backs to her, and dove out the window, dropping several feet into the shrubbery. As she ran along the side of the building, she searched for another entrance. She finally found an open window, and she hoisted herself through it.

She made her way back to the hallway that led to the room where they'd delivered the rug. She knocked quickly, opened the door, and was already inside before Cleopatra had a chance to respond.

Xanthe's jaw nearly hit the floor. There was Xavier lying on the sofa while Cleopatra fanned him with an ostrich feather. Cleopatra's hair was undone, tumbling in copper waves around her shoulders.

"What the heck is going on here?" Xanthe demanded, forgetting for a moment who she was supposed to be.

"Oh, great Isis, thank you for bringing your brother, the mighty Osiris. He has given me hope in this dark and uncertain time."

"Oh, is that what he was doing?"

"He said I was favored among the Gods, and promised his protection."

"Osiris should remember that there are some things best left unsaid," Xanthe stated pointedly, and Xavier knew what she really meant. *Back off, Xave, she's mine.*

"Yes, dear Isis, but favors should be showered upon those who honor us so well," Xavier answered smugly. *That's what you think.*

Xanthe shot him an evil look. "I've showered enough 'favors,' brother. I have told her of her bright future, and it has come to pass. She is queen." *I'm warning you, Xave. Stop what you're doing. This is my territory.*

"And I will remain queen?" Cleopatra pressed. "My brother, Ptolemy, will not succeed in getting rid of me?"

"No," Xanthe assured her. "He will not. This man Caesar, whom you have just met, he will protect you and empower you." She tried to communicate to Xavier with her eyes that they needed to talk, but he was oblivious to her meaningful looks, being far more interested in one-upmanship.

"You will bear a child by him, his first and only son," Xavier said, smiling slyly at Xanthe. She got the message. *You're not the boss of me.*

Xanthe glared at him. *Unbelievable,* she thought. *He's doing it again, just like he tried to do with Rowan. He's stealing Cleopatra from me.*

"Then we will rule together, two great kingdoms brought together as one, Rome and Egypt!" Cleopatra said slowly, her eyes bright.

"Not so fast," Xanthe cautioned. "Caesar will die...and you'll have to fend for yourself."

"But who will rule Rome then?"

Xavier started to say something, but Xanthe grabbed his arm, interrupting him. "You know what? We have to go. I'm afraid Osiris has an appointment with some mummies in the Underworld. Come along, brother dear..."

"Goddess! Tell me the rest! How will I survive once Caesar is gone? I must know!"

"You'll figure it out!" Xanthe called behind her, pulling Xavier out the door.

Xanthe dragged her brother along the hallway, out of the palace, and down the steps. Once outside, she pulled him around the corner and practically shoved him into a cypress tree.

"Hey, stop being so rough! Isn't Cleopatra amazing? She's got a great vibe. When she looks at you it's like you've been hit with a two-by-four... *pow*!"

"Shut up!" Xanthe snapped. "Just shut up! I'd like to hit you with a two-by-four you... stupid fathead!"

"What are you talking about?"

"While I was running for my life, you were busy stealing my friends. What were you doing in Cleopatra's room?"

"Hey, she invited me in."

"And you had no say in the matter."

"Do you want to know what happened or do you want to just keep yelling at me?"

Xanthe fixed her eyes on him. "Okay, what happened?"

Xavier ran his hand over his head. "I took Octavian to his room. He was sick as a dog. He said his stomach was flipping the entire trip over from Rome. He's having a terrible time. He hates it here—all the lush decor, the dancing, the music, the incense. He likes things pretty plain from the way he was going on; you know—a vanilla kind of guy. So I asked him why he came, just to make conversation. He said Caesar brought him here to observe."

"To observe what?"

"To observe Caesar's leadership. He's Caesar's heir—his nephew, but also his adopted son. And that's when I realized this is *the* Octavian. I was fooled by the way he looks, you know, so scrawny, but it's him all right." Xanthe looked at

Xavier, unimpressed. "You don't know what I'm talking about, do you?"

"No."

"Oh, come on, Xanthe. Didn't you study Roman history at all for the oration contest?" Xanthe blinked, surprised. It didn't occur to her to study Roman history to prepare for a speech contest. Maybe Xavier actually did put more effort into his speech than she did.

"Just say what you have to say, Xave," Xanthe snarled.

"When Caesar dies in forty-four B.C., he passes his leadership to Octavian. It's the same Octavian that's going to battle Mark Antony, Cleopatra's future boyfriend, for Egypt. Octavian wins that battle and changes his name. Xanthe, this pathetic teenager is the future Augustus Caesar!" Xanthe just stared at him. "Hello? *Augustus Caesar?* The first and greatest emperor of Rome?"

"Here we go. More Roman worship."

"C'mon, Xanthe! This is the guy who expanded Rome's borders, commissioned the building of the Pantheon, the Forum, the aqueducts, and other important civic structures! He's a supporter of the arts, including poets like Virgil and Ovid! A great peacekeeper among the provinces! The guy who charged heavy taxes, prompting Jesus Christ to say, 'Give to Caesar what is Caesar's, and give to God what is God's!' The man after whom they named the month of August! I'm telling you, Octavian is going to be one of the most important people in human history!"

"You still haven't explained what you were doing hanging out in Cleopatra's room," Xanthe snipped.

"After Octavian told me he hated Egyptian food, he threw up. I went to get Caesar to let him know his nephew was pretty sick. When I got to the room, I told the guard my business, Cleopatra invited me in, I told Caesar about Octavian, and he left. Cleopatra couldn't have been more friendly, after I told her I was your brother."

"You told her you were Osiris. The God."

"She seemed very grateful that I came all the way from the Underworld to honor her with my presence."

"Yes, I could see that."

"Hey, this was *your* idea."

"I don't want to talk about it. Let's just get back to the temple. It's almost sunrise."

As they raced through the agora, Xanthe heard a plaintive, muffled mewing and looked down to see the cinnamon-colored cat, emerging from behind one of the carts with a mouse in its teeth. She scooped up the troublesome kitten and tucked him into her arm, knocking the mouse away. Apparently the rodent was only stunned, and it scampered off.

Xanthe was just a hairbreadth away from exploding at Xavier. He'd ruined her last meeting with Cleopatra; screwed it up completely. She never got a chance to properly say goodbye or tell her that this had been their final meeting. How she was going to do it now, she had no idea.

Had Xavier been less pleased with himself, he might have

noticed the slight chill in the breeze and recalled that he had left his vest behind in the palace. Had Xanthe been less consumed by jealousy, she might have noticed a hunched figure duck into the shadows as she and Xavier left the palace grounds.

Far away, in another time, at the onset of the silver hour, Gertrude Pembroke sat in darkness, listening to their racing heartbeats. With a tap of her finger, she heard the sound of their feet stomping on packed dirt, the sound of the ocean waves nearby, seabirds cawing. The children were not speaking to each other, but she had a pretty good idea what was going on. As she switched the dial, she picked up Xanthe's voice muttering, "Idiot. Fathead. Arrogant jerk. Bone-brain. Slug." She clicked to Xavier and heard, "Dummy. Loser. Smarty-farty. She-monster." She heard another sound as well, one not picked up by the alleviator keys, but coming from a deeper source—the groan of the universe as it pushed forth a new branch. And then, with a crackle like a candle flame snuffed out, the two voices vanished.

+ CHAPTER FOURTEEN +
CITY OF THE DEAD

Back in 58 B.C., Xanthe and Xavier trudged to the inn in silence. The streets were still quiet as the rising sun cast its rays over the empty marketplace and the wide avenues that led there. The twins were both tired, but more than that, Xanthe was sick of Xavier's meddling. She'd just about had it.

As soon as they reached the inn, however, they both knew something was wrong. The shutters on the windows were unhinged, and the funny sign out front had been broken. The cinnamon-colored cat leaped from Xanthe's arms and cautiously sniffed the open door, the hair along his spine standing rigidly.

"I don't like the looks of this," Xavier muttered. He peered in the window, then quickly ducked down.

"What?" Xanthe said, huddling next to him.

"It's a mess in there. The furniture is turned over, and the sofas are ripped up."

"It sounds pretty quiet," Xanthe said, after a moment. She peeked into a window. "I don't think there's anybody in there. Even the cats are gone! Let's check it out."

Xavier nodded. They slipped inside and carefully made their way through the living room to the kitchen, where they found an even bigger mess. The pantry doors had been thrown open and all the food pulled onto the floor.

Xanthe's bare foot slid in a puddle and when she looked down she saw several large, dark spots all over the tile. "Xave...I think it's blood," she groaned.

"Oh no," Xavier said. "This is horrible." He knelt down and put his fingers in one of the dark pools, then brought his fingers to his nose and sniffed. His worried expression changed to relief. "Good grief, Xanthe, it's honey. *Honey*, you knothead." The cinnamon-colored cat sniffed at the puddle, then bolted from the room yowling for his friends.

Normally Xanthe would take exception to the knothead remark, but she was distracted by the bigger question: Where *was* everybody? She and Xavier ran upstairs to the bedrooms but they were empty; no sign of Agatha, Rowan, or Nina.

"What do you think happened to them?" Xanthe said.

"I don't know," Xavier said grimly. "But it looks like somebody was looking for something."

"We should've been here."

"Maybe it's lucky we weren't here. Maybe if we had been here we would be...wherever they are."

"You were going to say 'dead.'"

"We don't know what happened," Xavier said.

Agatha's suitcase had been forced open and her belongings strewn about. Xanthe found the leather bag the old woman had been using as a purse, and took it with her. They crossed the hall to Nina and Rowan's bedroom, which had also been ransacked. Nina's lyre had been tossed carelessly into a corner, so Xanthe picked it up as well.

"Let's get out of here," Xavier said. "Until we know what happened, I think we'd better keep our distance."

Xanthe agreed, so they quickly went to their room to see if they could salvage any of their belongings. She found her extra *kalasiris*, folded it carefully, and put it in Agatha's bag. Her makeup kit had been opened but not ruined; the jewelry box, on the other hand was gone. She was glad she at least had the jewelry she was wearing. It was then that she remembered the jewelry that she'd left in the satchel behind the Poseidon statue in 48 B.C., and silently scolded herself for forgetting it. She made a mental note to pick it up at the next golden hour.

She followed Xavier down the stairs and into the garden, stuffing Nina's lyre into the bag. "Where do you think we should look for them?"

"Well, let's think logically. First of all, we don't know why the inn was searched. Maybe it had nothing to do with us. In that case, Nina and Aunt Agatha would be on their way to the marketplace to set up the honey stand."

"I think we should assume they're in trouble. Just because . . . I think they are. No one left a note for us or anything. Everybody seems to have left in a hurry."

"Yeah, you're right. Okay, then how about checking the alleviator at the temple?"

"We just came from there, Xave. If they were waiting for us, they'd have seen us. I have a sinking feeling that they got worried and they went looking for us, and something awful happened." When she finally pushed the lyre into the bag, the strings twanged in protest.

"Hey, that's my lyre!" a tiny voice echoed behind them. They both turned, but there was nobody there.

"Shhhhh!" said another voice, echoing just as loudly.

"It's them!" Xavier cried. "Nina! Rowan! Where are you?" There followed a confusing clamor and a great deal of splashing.

"We're down here!" called Rowan. "Here in the well!"

The twins hurried to the well and leaned over the edge as far as they could, straining to catch a glimpse of their friends, but it was no use. "We can't see you!" Xanthe shouted.

"Keep it down," Rowan called back. "Is there anybody up there with you? Are the soldiers still there?" The twins glanced around nervously.

"No!" Xavier shouted back. "There's no one here."

"Pull on the rope," Rowan yelled. "Pull Nina up!"

Xanthe and Xavier tried cranking the handle, but it was simply too difficult. Xavier thought it might be easier if they detached the rope, and this seemed to work better. After several minutes of tugging and heaving, they saw Nina's dirt-smudged face appear over the edge of the well. She grabbed on to the side and hoisted herself up.

"Thanks," she said, squeezing water out of her tunic. "Let's get Rowan up here." They tossed the rope back down, and then the three of them inched him up, bit by bit. Xanthe's shoulders burned, and she was sure her arms were going to fall off. Suddenly, her foot skidded in the gravel and she crashed on her behind, releasing the rope. She watched in horror as Xavier and Nina hurtled toward the mouth of the well, the free end of the rope slithering after them.

Xanthe reached for it, clawing the dirt desperately. She caught the end but it zipped across her palm, tearing her skin. Nevertheless, she clenched her hands tighter, digging her heels into the dirt, until finally...they stopped. She looked up. Xavier had been pulled halfway into the well and Nina was on her back with both hands around Xavier's ankle.

"What happened?!" Rowan cried from below.

"We're okay," Xavier called back. "We'll have you up in a moment." They tried again. Despite her bloodied hands and her scratched-up feet, Xanthe steeled herself, and this time they managed to pull Rowan up. He, also, was drenched, and had a large bruise on his cheek.

"We've got to find Aunt Agatha," Rowan said. "She's been arrested."

Xanthe gasped. "Why? What for?"

"For stealing books," Rowan answered. "Actually, she wasn't who they were looking for. It was you, Xave." He crossed his arms and looked at Xavier squarely. "Did you take something from the library?"

"Me? No! Of course not!"

"Something like a short poem? By Plato? The Greek

philosopher?" Instantly all the blood seemed to drain from Xavier's face.

"Uh-oh. Maybe I did take something, but it was an accident! I left the library in a hurry yesterday because I wanted to follow...meet...Xanthe before she made her drop. I guess maybe I tucked it in my vest pocket."

"Theodictes came looking for you with some goons. He asked Aunt Agatha where you were and she said she didn't know. He thought she was covering for you. Then he asked where I was, and she wouldn't tell him that, either. I guess he thought maybe she'd hidden it somewhere in the inn, so they tore the place apart."

"When they broke the jars of honey, I thought Dionysius was going to have a heart attack," Nina added. "He cried like a baby."

"Anyway, Nina and I were crouched at the top of the stairs and overheard everything. We jumped out the window, and then, because the place was surrounded, we hid in the well. We heard Theodictes say that since Aunt Agatha had vouched for your trustworthiness, they were going to lock her up until you or the stolen item was found. So where's your vest?"

"I put it in the satchel...which I didn't bring back," Xanthe murmured.

"Well, we can pick it up from the Owatannauk at the next golden hour." Rowan squeezed his soggy tunic. "Man, I've been soaked so many times on this trip, I should've just worn a bathing suit."

"It's not at the Owatannauk," Xanthe said, clearing her throat. "But I know where it is."

"Can you get it?"

"I don't know." She started digging a hole in the dirt with her toe.

"Where were you guys, anyway?" Nina blurted. "We were really worried about you! The golden hour came and went and you never showed up!"

"Xavier went with me to the Owatannauk," Xanthe said. "Then we got caught up in something, and, before we knew it, the hour was over so we spent the night." That seemed to satisfy Nina, but Rowan frowned. "Look, we're sorry," Xanthe said. "But we'll figure out how to get Aunt Agatha back. Don't worry."

"I'd feel better if I knew she was okay," Rowan said.

"I know my way around the city pretty well," Xanthe said. "I think I know where the jail is. Come on."

She led them along the backstreets into Rhakotis, where the fourteen-year-old Cleopatra had taken her. As they reached the city wall that separated Alexandria from the open desert, they found the cube-shaped jailhouse. Xanthe noticed the narrow, barred windows at the base of the building, and she motioned to the others to follow her. As they approached the building, a foul smell nearly knocked them backward.

Rowan covered his nose. "I guess by now we shouldn't be surprised that ancient prisons weren't very clean."

Agatha was in the basement, in a corner cell. They couldn't

see her through the window because the cell was dark, but they recognized the humming.

"Aunt Agatha!" Rowan said. "It's us! We're here!"

"Oh, my goodness, it is you! I'm so glad to see you all! I was so worried about you two," Agatha said, coming to the window and peering at Xanthe and Xavier. She looked tired and drawn. "I hope you're not in any trouble."

"Aunt Agatha, *you're* the one in trouble!" Nina pointed out. "This is awful!"

"Yes, it is rather filthy down here," Agatha said, looking around. "And the food isn't very good. But I've seen worse."

"There's *got* to be something we can do," Xavier said.

"Yes, there is. Keep yourselves safe. At the golden hour, go to the Owatannauk and find Gertrude. She'll take if from there."

Gertrude. Xanthe groaned. She wondered if her vital functions had summoned the old woman to the black room to listen to her petty arguments with Xavier and her incriminating discussions with Cleopatra.

"Who are you talking to?" a harsh voice snarled. A guard stationed in the basement hit the bars of Agatha's cell with a stick. The foursome scrambled away from the window, but it was too late. They were spotted.

"They're up there!" the guard yelled. "She was talking to them! After them!" In an instant, the children heard a commotion of footsteps.

"Follow me!" Xavier shouted. He turned and sprinted down the street. Rowan and Nina flew after him.

Xanthe groaned. *Xavier has no idea where he's going,* she thought, but she followed anyway. The grid-like design of the streets was working against them. Winding, confusing streets would have provided someplace to hide, but these streets were wide open.

Xavier led them across the canal and toward the westernmost edge of the city, to the Gate of the Moon, one of the city's exits. Xanthe prayed he wouldn't go beyond the wall. Once outside the city, there was really no place to hide; they'd be sitting ducks. She turned and saw the guards only about a hundred feet behind them. Xavier made a sudden turn and raced down a set of stairs. Xanthe's heart sank when she realized where he was going.

The Necropolis. "*Necro,*" meaning "dead," and "*polis,*" meaning "city." A city of the dead. An enormous underground tomb.

"Xave! What are you doing?!" she screamed. She could barely see him as he disappeared into the dimly lit entryway.

"Hiding!" He yelled back. *Well, duh.*

As she entered the tomb, Xanthe heard the others' footsteps scatter in different directions. She was on her own. Fortunately, a few torches flickered in some of the alcoves, casting hazy light through the tunnels. As she darted through a passageway, she glimpsed tile pictures of flowers and pastures with oxen on the walls. Overhead, cherubs and dolphins played in carved reliefs. Incense drifted in the air, and fresh flowers filled vases set before statues of the dead. Xanthe spotted a table and some chairs in one of the alcoves and it occurred to her that in this culture, where loved ones still ate dinner with their dearly departed, the line between life and death was a thin one. She ran.

She turned one corner, then another, and another, and soon found herself in a whole different area. These tombs weren't as fancy, just big square holes carved out of the dirt walls. The holes held mummies, shelved in hundreds of body-sized recesses. Some were wrapped, others were bare skeletons, watching her with vacant eyes and predictably leering grins.

She left this room and ran to the next, which looked exactly the same. There was a door at the end of it, and she ran through that, finding herself in a similar room. She couldn't tell if it was the same one she'd been in before, or if it was entirely new, but she realized she was stuck in a maze and had no idea where she was or how to get out.

Something tickled her neck. Xanthe froze, her heart beating wildly. An arm had dropped from a cubbyhole and was reaching toward her, the hand, the fingers moving closer, and now the whole body rolled slowly from the hole.

She screamed.

"Xanthe! Shhh! It's me!" a voice squealed from the recess. Xanthe blinked. It was Nina, who had wedged herself behind the skeleton. "Climb up and hide behind a body!"

"Oh, God, I can't. It's too small."

"Do it!" Nina said urgently. "They're coming! They heard your scream!"

Xanthe could hear the guards converging on the room. She took a deep breath and climbed up the cubbies as high as she could go, then slid into one of the niches, squeezing behind the wrapped body that lay within.

Two guards arrived at the same time, their swords drawn. The walked slowly around the small room. Xanthe could only see the tops of their heads go by. Her body was already shaking from the boxed-in feeling. She had a sudden desire to burst out from the hole, to stretch out, to fly...but she had to stay perfectly still. The wisps of dust swirling in the air didn't help. *I can't breathe*, she thought. *I can't breathe, I can't breathe...*

Then her nostrils twitched. She had to sneeze—a big nuclear blast kind of sneeze. It burned the bridge of her nose, bringing big fat tears to her eyes. Somebody had once told her if you chanted the word "grapefruit" it would keep you from sneezing. It sounded unlikely, but she tried it anyway, whispering the word over and over in desperation.

"There's nobody here," one of the guards muttered. A third guard joined them at the doorway, and growled something that Xanthe couldn't hear very clearly, and the other two followed him out. An entire minute went by. She couldn't hold it any longer.

"Grapefruit!" she heaved with a burst of dust from her nose.

"Stay put!" she heard Nina whisper. "We've got to be sure they've gone."

They both stayed where they were. For Xanthe, those minutes, waiting as the guard's footsteps became fainter and fainter, were pure agony. Then she heard lighter footsteps.

"Hello?" Rowan whispered.

"Anybody here?" Xavier asked.

Xanthe shoved the mummy that had sheltered her out of the hole and it landed with a clatter of bones on the dirt floor, raising more dust. She leaped out after it, breathing heavily. Soon Nina clambered down, brushing herself off.

"Do you think they're gone?" Nina asked. "They must know we're still in here."

"But not where," Rowan said. "They probably got as turned around as we did. This place goes on for a while. It's huge."

Xanthe looked at the bundle of bones on the floor and shuddered. "Somebody help me put this guy back where he belongs." Xavier and Rowan helped her lift the mummy into the hole, and she felt a little better. She didn't actually believe in curses from mummies, but why tempt fate?

"So now what? How do we get out?" Rowan said, wiping mummy dust from his hands.

"If you put your hand on one of the walls and walk in one direction without taking your hand off the wall, you will eventually find the end of any maze," Xanthe said, remembering Gertrude's advice. They all looked at her. "It's true!" she said. "But it might take a while."

Rowan shrugged and placed his right hand on the wall. "I think it's this way. Anyone disagree?" Nobody had any better ideas, so they followed him as he wove through one room after the another. It did take a while, but after three hours and no guard sightings they were out.

+ CHAPTER FIFTEEN +
# A WHOLE NEW WORLD

"NINA AND I THINK YOU OWE US AN EXPLANATION,"
Rowan said.

This was the moment Xanthe had been dreading. "Yes. I
know." She'd been stalling the entire time they were finding
their way out of the Necropolis, but now she had no choice
but to confess. She took a deep breath.

"Okay, here it is," Xanthe said. "Xave and I took an
unscheduled trip. That's why we weren't back at the golden
hour. I don't know why he took the poem. He must've had a
brain cloud or something."

"No, I was just so focused on catching you in the act I forgot I was holding it," Xavier snapped. "I stuffed it in my
pocket without thinking—"

"What do you mean, 'catch you in the act'?" Rowan interrupted.

"This wasn't Xanthe's first 'unscheduled trip.' She's done it a few times. Didn't you wonder why she was so spaced out all the time?"

"Don't try to pin this on me," Xanthe said. "I wasn't the one who took the poem. If you'd kept to your job instead of sneaking after me, we wouldn't be in this mess."

"Hold on a second. Where exactly did you go?" Rowan asked.

"I hopped a few years into the future. I...went to see Cleopatra." Xanthe braced herself for the inevitable blowup, but Rowan just stared, shaking his head. When he finally opened his mouth, she expected a scream. Instead, his voice was quiet, which was almost worse.

"I don't believe it. This was our chance to show the Board we could be trusted, that we could be responsible..." His voice trailed off.

Xanthe looked at her feet, ashamed. "Sorry, Rowan. I don't have a good excuse," she said. "It was a stupid idea." Rowan wouldn't even look at her. She felt his disappointment weigh on her like a lead coat.

"I can't believe you've been doing all this stuff and keeping it from us," Nina said. "It's almost like you don't trust us."

Xanthe said nothing. They were right, of course.

"Okay," Rowan said after a long, agonizing moment. "I think we can still salvage this trip. Aunt Agatha doesn't really know what happened. We may be able to snow her a bit. Once we get Aunt Gertrude on the case, I'm sure she'll find a way to get Aunt Agatha out. Hopefully we've saved enough scrolls from the warehouses to satisfy their client." He shot

Xanthe another disappointed look that stabbed her right in the heart. "C'mon. It's the golden hour. Let's do what we have to do."

The foursome shuffled into the temple, lost in their thoughts. After a few minutes, the alleviator appeared and they stepped inside. Xanthe took one last look at the painted columns, the flickering torches, and the beautiful statue of Isis, wondering if she'd ever see them, or any part of Alexandria, again. She was so consumed with regret, she didn't notice she was taking part of Alexandria with her.

They arrived at the Owatannauk sullen and depressed. As they left the alleviator and walked down the hall, Xanthe hung back. She felt like she had betrayed everyone. How could she have let her rivalry with Xavier distract her from their mission? She was so focused on beating him, she'd lost sight of what was truly important: passing the test and becoming frequent fliers. *Too busy looking at yourself in the mirror*, she thought, glumly. *You lost the path, and dragged everyone else down with you.*

Something darted between her legs, causing her to trip and fall. It was the cinnamon-colored cat. "Oh, no," she said. "Not again."

Rowan turned and came back to help her to her feet. "That's Dionysius's cat. He must've followed us without us noticing. I guess he's loyal to you." Xanthe detected a note of irony in Rowan's voice.

"Rowan, I know there's nothing I can do to make up for it,

but for what it's worth, I'm sorry. I blew it. I just wasn't thinking."

"You and Xave have something going on between you. I wish you'd just stop it."

"I do, too," Xanthe muttered. "It's not as easy as all that."

As they got to the lobby, they found Otto behind the desk, hands folded with his usual pleasant smile. "How may I help you?" he said.

"Is Aunt Gertrude in the back?" Rowan asked. "Is she in the resort at all?"

"No, I'm afraid not," Otto said, still smiling.

"Did she take one of the alleviators somewhere?" Nina asked quickly. They all knew by now that to get a straight answer from Otto, you had to ask a direct question, sometimes several.

"No, she did not," Otto said.

"Have you summoned her here for any reason today?" Xanthe asked.

"I have not."

"She must be at her house," Xavier said.

Xanthe said nothing. She was secretly glad that Gertrude had not been in the hotel; it meant that she had not been listening in on their conversations, and might not know the extent of Xanthe's transgressions. They might still have a chance to get out of this mess without anyone on the Board of Directors being the wiser.

The four children, followed by the four-legged stowaway, left through the subterranean garage, walked through the tunnel and the holographic boulder, and down the rough private road that fed into Main Street. It had started to drizzle, and Xanthe was freezing. Suddenly, she felt a wool cloak around her shoulders. It was Rowan's.

"Take it off," she said. "I don't deserve it. Just please don't hate me."

"I'm not taking it off, and I don't hate you. You're more important to me than becoming a frequent flier, Xanthe. I'm surprised you didn't know that. We'll figure out a way through this. It's just that... We've all got to stick together. I feel it in my gut, you know? The four of us make a great team. I felt it on our last trip. We would've been killed, easily, if we hadn't worked together. Nobody here can go it alone. Not you, not Xave. You guys are smart, but you're not perfect." He lowered his voice. "Even though Xave wants us to think he is."

"You noticed that?" Xanthe said, a small laugh escaping.

"Has trouble admitting when he's wrong, doesn't he?" Rowan said.

"All the time."

"Nina's the same. Perfectionists. Thank goodness I'm a mess and proud of it."

"Me, too." Xanthe felt a little better. "You know, Xave's my best friend, but honestly there are times when I can't stand him. I can't explain it..."

"You don't have to. I have a sister three years younger than me who's cut three CDs, played in concert halls all over the country, has a shelf full of trophies, and is about seventy-five percent cuter than me. Believe me, I know what you're talking about."

"I thought this trip to Alexandria was going to be amazing. I was so psyched. But then Xavier showed up and started stealing you away..."

"'Stealing me away?' Do you know how dumb that sounds?"

"Yes. But at least it's the truth."

They were walking close to each other so as not to be overheard. To Xanthe's shock, she felt Rowan's fingertips brush her hand. She thought it was an accident, but he didn't move away. "There's Main Street," Nina said, running past them. She stopped suddenly. "Hey, something weird is going on here."

"What is it?" asked Rowan.

"I can't...I can't move past the Stop sign."

"That Stop sign is for cars, not for people," Xavier joked.

"I'm serious! I can't take a step farther!"

"That's ridiculous." Xanthe wandered easily into the intersection.

"Yeah," said Xavier, following her. "What are you talking about?"

"She's right, there's something stopping us," Rowan said. He spread his hands and pushed on what seemed to be an invisible shield. "There's a...a force field or something." He threw his body against it. Whatever it was propelled him backward and he fell to the ground. He rammed into it again. "I don't understand! We can't get past it!"

Rowan's voice sounded thin. A prickly feeling spread over Xanthe like a fever.

"What's happening?" Nina said, her voice as light as the breeze. Xanthe gasped in horror. Nina had become transparent. Xanthe could see the hotel right through her. Through Rowan, too.

"Rowan! Nina! You're disappearing!" Xavier yelled.

Then Xanthe realized the sun was already a deep blood-orange, and that sunset had begun. In a matter of seconds, the hotel transformed in front of her eyes, its colors fading, its windows breaking, the entire building slumping under the weight of the ages. Grass and flowers shriveled into dry clumps and the breeze ceased, as though a fan had been turned off. The cinnamon-colored cat hissed and flew into the brush by the side of the road. And as Xanthe watched, disbelievingly, her friends faded away.

"Where did they go?" Xavier whispered hoarsely.

"I don't know."

"What are you going to do?"

"Don't you mean what are *we* going to do?" Xanthe said, turning on him.

"You're the one who got us into this."

Xanthe erupted. "Oh, no you don't, Xavier Alexander! You're just as much to blame. If you hadn't been so keen on following me, you wouldn't have stolen that poem."

"I *had* to follow you! You made me! Teasing me with those secretive looks and that stupid smile. How long was I supposed to put up with that?"

"You wouldn't have to put up with it at all if you'd stayed in Washington, D.C.! What are you doing here, anyway?

Couldn't stand that I was going to do something interesting without you?"

"You would've liked that, huh? Coming back from ancient Alexandria and lording it over me, trying to make me jealous."

"Sounds like you *were* jealous."

"*You're* the one that's jealous, Xanthe. You can't stand the fact that I beat you in the Cicero contest. It's just been eating away at you, hasn't it? I'm better than you at math and science, and now even history, too. Well...deal with it!"

"Get out of my life!" Xanthe screamed. "You stupid jerk!" She balled up a fist and hit him in the shoulder as hard as she could. Now on top of everything else her knuckles hurt.

She turned and ran. She had to get away from him. Either that or kill him.

"Hey, where are you going?" she heard him call after her, but she kept running and running and running.

Crying while running makes your throat burn. She kept choking on her own spit, and had to slow down to catch her breath. Rowan and Nina had disappeared. Aunt Agatha was in jail, Aunt Gertrude would never trust her with anything again, and Xavier was being a jackass. He sure could pick his moments.

As she jogged to the town center, she noticed that the town looked different. Small things had changed. The mannequins in the window of the dressmaker's shop no longer wore wool coats. Instead, they modeled long woolen tunics in bright, bold patterns, over which were draped hip-looking capes and brightly patterned togas. The jewelry store displayed its usual watches and rings, but among them were scarab bracelets, falcon pins, and a golden cobra coiled to fit the upper arm. Next to a tray of gold crosses sat a similar tray of ankhs, the Egyptian symbol for life. The tree nursery where Gertrude bought most of her vegetable seeds had disappeared altogether, replaced with a square, modern building.

Curious, Xanthe wandered inside. Pictographs covered the walls, and statues with animal heads stood stiffly in the alcoves: Bastet, Thoth, and Horus...these were Egyptian Gods. She was in a modern Egyptian temple. In the very center of the temple stood a serene statue of Isis.

Xanthe turned and ran outside. More changes flashed past as she bolted down the street. The burger place advertised deep-fried flamingo tongues. Cats were everywhere, slinking around alleys, disappearing into shrubbery. By now she knew she was not in the Owatannauk, Maine, that she had left. She had done the very thing she had been warned over and over not to do. She had changed the future and started a different branch of time. Now, stranded in this new world, she had no way of reaching the old one. She could not go home.

There was only one thing to do: visit the Sisters' house and get help. But not yet. There was one stop she wanted to make first.

When Xanthe walked up the driveway to Nana's cottage, she almost didn't recognize it. It was so quiet. It was the same house all right; it was certainly the same mailbox with "Alexander" painted on the side. She recognized the rhododendron bush that Nana had planted, and there was the same old wicker rocking chair on the porch. But where were the birdhouses? The front lawn was bare. Xanthe rang the doorbell, but nobody answered, so she walked around to the back. There she saw an amazing sight.

Laid out behind a white picket fence was a miniature alpine town made of a dozen dollhouse-sized buildings. Living in the town was a happy community of rabbits. Rabbits of all sizes and colors hippity-hopped along scaled-down dirt roads. Small pine and fir trees, as well as flowering bushes, completed the effect. Xanthe was so enchanted that she didn't notice Nana coming out from her workshop, holding a miniature clock-tower.

"Yes, may I help you?" she said. Xanthe turned and Nana's eyes grew big as saucers. She staggered and dropped the tower, which broke. "Who are you?" she whispered.

"It's me, Nana, Xanthe."

"It can't be." Nana crossed herself several times.

"Please, I don't mean to frighten you," Xanthe said. "If you just let me talk to you, I can explain what's going on. Just tell me one thing: Do you know about the Twilight Tourist Program at the Owatannauk Hotel?"

Nana gaped at her. "Who told you about that?"

"So I guess the Xanthe and Xavier in this world don't know it's a time machine?"

"What are you?" Nana whispered. "A demon taking over my grandbaby's body?"

Xanthe took a deep breath. "Nana, listen to me. I really am Xanthe, I'm just from an alternate universe. In my universe,

Xave and I know all about the Owatannauk and the alleviators and the Board of Directors. *Everything.* I went back in time to Egypt, but something happened and...oh, I don't know, somehow Xave and I changed something in history, created a new branch in time, and now we're both stuck here. I came here hoping you could give me some advice. I may not be your real granddaughter, but I really am your granddaughter. You see?"

Nana opened and closed her mouth a few times but nothing came out. Finally she shook her head. "Come inside."

"I guess I have to believe you," Nana II said, slicing up an apple and placing it on a plate in front of Xanthe. "There's no other explanation. You look exactly like her. Taller maybe, filled out a bit, but you're Xanthe all right. Funny, we always knew this could happen. I just never thought I'd see it happen to someone I knew. A visitor from an alternate universe. That is something truly unusual."

"You did seem a little shocked."

Nana II laughed. "Oh, yes. Well, I never thought I'd see you again, at least not in this world. Baby girl, we put you into the ground when you were ten years old."

Xanthe nearly choked on the apple. "I'm *dead* in this universe?"

Nana II nodded sadly. "Yeah, an unfortunate accident. You got stuck in a window seat playing some game—hide-and-seek, or something."

"You know, I did get stuck in a window seat when I was

ten. I couldn't get out until Xave found me. He got Dad, and Dad broke the seat apart."

"Is that how it went down with you? Well not in this case. My little Xanthe was stuck and Xavier didn't lift a finger. In fact, he put some heavy blankets on the seat to make it harder for you. It was supposed to be a joke.... He said he was getting back at you, I don't really know what it was all about. But you were in there too long, baby. You suffocated in that window seat." Nana II dabbed at her eyes with a dish towel. "Andrew and Helen weren't even home."

"Why would your Xavier do something so mean?"

"You don't know?"

"No."

"You sure?"

Xanthe frowned and shook her head.

Nana II leaned forward, keeping her eyes on Xanthe. "Because my granddaughter could be as mean as a wet cat when she wanted to, rest her soul. If she had a chance to make her brother look bad, she took it. Every time he tried to get ahead, she smacked him down. And he'd pick on her, too. Back and forth, back and forth. It made me sick to watch 'em. I knew something like that would happen."

"Why would you think I'd know why Xavier would be so mean?"

Nana II took her pipe from her pocket, tapped it on the table, then tucked it in her teeth. "Because you've got a guilty conscience."

"Oh, no. You've got me all wrong," Xanthe protested. "You really barely know me."

"I know you," Nana II cackled. "I know you well enough. You're too clever for your own good. That's why you're stuck here." Xanthe stared at the old woman, but she just lit the pipe and sucked until she got it going. "Why don't you sit awhile, tell me what you've been up to? You may not be my Xanthe, but you're close. I'd like to know what might have happened to her if she'd . . . survived."

"I'm sorry," Xanthe said. "I'd love to talk, but I don't have much time. I've got to figure out how to straighten out this mess I've made. Otherwise . . . I guess in the other world, my world, I'll have disappeared, and my Nana will be just as heartbroken as you were. This is very confusing, I know."

"Yes it is," Nana II agreed. "And I suppose it would create quite a stir if anybody around here was to see you and recognize you. They might think you were a zombie or something. You know the Sisters? Gertrude Pembroke and Agatha Drake? They live behind that big curio shop—you know the one I'm talking about?" Xanthe nodded. "Talk to them. They may be able to do something for you."

"You really think so?"

"Nope, but I don't have any other ideas." This Nana was very much like the Nana she knew. Maybe too much.

"Thanks." Xanthe started to leave but then turned back. "Nana, what happened to Xavier? I mean, after I . . . your Xanthe died?"

"He's angry. Doesn't talk much. Doesn't have any friends. He's messed up all right. It just goes to show, sometimes decisions we make or actions we take, even as children, can make a big difference."

Xanthe nodded grimly and rose from her seat. Nana II saw her to the door. Even with her back to the house, Xanthe knew that the old woman was crossing herself and muttering, and she didn't blame her.

The Sisters' house appeared to be the same in either universe. Their curio shop had not changed, nor had their makeshift house in the back; it looked as rickety and unstable as ever.

Xanthe knocked on the door. After a moment, Agatha answered it. Agatha II looked almost exactly like Agatha I, but with a few slight changes. She had a chin-length haircut, unevenly trimmed, and wore a loose tunic, reflecting the same Greek influence that Xanthe had seen in the dress shop window. True to form, the outfit was hot pink and belted in uneven drapes so that she looked like a lopsided birthday cake.

"Yes?" Agatha II said. "It's a little late to be selling magazines, don't you think?"

"Oh, I'm...so sorry...to bother you," Xanthe stammered. "But I'm not selling magazines. I'm Nana's...Annabelle Alexander's granddaughter."

"Well, now. That would be a neat trick, wouldn't it? Annabelle told me her only granddaughter passed away several years ago. She has just the one grandson now."

"Here I am," Xavier said, emerging from behind the

hedges. "Where have you been?" he asked Xanthe, who jumped, startled. There was an odd tone in Xavier's voice, and he looked upset. Xanthe wondered what was wrong, but it would have to wait.

Xavier turned to Agatha. "I'm Xavier, and this is my twin sister. We could really use your help."

"You two get along much better than your grandmother led me to believe," Agatha II said, amused. "Why don't you come on in and tell me what all of this is about."

She led them to the kitchen and gestured for them to sit. "Try some blueberry scones. They are incredibly flaky!" She pushed a plate of scones and butter toward them just as Gertrude II entered the room. She stopped, surprised at their presence, and then did something truly bizarre—she smiled.

"Who do we have here?"

"Believe it or not, these are Annabelle's grandchildren. *Both* of them," Agatha II said meaningfully. "I was just about to find out the nature of their visit."

Gertrude II's style of dress was exactly the same as Gertrude I's, except she favored lighter colors: She wore tan slacks, clogs, and a pastel-pink striped shirt. Instead of the braid, however, she wore her long hair down about her shoulders, and her face was softened by bangs. She seemed much more relaxed.

"This should be interesting," Gertrude II said, taking a seat at the table.

"I'm going to start from the very beginning," Xanthe said. She proceeded to tell the Sisters everything that had happened since the trip to Alexandria, with help from Xavier.

They both left out the part about the trip being a test for frequent-flier status, possibly because they didn't want to be reminded of it themselves, and they also left out their fight. After they finished, the two aunts clapped their hands gleefully, like preschoolers at a puppet show.

"This is fascinating! Two people from an alternate universe who apparently know our alternate selves!" Gertrude II exclaimed.

"Yes, it is a pip!" Agatha II chirped. "Oh, do tell, what do our counterparts look like? Are we the same? In your universe, I mean?" She slapped a spoonful of blackberry jam onto a scone and spread it around with the bowl of the spoon.

"Well, there are some slight differences, but yes, you seem pretty much the same," Xanthe said. She wasn't about to tell Gertrude II how stern and humorless her alternate really was.

"I was hoping I was a few pounds lighter in another universe," Agatha said, poised to take a bite. She thought better of it and placed the scone on the plate. She gazed at it wistfully, then suddenly her eyes brightened. "But Gertrude! Do you know what this means? The theory of time travel behind the alleviators is correct! Time really is like a branching tree! There could be billions of such branches, all stemming from changes made by time travelers!"

"Yes, yes, but that raises an interesting question: Is time supposed to be one straight trunk that extends infinitely, and these branches are accidental side trips? Mistakes? Or are all the branches equally valid? I must confess, Sister, it would be very disheartening to think I've lived all my life on an inconsequential branch, rather then the one true primary artery—"

"Excuse me," Xavier interrupted. "But what are you talking about?"

"Just questions of religion," Gertrude II said. "Whether or not the universe has a direction. Whether there is a will of God—or Gods, if that's what you believe."

"Gods...Are you talking about the Egyptian religion?"

"Yes," Agatha II said. "It's not our belief, but it's fairly popular."

"We must've changed something that helped the survival of that religion," Xavier said. Xanthe noticed he'd said "we" and softened, grateful for that small gesture.

"Nana said that you might be able to help us figure out a way to get back," Xanthe said. "And help us figure out what happened to Rowan and Nina."

"Who and who?" Gertrude II asked, biting into a scone.

"They're the brother and sister that went with them to Alexandria," Agatha II answered.

"Wait, you've never heard of them before now?" Xavier asked. He looked at Xanthe. She shook her head and frowned.

"No," Gertrude II shrugged. "Should we have?"

"Yeah!" Xavier said. "You're their great-aunts! You were their mother's godmothers...Gabriella Popplewell. This doesn't ring a bell?"

"No, it doesn't, but it *is* interesting," Gertrude II said, thoughtfully. "I wonder if...Is their family from the region you visited? Egypt?"

"You know, Rowan told us his mother was Greek, and we were in Alexandria, Egypt, around forty-eight B.C.," Xavier said.

"And the Greeks *were* running the country at that time," Xanthe added.

"Well, I think I can tell you what happened to your friends," Gertrude II said matter-of-factly. "They simply don't exist in this universe. They were never born. We can check a database to see if their names show up anywhere, but I can almost guarantee I'm right."

"You see, my dears, one can visit the past in the alleviators, but it's impossible to travel to a future where you don't exist," Agatha II said. She was picking pieces off the jam-covered scone and had eaten about a third of it.

"I'm afraid the fate of your friends, Rowan and Nina," she continued, "is the same as the fate of all the others who have lost their place in time. They are not of this universe. Subsequently, they've become phantoms of the resort." Now two-thirds of the scone had disappeared.

"Not of this universe ... How many universes are there?" Xavier asked.

"Nobody knows," Aunt Gertrude II answered with a shrug.

"Aunt Gertrude, is it possible that the universe Xavier and I came from is also some alternate universe created by somebody's mistake?"

"I didn't want to be the one to say it, but it is entirely possible."

"Let's not get so gloomy!" Agatha II popped the rest of her scone in her mouth. Bits of the pastry flaked onto her tunic, which she brushed off. "Life goes on, whatever universe you're in. Your problem is getting back home. I suggest we focus on that, and leave philosophy to the philosophers."

"Well, there's only one solution," Gertrude II said, clapping her hands suddenly. "You must take the alleviator back to Alexandria, forty-eight B.C., and undo whatever damage has been done. You've got to keep your universe from creating this new branch."

"How will I know where things started going off course?"

"For that," Gertrude II said, grabbing her poncho, "we'll need a trip to the library."

"Perhaps," Agatha II said. "But first I think a good long rest is in order. We can go tomorrow after a good, hearty breakfast. You two look exhausted. Why don't you go upstairs and lie down in the guest room."

But upon the mere suggestion of rest Xanthe had already collapsed on the couch, her eyes fluttering to stillness. She stayed there until morning.

+ CHAPTER SIXTEEN +
PHANTOM WORLD

AGATHA DROPPED XANTHE AND XAVIER OFF AT the library bright and early. Though weary from the time travel jet lag, both had rested uneasily knowing their friends were in limbo. They hoped Rowan and Nina understood that they were working on a solution.

Jenny O'Neill II provided them with a stack of books on Alexandria, Egypt, and Roman history, and they dove in. Xanthe quickly found the point in history where they'd arrived in Alexandria, with Cleopatra Tryphaena's disappearance and the ascension of Berenice. She flipped ahead to the return of Cleopatra's father and his death, Cleopatra's rise to the throne, and the arrival of Caesar.

"Here we go, Xave," she said, pointing. "Cleopatra is smuggled into the palace in a rug. Ptolemy the Thirteenth, her younger brother and co-ruler, finds out the next morning and throws a tantrum because he realizes she's allied with Caesar, and...wait a minute. I think this is where things go screwy. Didn't you tell me that Octavian becomes the first emperor of the Roman Empire?"

"Yeah, after Caesar's death."

"Well, not in *this* universe. Octavian dies from a snakebite, soon after Caesar meets Cleopatra. He never gets back to Rome. Caesar blames Ptolemy, kills him..." She flipped to the back of the book. "Huh? Mark Antony isn't even mentioned in the index of this book."

Xavier nodded, looking through a biography of Julius Caesar. "It says here that Caesar dies at the ripe old age of seventy-eight. On March fifteenth, he narrowly escapes being assassinated by members of the Roman Senate. He commands his legions to slaughter the people who planned the attack, but he still remains hugely popular. He is the one crowned emperor, with Cleopatra as his empress, because she never kills herself." He scanned further through the book. "Then when Julius Caesar dies, their son, Caesarian, is crowned both emperor and pharaoh, and it goes on from there. Caesarian spawned a dynasty of his own that lasted several hundred years."

"So I guess in this universe, Cleopatra had a much greater influence on history."

"Octavian's death is the turning point," Xavier said. "But how on earth are we going to keep him from getting bitten by a snake? And how could we have caused it?"

"I don't know, but we've got to try to protect him."

• • •

Before heading out to the Owatannauk, Gertrude II and Agatha II joined the twins for dinner at Hilda's Coffee Shop and Grocery, whose menu included such downhome delicacies as fried pigeon and rabbit pie, as well as her famous soups. Xanthe stuck to the grilled cheese sandwich, while Xavier played it safe with the fish chowder.

"You know, even if we can change things back to the way they're supposed to be—so Rowan and Nina can exist—we still have to go back and rescue Aunt Agatha," Xavier said between spoonfuls of soup. "I mean, *our* Aunt Agatha."

"I know, I was thinking the same thing," Xanthe said. "I hope she's okay. I don't even think she had a chair in her cell."

"Oh, I'm sure she's ... I'm ... fine," Agatha II tittered. "I'm quite resourceful. In any universe, I believe I would have a good head screwed onto my shoulders."

"My goodness, yes." Gertrude II laughed. "If anybody can navigate through the perils of time travel, it's Agatha. I may be the Time Detective, but if it wasn't for Agatha, I wouldn't be here today. She rescued me from a rat-infested hellhole where I'd already spent thirty-six days, accused of heresy during the Spanish Inquisition. I would've died there for sure, or been burned at the stake. I am forever in your debt, dear Sister."

"Ooh, yes, that was grim, wasn't it?" Agatha II said. "Don't talk about those horrible times, Gertrude. That was long ago."

Xavier stopped eating. "How could you spend thirty-six days in a cell if your alleviator key disintegrates after seven?"

"I didn't have a key," Gertrude II said. "I was just an ordinary nun, ministering to a small village on the outskirts of

Seville. The Inquisition was very strong at that time, arresting people on the flimsiest of pretexts and torturing them until they confessed to being enemies of the church. Then, after forcing the prisoners to name other supposed enemies, they'd execute them." She sighed. "It was hard to be a nun then. Very hard ... I stood by and watched a lot of innocent people go to their deaths. After a while, I couldn't stand myself for not speaking out, so I did. It wasn't long before I was snatched up and thrown in jail with the rest of the so-called heretics."

"Hold on," Xanthe interrupted. "You were living in Spain during the Spanish Inquisition? But that's like ... wasn't that in the fourteen-hundreds?"

"It was fourteen ninety-two to be exact," Agatha II piped in. "I was poking around Seville at that time, following Christopher Columbus. Fascinating explorer! I took this trip about five years after the Owatannauk had been constructed and Archie had just invented his first alleviator."

"You mean Archibald Weber? You knew him personally?" Xavier asked, eyes wide.

"He was a history student of mine when I was a brand-new teacher at St. Augustine Academy for Boys. I always knew there was something special about him, and I think he liked my, shall we say, 'unconventional' teaching style. The principal didn't, but that's another story. Anyway, we remained good friends after he graduated and after I moved on to a different job as a private secretary. I was a regular at the Owatannauk during its heyday."

"So you were one of the first people to use the alleviators?"

"That's right. It was very different then. Not so many regulations. So there I was in Seville, and, being a nun myself, I
sought out the local church. That's how I met Gertrude."

"We immediately hit it off," Gertrude II said. "Agatha was
like a breath of fresh air in a rather frightening time."

"There was something about Gertrude, her intensity, her
strength, her purity of faith..."

"Oh, stop!" Gertrude II laughed. "You just wanted a chess
partner and I had the only board in town." Agatha II fell into
a fit of giggles.

"At any rate, we spent a lot of time together," Agatha II
continued after settling herself. "I was there when the church
police broke down her door and carted her away, and I
attended her trial. It wasn't much of a trial, really, just a lot of
crazy accusations, and she was as stubborn as you'd expect her
to be. I knew that she was going to be tortured. I couldn't bear
to think of what they might do, so I appealed to Archie. He
granted me a favor, as an old friend. He gave me a second key. I
alleviated into the torture chamber where Gertrude was
chained up, poor thing—"

"And you came just in time. The guards were just about to
brand me with an H, for heretic, right on the back of my
neck." Gertrude II shuddered. "Thank God I was spared that.
Agatha appeared in a blaze of light, like an angel..."

"Or a devil, depending on your point of view," Agatha
giggled to herself. "Those guards dropped the brand and
screamed that they'd seen Satan himself. It gave me enough
time to push Gertrude into the alleviator and disappear. I

brought her back to the Owatannauk, and we have lived here to this day."

"Of course it took me a while to get used to the idea of living in the future," Gertrude II added, "but as you can see, I've learned to adapt."

Xanthe and Xavier looked at each other, wondering if they had really heard what the Sisters had said correctly.

"But that means you are from the Middle Ages," Xanthe finally said, pointing to Gertrude II. She turned to Agatha II. "And you are from Victorian times? Late eighteen hundreds?"

"This happened right around the turn of the century, I think," Agatha II said, squinting as though trying to remember.

"So, Aunt Gertrude, you're over five hundred years old? And you, Aunt Agatha, you are over two hundred?"

"Oh, goodness, I'm not that old! I'll only be a hundred and ninety-eight this December," she said, her eyes twinkling.

"I'm surprised your Agatha and Gertrude never told you how they met," Gertrude II said.

"But how can you be so old?" Xavier asked. "You don't look it."

"Thank you, my dear, but surely you realize that when you time travel, the process of aging is suspended during the period that you spend in the past," Gertrude II replied. "We have been getting older, just a lot more slowly than most— probably because we spend so much time poking around in history. Now we should go," she said, taking the check from Hilda. "The golden hour is almost upon us."

• • •

Xanthe ran up the rotting stairs into the hotel lobby, ahead of Xavier and the aunts, coughing from the dust. She wanted to be there before Rowan and Nina materialized. *They must be terrified*, she thought. She pictured them drifting through nothingness like lost balloons. She hoped they knew how sorry she was, but, most of all, she hoped she found them within the hour, before they disappeared back into the unreachable void.

As the rest of the group entered the lobby, life rushed upon the hotel like a storm. This time, Xanthe and Xavier had both braced themselves against something. Even though it always made Xanthe's stomach feel a little squirrely, she never tired of watching the building spring into shape.

"Xanthe! Xavier! Over here!" Rowan waved from the top of the curved staircase. He scampered down as Nina slid down the bannister. Xanthe and Xavier hurried to meet them at the bottom. They grabbed each other in hugs. Rowan and Nina were solid and warm.

"You're here! You're here!" Xanthe squealed. "Oh, man, I was so worried. When you guys disappeared…I thought…" Tears had formed in her eyes. She shook her head, laughed, and squeezed them both tightly.

"We're okay," Rowan said. "We could see you going crazy, and we tried to call out to you, but it was like a veil suddenly dropped and you sort of…faded. Actually, the whole outside world beyond the Stop sign faded. We could still see you, but you just looked like outlines in a coloring book. No matter how much we yelled and screamed you couldn't hear us."

"There was nothing to do but go back to the hotel," Nina said.

"Even though it was back to being rundown?" Xavier said.

"Not to us. It still looked like this," Nina said, sweeping her hand at the clean, bright lobby.

"We think we know why this happened to you," Xanthe said hesitantly.

"We know, we know," Rowan said. "We're in an alternate universe where we weren't born. We know all about it."

"Oh." Xanthe expected them to be a little angrier. "I'm really sorry. We really screwed it up for you guys."

"Don't kid yourself, you guys screwed things up for yourselves, too. You can't live in this alternate universe any more than we can. You can't risk running into yourselves, remember?"

"Actually, that won't be a problem for me," Xanthe muttered. "Xave and I went into town and I dropped by Nana's house, although it wasn't really *my* Nana, it was *this* universe's Nana. Anyway, she told me that in this universe, I died when I was ten. But it's a long story. We don't have time for it now."

Xavier seemed to disappear into his thoughts for a moment, but then snapped back. "We think we did something that affects Octavian in forty-eight B.C.," he said. "He's Julius Caesar's nephew and adopted son, *and* he's the future Augustus Caesar. I'm not sure what it was, but we've got to go back and reverse it in order to get everything back on track."

"Sounds like a plan," Rowan said. Nina nodded.

"Excuse me," Xanthe said, "but I thought you guys would be furious. What's wrong with you?"

Nina looked like she was about to burst. "We didn't have time to be mad. As phantoms, we've had the run of this whole resort. It's so totally mind-blowing!"

Rowan grinned. "We've been to the lake, on the squash courts, in the sauna, at the stables...Did you know they have an entire equestrian center here? We heard an art historian talk about French impressionism in the Evergreen Reading Room, had lunch at the pool cabana and dinner in the big restaurant!"

"And we met some other kids who clued us in to what had happened to us. It's what's happened to everybody here," Nina said.

"Sounds like a party," Xanthe said. "I hope we didn't ruin it for you by showing up."

"Be serious," Rowan said. "This is a prison. A nice one, but still, people are stuck here. The only other option is to find a place in history that you like, go there, and stay there."

"Of course, if you do that you're beyond the reach of the Owatannauk's search-and-rescue team," Gertrude II interrupted. She had walked over from the concierge desk with Agatha II, after talking with Otto. "If you choose to live in the past, you will no doubt affect history and consequentially start a whole new branch. Out of my territory."

"Just like we're out of the territory of *our* Gertrude," Xanthe mused.

Gertrude II extended her hand to Rowan. "Hi, I'm Gertrude Pembroke, and this is Agatha Drake. You must be Rowan and Nina."

Rowan shook it, obviously disturbed that she didn't recognize him.

"Okay, we should go," Xavier said.

"Ooh, wait, I forgot my lyre," Nina said. She darted to retrieve it.

Xanthe turned to Agatha II and Gertrude II. "Thanks for your help. It was nice to meet . . . these other versions of you."

"Likewise," Gertrude II said. "Good luck. I hope you fix what you changed and find your way back to your own universe. I'll be listening from my station, so don't hesitate to ask for help. And incidentally . . ." She leaned forward, conspiratorially. "If the Gertrude in your universe is anything like me, she's going to be incredibly disappointed with this turn of events," she said.

"I know," Xanthe sighed. "What can I do?"

"Try giving her these," Gertrude II said, handing Xanthe a small paper bag. Xanthe looked inside. It contained horehound drops, the bitter brown candy that Gertrude loved, which gave her breath a distinct medicinal smell. "Tell her that those of us in the alternate universe bid her warm greetings. Tell her we are alive and well."

"I just thought of something," Xanthe said. "If we succeed,

and we're able to get back on track, you won't be alive and well. This universe will disappear, and so will you."

"I suppose that's true, but it's only a theory," Gertrude II said with a grim little smile. "Quite a power, isn't it? To create and destroy whole universes? Not something to be taken lightly."

"Ah, Sister," Agatha II said, putting her hand on Gertrude II's shoulder. "They have enough to worry about without adding our existence to the pile." She turned to Xanthe. "Don't worry about us. If our universe disappears, we won't even be born yet. Now go. And good luck."

Xanthe followed Xavier, Rowan, and Nina into alleviator number five and braced herself as Xavier set the temple's coordinates and pushed the button for 48 B.C., the year of their last encounter with Cleopatra, but one day later. As the pitch of the alleviator's hum rose higher and higher, she tucked the bag of horehound drops into her *kalasiris*. She had left the mischievous cinnamon-colored cat with the Sisters for safekeeping, though how safe he'd be in a doomed alternate universe was admittedly debatable. The next thing she knew, she was splayed on the floor of the alleviator, and Xavier was helping her to her feet.

She was about to step into the temple when Xavier yanked her back. "Wait!" he whispered. "Somebody's out there. Look, behind that pillar...a shadow. And there's another one!" Xanthe peered through the open door. Sure enough, there were people back there. She could hear murmuring and rustling sounds. She pressed the button to shut the doors.

"Something tells me that's not Cleopatra," Xanthe said. She turned to Xavier. "Listen, you and I should go first as bait, and find out who is hiding behind the pillars. Once we're out of the temple, then Rowan and Nina can follow. Nobody knows who Rowan and Nina are, and we can use that to our advantage."

"Good idea," Xavier agreed. "It's like you read my mind."

Xanthe turned to Rowan and Nina. "If we get separated, we'll meet you in the botanical gardens near the museum."

Xavier squeezed her hand. "Remember, we're Gods. Time to toss some thunderbolts."

"You said it," she agreed, opening the alleviator doors. "Let's go!"

CHAPTER SEVENTEEN

THE CHALLENGE

As soon as Xanthe and Xavier stepped into the temple, they were surrounded by guards and put under arrest, charged with treason. They didn't argue, but went quietly. Xanthe thought they might have been able to put up a good struggle, since several of the guards appeared nervous, shaken by the twins' sudden appearance. But it wouldn't have done them any good to get injured, and Xanthe suspected the guards would take them right where they wanted to be anyway.

Sure enough, they were escorted to the palace and into what appeared to be a throne room, richly decorated in green and purple silks. Ptolemy entered, followed by Photinus. The boy king slumped on the large golden seat while his adviser paced a circuitous route around the room, glowering at the twins. Eventually he ended up in front of them, so close that Xanthe could smell the oil in his hair.

"So. You came back," he said to Xanthe. "I wondered if you

would. I was under the impression that you made an appearance only once every few years."

Xanthe said nothing. Photinus narrowed his eyes.

"The queen thinks you are a Goddess—the Goddess Isis. I, on the other hand, don't. I don't know who or what you are—thief, enchantress, or fraud. It doesn't really matter to me. I do know that the queen listens to you and will take your advice. Is that not so?"

Xanthe knew he was trying to get her to speak, so she didn't, out of pure stubbornness. Photinus's hand shot out and slapped her. Xanthe gasped, holding her cheek.

In a flash, Xavier kicked Photinus squarely in the nose. The man collapsed in a heap, and two guards fell upon Xavier, holding him back.

"Hands off!" he roared, ramming one in the gut with his elbow and punching the other in the nose with the heel of his hand. They staggered back, gasping, not quite sure what hit them. *Never mess with a black belt*, Xanthe thought to herself.

"You dare place your mortal hands on us?" Xanthe spat, standing over Photinus. "Keep your distance, or the next time we will turn you to dust!"

"I believe you can bleed like any mortal," Photinus said shakily. "And I'm willing to test my theory, right now, unless you do as I ask!"

"And what, pray tell, is that?" Xanthe said.

"Order Cleopatra to break her alliance with Caesar. She must abdicate the throne to her brother, Ptolemy the Thirteenth, to rule Egypt alone."

"Their father willed that they rule together."

Ptolemy pounded the throne. "*She's* the one who won't share! She won't include me in anything! She minted coins without my face on them, as though I didn't even exist! But she underestimated our people—the Alexandrians and the Egyptians want a king. They suffered under her. Nobody came to her aid when I had her banished. But somehow she snuck back into Alexandria!"

"Yesterday morning she revealed herself, clinging to Julius Caesar like a barnacle on a ship," Photinus said, his mouth twisted as though he'd sucked a lemon.

"She's a snake!" Ptolemy sat down with a great scowl on his face.

No, she's a cat, thought Xanthe.

"You are too late," Xavier said. "The alliance is made. Caesar and Cleopatra are together. It is as it should be."

"We'll soon see about that," Photinus said, focusing his attention on Xavier. "But that brings us to the question of you. I thought you were a servant, but then I overheard you talking with...I'll call her 'Isis' for lack of anything better. I heard 'Isis' call you 'brother,' which would make you Osiris, I believe?"

Xavier leveled a piercing stare at Photinus, who shrank back. *Xave really is gifted at this,* Xanthe thought. *He's such a chameleon, he's comfortable inside anyone's skin. Even a God's.*

"What is your point?" Xavier said evenly.

"Fascinating story, the legend of Isis and Osiris," Photinus said, taking interest in the grape bowl. "Seth, the God of destruction, overcome by jealousy, kidnaps Osiris and nails him into a chest. Then after Isis rescues him and breathes life into him, Seth rips him to pieces and casts them into the river for crocodile food. Isis finds all the pieces but one, and again brings Osiris to life, to become ruler of the Underworld." Photinus slid Xanthe a look. "You may find you'll need to use your rejuvenating skills again, very soon, 'Goddess.'" He snapped his fingers at a nearby guard. "Get the queen," he said.

Cleopatra entered the room within minutes. "What is the meaning of this?" she demanded. "I will not be summoned like a common servant. Not by the likes of you, Photinus." She stopped when she saw Xanthe and Xavier. "Why are they here?"

"They have something to tell you," Photinus said. "A small piece of advice."

"I'll give no such advice," Xanthe scoffed.

"Forget it, then," Photinus snapped. "We don't need you." He turned to Cleopatra. "Give up the throne to Ptolemy. Julius Caesar has no business in Egyptian politics. He'll be paid what your father owed him, but after that he must leave. If you don't break your alliance with him, his nephew Octavian will be killed."

Xanthe gave Xavier a look. They'd only just arrived and Octavian was already in danger.

"What do I care what you do to Octavian?" Cleopatra scoffed. "He is nothing but a fair-haired boy with a weak constitution."

"That's not what I heard," Photinus sang, turning his gaze to Xanthe and Xavier.

Xanthe broke out in a cold sweat. Photinus must have overheard her and Xavier arguing after they'd left the palace. He'd heard them talk about Octavian's future—whether or not he believed they were Gods, he knew at the very least that Octavian was important to them.

"Octavian is under Caesar's watchful eye. Do you really think he'll let an attack on his nephew go unanswered?" Xanthe said coldly.

"The attack has already happened. Caesar's 'watchful eye' was not open at the time, due to his being . . . distracted . . . by you, dear Queen." Photinus snickered. "And I'm sure it won't take much to convince him that your distraction was part of this plot against his beloved nephew."

"That's absurd!" Cleopatra cried. "Caesar would never believe such a lie! In fact, I'm going to tell him right now!" She spun on her heel and headed for the door.

Xanthe ran after her. One thing she knew was that they had to save Octavian without Caesar knowing about any of it, or history would surely change again. She caught the queen before she reached the door and pulled her aside.

"Queen Cleopatra, Photinus is right. Caesar must not hear about his nephew's capture, or he will blame you for it."

Cleopatra frowned. "You see this?"

"Yes, I see it, and if anything happens to Octavian, Caesar will become depressed and leave Egypt for good. You'll never see him again," Xanthe lied. "And it will leave you vulnerable. Ptolemy will prevail."

"So what must I do? Either way—I lose the throne!" Cleopatra glanced at Photinus, who smiled smugly. "I'm going to poison that horrible creature," she said. "He has been a thorn in my foot since my father died. Ptolemy, too. I should get rid of them both."

"No, no, that's no good, either," Xanthe cautioned, worried about Cleopatra causing more changes to history. They needed a way to force Photinus to reveal the location of Octavian before another day went by. She looked desperately at Xavier. He stared back at her intensely, then, much to her relief, a smile spread across his face.

"I have another way to solve this matter," Xavier said, striding to the center of the room. "I propose a challenge."

Ptolemy sat up straight, his interest piqued. "A challenge to determine who will rule Egypt," Xavier continued. "Cleopatra, with the aid of Julius Caesar, or Ptolemy the Thirteenth and his Regency Council."

Xavier, you're brilliant, Xanthe thought. She had seen for herself how much the Ptolemies enjoyed challenges. And from the eager looks on their faces, Cleopatra and her brother were no different. Now the young king was on his feet.

"Yes! A gladiatorial battle in the amphitheater!" Ptolemy declared, turning to his sister. "And since you seem to love the Romans so much, let it be fought in the Roman tradition. A fight to the death."

"Each side will choose two champions," Cleopatra proposed. "Whoever survives, wins."

"And the champions can choose whichever weapon or weapons they wish," Xavier added.

Xanthe wondered how he could be so confident. She caught his eye and thought she saw him wink.

Photinus whispered in Ptolemy's ear. Ptolemy smiled. "Then it is decided," he said curtly.

Cleopatra nodded her assent. "And now that we have determined how we will settle our differences, you must tell us where you are keeping Octavian."

"Not so fast, dear Queen," Photinus said smugly. "We're going to hold him until the battle is over, to ensure that you keep your side of the bargain."

"How dare you question my honor!" Cleopatra snapped. "I can end this right now by marching over to Caesar and telling him you're holding his nephew hostage! It'll be *your* head on the platter this time, not Pompey's!"

"Do it, and no one will ever see Octavian again," Photinus countered.

Xanthe stepped between them. "Is Octavian in danger?" she asked Photinus.

"He's not dead, if that's what you mean."

"But he's sick," Xavier said. "He could easily take a turn for the worse."

"Then we must have the challenge before sunrise," Xanthe announced. She turned to Photinus. "And you must give your word that whatever happens, Octavian will not be injured."

"If King Ptolemy's champions fail, then Octavian will be released, and Ptolemy will submit to ruling with his sister and her...consort," Photinus said. "If Cleopatra's champions fail and she steps down, then Octavian will be on the boat with Caesar when he sails back to Rome. If, however, Cleopatra's champions fail and she does *not* step down, Octavian's life is immediately forfeit, and—" Photinus cut his eyes at Cleopatra. "The queen's own health will be in jeopardy. I do swear it."

"My champions will not fail. *You* will be the one on a boat looking for sanctuary, if any other country will have such a flea-wit."

As they continued bickering, Xanthe noticed a figure with wild black hair dart by the window, followed by a stocky figure, which dove into the bushes. They were like two guardian angels, Nina and Rowan. She felt a surge of confidence. They could do this.

After a few more minutes of posturing, Cleopatra, Xanthe, and Xavier left Ptolemy and Photinus and headed back to Cleopatra's chamber. In those last heated exchanges, they had decided that to keep the battle a secret from Caesar, Cleopatra and Ptolemy would not be present, and that Xanthe and Photinus would attend in their place. In this way, the royal siblings could distance themselves from the battle if Caesar, or anyone else, caught wind of it.

Once in her room, Cleopatra offered Xanthe and Xavier food, but they declined. She took a seat and motioned to a servant, who set about preparing a footbath.

"I'm surprised to see you, Goddess," Cleopatra said. "But I am pleased. I thought you could only come once every few years."

"Usually that is true," Xanthe said. "But I sensed your need, so I returned with my brother. We will see you installed firmly on the throne before we leave."

"I am glad of it. But still I am worried. Photinus has the best fighters in the Alexandrian Army. Some of them can crush a man's skull in their bare hands. I would ask Caesar for two soldiers for this contest, but if I do he will ask questions. Also, Photinus cannot be trusted. The fact that he and Ptolemy agreed so readily to the challenge worries me. They will not play fair."

"That's all right." Xavier laughed. "We're Gods. We don't plan on playing fair, either."

As they walked through the botanical gardens, Xavier laid out his idea to Xanthe, who again was amazed by her brother's logic. All their lives she had taken the lead, making the decisions and ordering him around. She had to admit, he was more than capable of putting together a decent plan. But they'd need Rowan and Nina's help, and convincing them might take some doing. They came upon the Popplewells near the entrance to the zoo. Xavier immediately started filling them in on everything that had happened since their capture.

"We heard you suggest the challenge," Rowan said. "Great idea. Caesar is bound to have some huge muscle guys who can beat anyone they've got. He may even have some soldiers that were former gladiators..."

"No, Rowan, you don't understand," Xavier interrupted. "Caesar can't know about this. I told Cleopatra that we would provide the champions ourselves."

"But who do we know who can fight?"

"You and me."

"I'm sorry, you and *who*?"

Nina put down her lyre. "Quit kidding around," she said. "Who do you have, really?"

"I'm not kidding. Rowan and I are going to fight the gladiators."

"We can't force you to do it, Rowan," Xanthe said. "But it makes sense."

"No it doesn't! It's insane! Xave might be a karate king, but I can barely do ten pushups! Just lifting one of those big swords will snap my wrist!"

"That doesn't matter," Xavier assured him. "Rowan, have you ever read any Greek or Roman myths? One thing you see happening over and over is the Gods meddling in human affairs. They get jealous, they pick favorites, they choose heroes. Heroes like Jason, Odysseus, Hercules, Perseus, Theseus..."

"I get the point. Gods help heroes. What does that have to do with anything?"

"I'm getting there. Gods help heroes by giving them magical gifts, like winged sandals, unbreakable swords, invisible cloaks, flying horses...Get the picture? And the heroes use these enchanted items to defeat their enemies. Xanthe and I are Gods. At least everybody here thinks we are. During the battle, Xanthe can provide us with magical gifts, or at least appear to."

"How?"

"I get it! The alleviators!" Nina squealed. "You're going to use the alleviators!"

"Actually, *you* are," Xanthe said. "The battle's taking place at the silver hour. While I wave my hands and mumble some hocus-pocus, you will be at the Owatannauk, sending things to Rowan and Xavier through the alleviator. Alternate-universe Gertrude can help her set the coordinates to land one in the arena, and it'll be like a direct pipeline." She turned to Rowan and Xavier. "Also, if you guys get in trouble, you can get out quickly by jumping into it and disappearing."

"The beauty of it is, since they already believe we're Gods, the magic is explained—maybe even expected," Xavier added.

"Wait a minute, what kind of stuff am I supposed to send?" Nina asked.

"The aunts' vault has all kinds of stuff," Xanthe said. "Again, Gertrude can help you. I'm not sure what the alternate Sisters have, but *our* Agatha and Gertrude had all kinds of cool weapons in theirs."

"What if there are no weapons?"

"Are you kidding? Those pack rats? I can guarantee there's something you can use in there." Xanthe placed a hand on Nina's shoulder. "You'll just have to be creative."

Rowan mulled it over, then shrugged, resigned. "Okay, I'll do it. But what if the fight goes past the silver hour and the alleviator disappears?"

Xanthe shrugged, too, at a loss. "Make sure it's a fast fight."

"It's decided then," Xavier said. "Now let's get some sleep. We're all going to need it if we're going to pull this thing off."

Xanthe held out her fist. Xavier did the same. Rowan and Nina joined in, and they pounded their fists together in solidarity. In her mind's eye, Xanthe had a vision, a quick flash into the future. This was the first time they'd ever made this gesture, but it would not be the last.

+ CHAPTER EIGHTEEN +
BATTLE

Cleopatra provided luxurious accommodations for her guests: a room with four ample beds, each with plump, inviting pillows and sumptuous linens. It brought them little pleasure, however. Xavier lay on top of the bedding, nervously slapping his knees together. Rowan tossed and turned so much he toppled over the side. Nina never even got into bed; she sat staring at the moon, twisting her hair into hopeless knots. Xanthe couldn't relax, either. After Rowan's third tumble, she suggested that they give up on sleep and instead talk about what they might face the next day. Deep down, she feared the only thing that would save them was a whopping dose of luck—but she kept this to herself.

Xavier was much more positive. He spun out information from his Cicero contest research, describing a typical gladiator battle.

"Inside the holding pen, Rowan and I will be given light

armor for our arms and legs, and helmets—just enough to protect us from minor injuries," Xavier said. "Also, we'll be wearing loincloths."

"Oh, come on!" Rowan groaned. "You're telling me all I'm going to be wearing is some kneepads and a diaper?!"

"Rowan, what you'll be wearing is really the least of your worries," Nina said. She turned to Xanthe. "Are you guys sure about this? I've been thinking about it and...it seems awfully dangerous."

"Look, I can't say it's safe," Xavier said, "but we have to do what we can to find Octavian and return him safely to Caesar. Otherwise we're stuck out of our own time for good."

"I don't want to be a phantom, Nina," Rowan said. "I prefer the life I know. It may be dangerous, but we've got to get back...or die trying."

"Okay, okay," Xanthe grumbled. "Let's keep things upbeat. Go ahead, Xave."

"So then they will offer us our choice of weapons," Xavier continued. "They'll probably have an axe, a straight sword, a trident and net, a lance, a curved knife, and a curved sword."

"Is one of the choices a rubber band? Because shooting pencils with rubber bands is the only weapon I've ever used in my whole entire life."

"Well, it doesn't really matter which weapon you choose," Xanthe said. "Hopefully Nina will send down stuff that the other gladiators won't be expecting."

"Like what? An old typewriter? A wagon wheel? A vintage hula hoop?"

"Happy thoughts, Rowan, happy thoughts!" Xanthe said, but she could see that Rowan wasn't buying it. "Look, I know you're nervous. We all are. But you've got to remember that Gertrude will be there. She's listening in, remember? She promised she'd do everything she could to help us. Even if *we* don't really know what we're doing, *she* does."

Rowan grimaced. "This is the alternate-universe Gertrude, though. Maybe she's not as good as the other one."

Xanthe shrugged. She didn't have an answer for that.

Rowan relented. "All right, I'll try not to be so negative." He turned to Xavier. "Then what?"

"After we choose our weapons, an official will inspect them to make sure they're sharp," Xavier continued. "Then we'll turn to face Xanthe—that is, Isis—and Photinus, who will be in the stands. Our opponents will do the same. At that point, we raise our weapons and shout courageously, 'We who are about to die salute you!'"

"My stomach hurts."

"I have faith in you," Xanthe said. "And we won't let anything happen to you. We're all in this together, you know."

Rowan closed his eyes for a moment and nodded. "All right. Let's do it. We've gotten out of tight places before, we can do it again."

"That's the spirit!" Xanthe said. With Rowan onboard, anything was possible.

"Whatever you do, don't run away," Xavier added. "Or the official will come out and whip you, or brand you with a hot iron."

"Xave!" Xanthe punched him hard in the arm. "Save it!"

"Sorry! I thought he should know!"

"Just hang out near the alleviator. Both of you." Xanthe said. "It's your source for weapons—and your escape hatch."

An hour before the match was set to begin, while the boys went to the arena, Xanthe took Nina to the alleviator in the Temple of Isis.

"I'm scared," Nina said suddenly. "I don't think I can do it."

"Of course you can," Xanthe said. "Gertrude will help you set the alleviator in the arena. All you have to do is find something in that vault that can defeat a gladiator."

"I mean, I don't think I can be away from Rowan right now. What if something happens to him?" Nina's eyes were shiny. "I can't lose him, Xanthe. I've already lost one person..."

"Look, Nina, I know what you mean, but we can't think about that right now. We all have to be strong, otherwise it's not going to work. Rowan doesn't need you to hold his hand—he needs you to use your head. And don't worry about Xave. He's taken a lot of martial arts classes, he knows a little about weapons, and I think he might be able to dazzle them with sheer personality. At least I hope so. But you know Rowan better than anybody. Only *you* know what he can use to beat these guys."

"I guess so," Nina bit her lip. "But honestly, Xanthe, we're talking about Rowan. He's wonderful. He's the best brother in the whole world. But skills? Fighting skills? He can beat anyone at a video game, he's memorized the *Star Wars* movies, he knows every detail of the Harry Potter books, he's a really good chess player..." She sighed. "I don't see much there to use."

Xanthe couldn't argue with that. Rowan's strength lay in his heart and soul, not his fists. The gladiator battle had seemed like a decent idea, but now, with only an hour to go, she had to admit it was a long shot.

"And we're all avoiding saying this," Nina continued, "but Rowan and Xave don't just have to *defeat* these guys, they have to *kill* them. I don't know if Rowan can do that. I don't know if he has it in him."

Xanthe just looked at Nina. "I don't either," she said finally. And now she had doubts about Xavier.

Photinus was already in the stands of the amphitheater when Xanthe arrived. As she took her seat, he motioned to his guard, who blew a single, prolonged note from a horn. The sound resonated throughout the arena. On cue, a lone figure dressed in a loincloth and light armor stepped hesitantly into the arena. He clutched a short knife, and, as he walked, his shield scraped the ground. It caught on a rut and he tripped, landing on top of it and sliding several feet in the dirt.

"Ah! A clown to entertain us!" Photinus said, clapping.

Xanthe cleared her voice. "That is our champion."

Photinus said nothing, but turned back to the arena with a smug smile.

Xavier followed soon after, carrying a spear. One end had

an iron blade, and to the other he had tied a short knife, so that both ends of the spear could be used for stabbing.

Good, Xanthe thought. He had used just such a pole to win a silver medal at a jujitsu tournament. She'd seen him sweep men much taller than him and three times his weight off their feet. She wondered how big Ptolemy's gladiators would be—they hadn't shown up yet.

"Where are your champions?" Xanthe said. "Or are you forfeiting the match?"

Photinus pursed his lips. "Hardly."

Just then, two mountainous figures entered the arena from the opposite side. One held a curved sword and shield, the other a trident and net. Both were bald, except for a shock of hair in the back, tied up with leather straps. Rowan and Xavier hesitated, then approached the stands, turning to face Xanthe and Photinus. The gladiators did the same. Xanthe and Photinus stood, and there was silence.

From the corner of her eye, Xanthe saw the alleviator materialize several yards away from the boys. She smiled.

Xavier and Rowan saw it, too. They raised their weapons.

"Those of us who are about to die salute you!" they declared with their opponents.

Photinus held up a white handkerchief, then dropped it. It fluttered to the dirt floor, and the battle was on.

Xavier immediately paired himself with the taller gladiator with the curved sword, leaving Rowan to deal with the one holding the trident. Xavier and his foe seemed evenly matched. The gladiator was much bigger, but Xavier was quick and relentless, parrying, swinging, and twirling the spear as only a true show-off can. Satisfied that her brother was holding his own, Xanthe's gaze shifted to Rowan.

Her heart sank. The stocky gladiator had already dragged Rowan down with the net and was jabbing at him with his trident, but Rowan avoided it, flopping around and rolling from side to side like a beached fish. He managed to jerk the net from the gladiator's grasp, then scrambled to his feet and ran, tripping several times, but finally untangling himself from the ropes. Unfortunately, he left behind his knife and shield.

"I think the goose is about to be cooked." Photinus chuckled.

Xanthe crossed her fingers so hard for luck she thought they might break.

Rowan made a mad dash for the alleviator. This was Xanthe's cue. She stood and made a great show of summoning her powers, waving her arms and muttering incantations. What she was really doing was praying that Nina had found something big and dangerous, like a hand grenade or a bazooka.

Rowan reached inside the alleviator and pulled out a barrel. Stenciled on the side in thick black letters was the word "pickles."

At first Xanthe thought she was dreaming, but there it was, a barrel of pickles. She wondered what he was going to do with a bunch of gherkins, when out rolled another barrel. This one said "nails." Then out came four that said "rum," followed by "gunpowder," "olive oil," "buttons," and "hardtack."

"Where did those come from?" Photinus demanded.

"I gave them to him," Xanthe announced. "It's a gift from the Gods." Photinus's mouth fell open. She gave him a curt smile and turned her attention back to the action.

The stocky gladiator flew toward Rowan, his trident raised. Rowan tipped over the pickle barrel and gave it a hard push with his foot. The gladiator leaped over this one deftly, but soon the other nine barrels were bouncing and careening toward him, and he became confused, jumping this way and that, but finally getting nailed by the one marked "nails." The barrel took a bad bounce, slammed against his head, and he fell backward, only to be run over by more barrels. While he was down, Rowan made another break for the alleviator.

Xavier's gladiator, distracted by the rolling barrels, soon found himself falling victim to Xavier's expert leg-sweep. Then Xavier stabbed him sharply in the shoulder.

"A hit!" Xanthe cried. But in the next moment, Xavier's gladiator was up, his sword skimming over Xavier's head. If Xavier hadn't already been bald, he would have been now.

Again Xavier twirled his spear, moving it so fast it looked like helicopter blades, but the gladiator brought his sword down on the shaft, cutting off one end. Xavier flipped it over to jab him with the other end, but that, too, was chopped off, leaving Xavier with nothing but a long wooden pole. *Oh, no, what can he do with just a stick?* Xanthe fretted. In a moment she found out.

Xavier held the pole over his shoulder and charged the

gladiator. At the last minute, he plunged the pole into the ground, vaulting over the gladiator's head and landing only a few feet from the alleviator. Xanthe was so impressed she almost forgot to make her magical gestures, but it really didn't matter. Photinus's eyes were locked on the action. He looked positively baffled.

Meanwhile, Rowan was already returning from the alleviator with a dark gray blanket. Again, Xanthe didn't think a blanket was much of a weapon, but she'd been wrong about the barrels and so waited anxiously as Rowan rushed over to the gladiator, who was groggily rising after being rammed by the "rum" barrel. Rowan tossed the blanket over him. He struggled for a few seconds, then collapsed. He didn't get up again.

Xanthe couldn't contain herself any longer. "In your *face!*" she shouted. "Go Rowan! Go Rowan! It's your birthday! Raise the roof!" She rotated her arms and swung her hips in celebration until she noticed Photinus staring at her, perplexed. She quickly regained her cool.

Then there was a flash of blue light and a sound like a gunshot. Everybody jumped. Xavier strode purposefully toward his gladiator. He threw up his hands and there was another fiery flash, this time green, and a loud *bang*. Then again and again and again, blue, orange, silver, *bang, bang, bang*. The poor gladiator stood petrified. From the look on his face, he had obviously heard rumors that he would be fighting the great God Osiris. This fire show was clearly only a hint of the dark powers at the command of this wrathful God. Xanthe could've told him that they weren't dark powers at all, just cheap fireworks, but she kept that information to herself.

The gladiator fell prostrate, begging for forgiveness. Xavier planted himself over him, allowing him to grovel for a bit, then nudged him roughly with his foot.

"Leave," he said. The man didn't need to be told twice. He leaped to his feet and fled from the arena without looking back.

Xanthe turned to Photinus, triumphant. "Your champions have been defeated. You have lost the match. Tell us where Octavian is." Photinus's nostrils flared in fury, but then his eyes flashed and a crazy laugh escaped from his mouth.

"It's not over yet!" He pointed to the entrance of the arena. From the shadows emerged another figure. He was muscular and lean, with a massive crop of golden hair surrounding his face. His eyes were yellow and hungry, and he moved with the stealth of a hunter. He was, in fact, a full-grown African lion.

"That's not fair!" Xanthe blurted. "You were only allowed two champions!"

"Consider him a weapon." Photinus cackled. He gathered up his toga and rushed up the stairs. Xanthe now saw the weakness of their plan. Photinus had always had the upper hand. If he refused to comply, or cheated, there wasn't much they could do about it. Xanthe would've gone after him, but something else distracted her. The alleviator had disappeared from the arena. The lion took a few steps, then crouched, eyes locked on Rowan and Xavier. Every second seemed like an eternity.

"Don't move!" Xavier warned Rowan. "If you run or act like you're afraid he'll think that you're prey and attack. Just stare back at him."

They sat like that for several minutes. Xanthe could see the boys were tiring. The lion, however, remained alert. His tail thumped impatiently.

Then he roared. The immense sound flushed every thought from Xanthe's brain, and she was aware only that her insides were quivering uncontrollably. The bellow blew Rowan and Xavier several feet backward.

And then the alleviator reappeared and another sound rang through the arena, but this one sweet, like the sound of a brook running over smooth stones. A small figure in blue stepped out.

An angel, Xanthe thought. *An angel's come down to save them.*

But it was Nina and her lyre. Nina was playing the same tune she'd learned from Kwame—a song that soothed the lion's soul. The cat's muscles relaxed. His eyes moved from the boys to Nina, and he remained motionless. And then, just when Xanthe started to wonder how long Nina could keep playing, an even stranger thing happened. Out of the alleviator poured rabbits. Rabbits of all colors and sizes, hopping, scuffling, kicking, scampering. His trance broken, the lion took chase. The terrified rodents careened every which way like manic pinballs. Then one found an exit and they all bounded after him, with the king of the beasts in joyous pursuit.

Then, out of the alleviator stepped Nana. Xanthe vaulted

over the railing and flew into the old woman's arms. Even though she knew this was actually Nana II from the alternate universe, hers was just the right face at the right time.

"Nana! I'm so glad to see you!" Xanthe cried. Nana II held her close. Xanthe could tell she was trying to make up for all the hugs she'd missed with the Xanthe who never grew past age ten. Then Xavier approached warily, and Xanthe remembered that this was his first meeting with this alternate Nana. On his face was an expression of remorse. And on hers, understanding. They were communicating something that Xanthe was not a part of, so she broke from Nana II's embrace and turned to Nina.

"And you! You were absolutely brilliant," Xanthe said. "You have to tell me how you did it."

"Don't give me more credit than I deserve," Nina said. "When I got to the Owatannauk, alternate-universe Gertrude and Agatha had already called Nana. So I had a lot of help."

"Gertrude filled me in on the whole mess," Nana II explained. "She called me up, told me she needed for me to be a pack mule and help haul stuff from the vault to the alleviator, so she could concentrate on listening. But it was this little gal here who picked out what to send down. I had my doubts about some of those things, but it looks like she did all right."

"She did better than all right." Rowan grinned with pride.

"Okay, you've got to tell me what you were thinking," Xanthe said. "Because from where I was standing, it looked truly bizarre."

"Okay," said Nina, savoring the attention. "Xavier was the easiest. First, because he already knows how to fight. I don't know him that well, but I know he's aggressive and he likes rockets and playing with fire, and he likes doing things with style."

"Is it that obvious?" Xavier said.

"Yes. Very obvious. So when I saw the firecrackers, I thought of you immediately. I would've loved to have given you one of those really big rockets—there were a whole bunch of them in the vault—but I was afraid once you set them off they'd either be too loud or too bright, and would attract attention. So I stuck with the small ones. And of course, the matches were provided by the Owatannauk Hotel."

"So that covers Xave, but what about Rowan? After our last conversation it seemed like you didn't have many ideas," Xanthe said delicately.

"Oh, go ahead and say it." Rowan shrugged. "I'm hopeless. We were all thinking the same thing, Xanthe. I was sure I was going to be creamed out there."

"That's where you're wrong, Rowan," Nina said, taking his hand. "You're not hopeless. One thing I always know is that I can count on you to come through in a pinch." She grinned. "And to recognize a video game when you see one."

"So what does that have to do with barrels of pickles?"

"Donkey Kong!" Rowan laughed.

"Donkey Kong?" Xanthe and Xavier said in unison.

"It's a video game that's been around forever," Rowan

explained. "I play it all the time. It's one of my favorites. See, there's this gorilla at the top of a series of platforms who keeps throwing barrels at this little guy, who tries to climb up the platforms to save a princess." Xanthe raised an eyebrow questioningly. "Hey, it's not supposed to make sense, but it's funny!"

"But I knew just knocking the gladiators down wasn't going to be enough," Nina continued. "Sooner or later Rowan would run out of barrels...and then, well, it would be 'game over.' So that's where I got the idea of the poncho. You see, I knew he couldn't kill anyone. It's just not his nature."

"Poncho? I thought it was a blanket," Xanthe said, lifting it off the gladiator. Upon closer inspection she saw it was indeed a cloak. Suddenly a wave of dizziness hit her and bright yellow spots filled her vision. Nina yanked the cloak back and dropped it to the ground.

Nana II put her arm around Xanthe to steady her. "Careful, baby, it's soaked with ether."

"There was a big bottle of it with some other old supplies," Nina continued. "Gertrude told me they were quack medical inventions used in the nineteen twenties, like a shock-therapy machine, a vibrating chair, and a magnetic belt! Anyway, she told me that ether was used to knock people out before operations. That's all I needed to hear. She lent me her poncho and I poured the entire bottle into it." She nodded at the gladiator, who was curled up in a ball. "That guy should be out for a couple of hours."

"And Nana, those rabbits could only have come from you," Xanthe said, looking into the old woman's kind eyes.

"Yes, indeed." She nodded proudly. "We all thought the battle was over, when Nina suddenly came running back hollering 'lion' so loudly that Gertrude heard her all the way in the security room. She grabbed that harp of hers and I ran to my truck. You see, I was taking a crate full of my rabbits to the vet. One thing about rabbits: They'll draw anybody's attention with all their scampering and hopping about—especially a lion's."

"Things couldn't have gone better," Xanthe said, "except Photinus took off, and now we can't make him tell us where Octavian is. Cleopatra was right. He's totally untrustworthy."

"Actually, I think we can get around that," said Nina. "But we've got to find him."

"I have the feeling he's going to lay low for a while," Rowan mused. "After Xavier's performance, he's probably reconsidering his belief system. Right now the Egyptian Gods must seem pretty awesome. If he thinks Osiris is out to get him, who knows where he'd be hiding?"

"What about Ptolemy? Do you think he knows where Octavian is?" Nina asked.

"What difference does it make?" Rowan said as they hurried out of the arena. "Ptolemy's not going to talk to us."

"Yes, he will," said Nina slyly. "I've got one last trick. And it's a brilliant one, if I do say so myself."

"Come on then," Xanthe said. "Cleopatra will get us in to see him."

"Actually...guys...I think I'm going to sit this one out," Xavier said quietly.

It was then that Xanthe noticed Xavier's hands were covered with blood. "Xave! What happened?!"

"I guess the sword scratched my back." Xavier turned to reveal a long gash and a trail of blood running down, collecting in the back of his loincloth. Rowan looked ill.

"Oh, my God!" Xanthe gasped. "Why didn't you say anything?!"

"I didn't know it was so deep. But I'm actually feeling a little lightheaded . . ."

Xanthe pressed the wound with her fingers, but couldn't stop the flow. "Xave, you've got to go to a hospital!"

"A *real* one!" Nina added.

"Oh, my. You'd better come back with me, before you lose too much blood," Nana II said, taking him by the arm.

Xavier didn't bother protesting. "Sorry, guys. I don't know how I'll catch up with you."

"Don't be ridiculous!" Xanthe ripped a long piece of cloth from her *kalasiris* and wrapped it around Xavier's back. A thin red line immediately soaked through. Xanthe gulped and turned to Nana. "Please look after him. Just . . . make sure he doesn't . . . you know . . ."

Nana II nodded. "I'll take care of him." She slung Xavier's arm around her neck, and led him into the alleviator. The door closed behind them, and they were gone.

Xanthe slumped onto the dirt. Rowan patted her shoulder. "He'll be okay," he said. "I can feel it." Xanthe nodded grimly and rubbed her stained hands. The blood might as well have been her own.

CHAPTER NINETEEN

THE RIDDLE OF THE SPHINX

Xanthe, Rowan, and Nina searched the palace for Cleopatra, but she was nowhere to be found. They explored the gardens and the zoo, but it wasn't until they overheard one of Caesar's soldiers remarking that Caesar's wife, Calpurnia, couldn't compete with the lure of Cleopatra's baths that the children realized she must be entertaining her guest in her private pool.

Apollonius, Cleopatra's loyal servant, knew that the queen was anxious to see the Goddess Isis, and so announced their arrival immediately, disappearing momentarily into the brightly tiled room. Xanthe peeked through the open door and spied the blue, green, and gold mosaic designs around the large rectangular pool. In the crystal water swam Julius Caesar. Xanthe caught a glimpse of his bare bottom. Calpurnia would not approve of this private party, that was for sure.

Cleopatra appeared at the door in a silk robe, and drew the

children into the nearby dressing chamber. "How went the battle?" she asked, eyes glittering.

"We won, Queen Cleopatra," Xanthe answered. "Our champions prevailed, although one was injured." Her voice caught in her throat, but she pressed on. "This is the other champion, Rowanus the Resourceful," she said nodding in his direction. Rowan wore a crooked smile, and his face was several shades of pink, like a Jell-O parfait.

"This is his servant, Ninae," Xanthe continued. "Cleopatra, it is urgent that we find Ptolemy and force him to reveal Octavian's location. Photinus escaped without telling us, and even with my great powers I am unable to find him."

"He's a slippery one." Cleopatra sighed. She turned to Rowan, who now wore a dopey, lopsided grin. "Thank you for your excellent skills," she said. "They must be great for so...compact a man."

"Thaggah, smi plurrr!" Rowan blurted, which Xanthe took to mean "Thank you, it was my pleasure." She rolled her eyes. *Boys.*

"Queen, we must hurry," Xanthe urged.

"Caesar will become suspicious if I disappear," Cleopatra said. "And my brother is unlikely to tell me anything. I am, after all, his enemy."

"Isis is wise and persuasive," Nina said. "She has ways of making him talk." Cleopatra looked quizzically at Xanthe, who nodded.

"It is true. Just lead me to him, I'll take care of the rest."

Cleopatra left the dressing chamber and, after several minutes, returned, dressed in less casual attire. "Follow me," she said.

The queen swept through the palace, with the time travelers in tow. Apollonius also followed, a constant shadow to the queen.

Nina quietly conferred with Xanthe and Rowan along the way. When they reached the final building in the line of palaces, one of Ptolemy's guards blocked Cleopatra's way to the king's quarters. After one fierce look from her, he realized he was no match for the willful queen and stood aside. She pushed the door open. Ptolemy was squatting on the floor, shooting marbles.

"How dare you enter my room!" the king sputtered, scrambling to his feet.

"Shut up!" Cleopatra barked. "Your champions have lost the battle, and your tutor has run off with his tail between his legs. It is therefore up to you to tell us where Octavian is."

"I'll do no such thing."

"Ptolemy, you are trying my patience. Do you want the wrath of the Romans rained upon you? Use your thick head! You're supposed to be a king! Act like it!"

Xanthe knew Cleopatra wasn't likely to get anywhere with that attitude. Whenever she'd talked to Xavier with that tone, it had only made him dig in his heels and become even more obnoxious. Accordingly, Ptolemy crossed his arms and lifted his chin stubbornly.

"King Ptolemy," Xanthe said gently, stepping between the two royals. "You have every right to be angry, for you have been wronged. Your birthright is to be king, and yet you've been treated disrespectfully by all who surround you." Cleopatra's eyes grew dark with mounting rage.

Xanthe shot her a look, hoping to keep the volatile queen quiet. "I would like to offer you a gift," Xanthe continued. "Consider it a gift from the Gods."

Ptolemy eyed Xanthe suspiciously as she took a small, silver, cylindrical object from Nina and handed it to him. As he turned it over in his hands, his expression softened, and a dazed, dopey smile spread across his face.

"Oh, great Isis, what magic is this?" Cleopatra murmured. Xanthe ignored the question. Cleopatra would never understand what a Verita-scripter was.

"In return for this gift," Xanthe continued, "I would be most appreciative if you would reveal to me Octavian's location."

"I don't know where he is," Ptolemy said sleepily. "Photinus wouldn't tell me. I'm weak, untrustworthy, and easily frightened. I threw a tantrum, and he got so disgusted with me, he finally told me, but in the form of a riddle. I hate riddles. Anything clever makes my head hurt."

"Why is my brother telling you all of this?" Cleopatra asked warily. "I've never heard him speak with such honesty."

"My spell has great power," Xanthe replied. "None can resist it." She turned back to Ptolemy. "And what is that riddle, young King?"

Ptolemy closed his eyes and hung his head, then his eyes fluttered open, and with glazed expression he recited:

"Three beds for one king are made,
Guarded well by lion's shade.
One below where serpents lie,
The second under watchful eye,
The third you'll find through passage high,
Where to the stars his soul can fly.
Find which room he made his bed,
Or be you cursed, among the dead."

"Do you recognize it?" Xanthe asked Cleopatra. "Can you solve it?"

Cleopatra pursed her lips and concentrated. Ptolemy had drifted off to sleep, clutching the Verita-scripter in his hands, murmuring a confession for breaking several vases in the hallway while playing ball. Nina delicately removed the pen from his loosened grip and slid it into her pouch with the lyre. Ptolemy turned over and started to snore.

"I am sorry," Cleopatra said finally. "It makes little sense to me. Except... that last part about the king's soul flying makes me think that it could be a tomb."

"A tomb..." Xanthe repeated thoughtfully. "That's a good guess. The part about the beds *could* refer to a final resting place."

"And the curse!" Nina piped up. "Everybody knows tombs are protected by curses."

"Do you know how many king's tombs there are in Egypt? Thousands!" Rowan said ruefully.

"Yes, but not all of them are 'in lion's shade.'" Xanthe tried to clear her head. There was something nagging her about that phrase. She knew the answer was there, but she couldn't concentrate. She was worried about Xavier. She needed him. Her mind was orderly, like a file cabinet. But Xavier's mind was a jumble, a flea market of facts and information. That kind of mind was best for riddles—one that bridged leaps of logic, finding connections in unlikely places.

"What kind of tomb would be in a lion's shade?" asked Nina. "A lion doesn't cast much shade. Unless it's a really big one."

Xanthe blinked. "Big lion? Oh, good grief. I think I know where he is! It's the Sphinx! It's got the body of a lion! The Sphinx guards the three Pyramids of Giza!"

"That makes sense," Cleopatra said thoughtfully. "It is rumored that the Pyramid of Khufu has many passages and chambers to confuse tomb robbers. The main entrance is blocked, but there is supposed to be a second entrance cut into the side by the frustrated robbers. They emptied the tomb of its treasure long ago."

"Where are these pyramids?" Rowan interrupted.

"A short distance from here, along the Nile River," the queen answered. "Perhaps a few hours from Alexandria—you're moving against the current."

"We should leave right away then," Xanthe said. "We'll need a boat."

"You can use mine," Cleopatra said. "However I must remain here. Caesar has already asked about Octavian's whereabouts and I've assured him that his nephew's being cared for by my doctors, but if he becomes more suspicious, I

may be most useful as...a distraction. And I do have a country to run. Apollonius will accompany you."

She called to the faithful servant, who had been waiting
outside the door. "Give the Goddess and her assistants anything they require," Cleopatra ordered. "They are going on a
journey. I want you to go with them and help them."

"Yes, my Queen." Apollonius stood and gave Xanthe a
slight bow. "Follow me, please." He turned and led the three
of them briskly down the hallway.

It was Rowan's idea to stop at the agora to purchase supplies
for exploring the tomb. Several torches would of course be
essential, with extra oil, as well as water and food. They didn't
know what kind of shape Octavian would be in, so bandages
and a knife might also come in handy. Xanthe was grateful
that Rowan was taking the lead, since she was having trouble
concentrating. Xavier's health weighed heavily upon her
mind. The cut on his back had looked bad. Had Nana II gotten him to a hospital in time? And what would happen to
Xavier if they actually did manage to find Octavian and
reverse the damage they'd done? Would he vanish with
Agatha II and Gertrude II and the rest of the alternate universe? She broke into a cold sweat.

Once outfitted for the trip, they all tramped along the pier,
passing rowboats and sailboats of all sizes. Xanthe noted that
the merchant ships were moored on a much longer pier far
from the palace—this appeared to be a private pier for the
royals and their personal friends.

"Here it is," Apollonius said, gesturing to the vessel at the far end of the boardwalk. "The queen's boat."

Xanthe couldn't believe her eyes. Cleopatra had traded the little wooden skiff of her youth for a sixty-foot-long luxury barge. Made of a dark, polished wood and covered in hammered gold, it shone with a light all its own. Twenty-four oars tipped with silver hung at rest on either side. The sleek, rounded hull swooped up to a prow holding an impressively large figure of an Egyptian queen fashioned from gold. She wore an elaborate headdress and a gown whose folds, though made of metal, seemed to flow and billow from an invisible wind. Her features were outlined in black paint, and the rest of her was decorated with gems, glass, and translucent shells. It looked like a gigantic carousel creation.

"Xanthe," Nina murmured, squinting at the figure. "It's you."

Xanthe stared in wonder. Indeed, it was a very close likeness. It made sense, of course. She was Cleopatra's vision of Isis, and the boat had been designed to Cleopatra's specifications.

As they boarded, Xanthe detected a hint of incense wafting from the purple silk sails flapping in the night breeze. Music filled the air. It was then that Xanthe realized, with some concern, that Apollonius was not the only one joining them on the trip. A quartet of musicians played flutes and lyres, servants awaited them with fans, while others held platters of exotic foods.

Rowan and Nina boarded and eagerly nestled into the rose-colored pillows. This was not at all what Xanthe had in mind, but it was too late to come up with anything else now, and she was afraid that if she dismissed the servants it would offend the queen.

"The foreman reports the slaves are ready, Goddess." Apollonius gestured to a muscular, bare-chested Egyptian man, who held two thick, padded sticks. "They await your command."

"Take us to the Pyramids at Giza," Xanthe ordered. Apollonius nodded to the slave, who disappeared down a set of stairs. In a few moments, the steady beat of a large kettledrum could be heard. The oars creaked as they reached out and dipped into the sea. Water swished with each stroke, in rhythm with the drum, and the barge started to move.

Xanthe barely remembered falling asleep. She had fought it, in fact, but the bed in the chamber set at the barge's bow was so fluffy and inviting, with its mountain of purple and rose pillows and its thick, soft coverlet, that after she dove into it (and bounced up and down a few times, for it was a perfect jumping bed), she, along with Rowan and Nina, must have succumbed to exhaustion.

Now that she was up, she ate the fruit and cheese provided by a servant girl, who never once lifted her eyes to look Xanthe in the face.

"I wish we didn't have to use slaves," Xanthe said. "I wish I could give them something for their hard work."

"I don't see any way around it," answered Rowan. "Our mission is to reach Octavian; this is the only way."

Xanthe shrugged resignedly and gazed out at the water.

The Nile was the longest river in the world, its source lying deep within the African continent, but it was also wide. Xanthe could barely see all the way across the silty brown current to the far shore. The river had only just begun to recede from the flooding season; the near bank was lush with green plants, bushes, and grass. Farmers sowed seeds, leading their sheep to trample them into the rich mud the shrinking river left behind. The only sign of the surrounding desert was the hot air blowing from the south. It got increasingly hotter as the sun rose higher and as they sailed further inland, away from the cooling winds of the Mediterranean Sea. Hippos surfaced along the river every once in awhile, wiggling their ears, then sinking in flurries of bubbles.

"Look!" Rowan cried, pointing. "There it is!"

Rising in the distance were the three enormous pyramids, which Xanthe instantly recognized as the famous Pyramids of Giza, another one of the Seven Wonders of the Ancient World. In front of them, resting on its haunches, was the Sphinx. Right now it hardly cast a shadow at all, but in the morning, its shadow would reach behind it, toward the pyramids.

Apollonius anchored the barge in the river, then helped Xanthe, Rowan, and Nina disembark into a small rowboat with the supplies. Once ashore, they saw a tent in the distance, which Apollonius informed them was a place where they could rent camels. It only took a few steps in the hot, shifting sands for the threesome to understand the wisdom of this idea. He suggested they also rent a ladder, for it was the only way to scale the smooth limestone casing of the pyramid. Xanthe had expected the pyramids to be shaped like steps, but now that she was closer she saw that the white gleaming sides of the structures were perfectly straight.

The tent turned out to also be a souvenir stand. The two merchants smiled widely, having recognized the royal barge, and immediately started hawking the miniature limestone pyramids, wooden pharaohs, and carved cats that crowded the shelves.

"All we need are three of your camels and a ladder," Xanthe said. She left it to Apollonius to examine the animals and handle the bartering with the younger merchant while she got directions from the older one.

Soon Apollonius returned with three belligerent dromedaries. As the children loaded their supplies, the two merchants brought out the ladder. Xanthe stared at it disbelievingly.

"*That's* the ladder? It has to be over fifty feet long!" she cried. "Isn't there a shorter one we can use?" The merchants looked at her perplexed.

"The entrance to the tomb is forty-one cubits up the side of the monument," Apollonius said. "You need a long ladder."

Xanthe couldn't argue with that, so they waited for the merchants to tie the ladder to the biggest animal, and then mounted the lumpy creatures themselves.

Xanthe turned to Apollonius. "This is where we part," she said. "We must do this alone." She was already uncomfortable with the number of people who had been added to this mission. The fewer people who knew about Octavian's kidnaping, the better. She kicked her camel and it started to move, but she remembered something and turned back. "In our absence, you may treat the slaves to whatever wine and food is in the boat, courtesy of Cleopatra, and with my thanks."

Apollonius raised his eyebrows, intrigued, then bowed, and left them to cross the desert sands alone.

The camels walked with a peculiar gait that rocked the children back and forth. It felt to Xanthe like one of those rides at the amusement park where after only a few seconds you feel like throwing up, but despite the jiggling in her stomach she was glad to have them, for with their wide feet they made very good time getting to the monuments.

As they passed under the Sphinx, Xanthe peered up at the red-tinted head (which she estimated to be larger than three stacked minivans), its smooth features beautifully balanced in an expression of eternal patience. It was easy to see why some people thought it could only have been constructed by aliens from outer space. How could man, a creature so flawed and weak, produce such a remarkable thing? She felt a warm rush of pride for her species. Only humans could reach inside themselves, touch a spiritual dimension, and create a master-piece. The Sphinx's wise expression said as much.

Xanthe noted that the Sphinx faced east. She wondered how many sunrises it had seen throughout the ages, and this reminded her that the next rising sun was the seventh since they first arrived in Egypt. By her calculations, that meant tomorrow's golden hour was the deadline before their alleviator keys ran out of power. They *had* to find Octavian and bring him back to Alexandria, meet up with Xavier, then jump to 58 B.C. to save Aunt Agatha—all within the next twenty-four hours. How they would manage to do that, she couldn't even begin to fathom.

The three pyramids appeared massive, timeless, immoveable. The red-hued one on the far left was considerably smaller than the other two. Xanthe was pretty sure that wasn't the one they wanted, but the other two looked roughly the same size.

"Cleopatra said Octavian was in the largest of the pyramids, the Great Pyramid of Khufu," she said. "The merchant said it was the one on the far right."

"But the middle one looks the biggest," Nina said.

"It's an optical illusion," Rowan broke in. "I read about it at the library. The middle one is built on higher ground, but the one on the right is the tallest."

They directed the camels to the right, passing large blocks of rubble, possibly from an ancient temple, and across a causeway that led back to the Nile. As they circled the base of the Great Pyramid, they noticed three small pyramids lined up next to each other, as well as several long pits. Rowan said that these were the tombs of King Khufu's wives, also known as the Queens' Pyramids. The pits used to hold boats for the pharaoh to use in the afterlife.

Finally, they reached what seemed to be the front of the pyramid and dismounted.

"Um, how exactly are we supposed to get inside?" Nina

asked, craning her head to see the top. Xanthe did the same. The pyramid was so enormous, its construction boggled the imagination.

"It's close to five hundred feet high," said Rowan. "I hope we don't have to climb to the top. The ladder's long, but it won't reach that far."

"The old merchant told me the door is kind of hidden," Xanthe said. "Let's get the ladder up and see what we can find."

After some maneuvering, they managed to prop the ladder in place. Since Xanthe was the one who got the instructions directly, she went up first. The ladder was fairly flimsy, and it took both Rowan and Nina to keep it steady, but Xanthe's balance was good and so she reached the top quickly. The merchant had described a hinged stone, with a hidden handle. She examined the stones intently. After ten minutes Rowan called up to her.

"Well? Any luck?"

Just at that moment, she noticed an area of the wall that looked more scuffed up and scratched then the rest of it, and then, as she peered further, something that looked like it could be a carved knob, jutting from a stone the size of a large dog door.

"I think I found it!" She stretched out her hand, but as she shifted her weight the ladder started to slide.

"Xanthe!" Rowan shouted, but it was too late. She grabbed the knob but lost her footing and the ladder came clattering down. Xanthe held the knob with both hands, trying to find something to brace her feet against, but the side of the pyramid was too smooth and slippery. It didn't help that Rowan and Nina, in frantically trying to put the ladder back up, kept whacking her backside.

They finally got the ladder back in place. Xanthe regained her footing and, after taking a minute to get her breath back, pulled hard on the stone knob. A door opened on a hinge. She eased herself into the hole feet first.

"Come on up! I'll hold the ladder from up here!" she said, grabbing the sides of the ladder. Nina came up and, with the ladder thus steadied at the top and bottom, she was able to reach the hole with no problem. She ducked inside, and Xanthe motioned to Rowan to start his climb.

As he ascended, Xanthe clutched the ladder tightly, feeling guilty over what she had not told the others. While they were picking the camels, the older merchant had warned her that moving the rock would bring upon them a strong curse. Only a few brave souls had ventured into the Great Pyramid since it had been plundered by robbers, but few had been able to pierce its heart, the King's Chamber. Some who had tried had succumbed to fits, while others lost consciousness and had to be carried out.

As Xanthe reached out to Rowan to pull him in, she struggled with her greatest fear—not of a curse or madness, but of being trapped in a small, dark space, like the window seat Xavier had rescued her from years ago. She tried to convince herself they were just entering a monument, not a tomb—a massive grave. Every nerve ending in her body was set to crawl out of the hole, but Xanthe was a girl with incredible powers of self-control.

Now Rowan and Nina were both inside the pyramid. The only person left to go in was her. Xanthe took three deep breaths, holding the last one as though she were going underwater, and ducked inside.

+ CHAPTER TWENTY +
THE HEART OF DARKNESS

In the darkness, Xanthe took a few short practice breaths, her chest rising and falling with effort. She wasn't sure if it was her own heightened anxiety or if the oxygen was in short supply, but it was definitely harder to breathe. She resigned herself to the discomfort, but she dreaded moving away from the exit.

That time came all too soon. Nina had already lit the torches with the matches she'd taken from the Owatannauk Resort. Their eyes slowly adjusted to the hazy light, and they started down the long tunnel in front of them. As they inched along, sliding once in awhile on the loose dirt, the smoke from the torches warmed the air, making it even more difficult to breathe. Xanthe tried not to notice that the ceiling was only a few inches above their heads, but a clammy chill was already spreading through her body.

Suddenly, Rowan and Nina stopped. "We've come to a

fork," Rowan announced. "One way continues down the way we were going, but there's a path that goes up."

"Do you think we should split up?" Nina asked.

"No!" Xanthe said, almost a little too quickly. "No. Cleopatra said there were a lot of tunnels in this pyramid. We can't afford to have anyone get lost."

"I agree," Rowan said. Then he put his hand to his mouth and called, "Octavian! Octavian!" There was no answer. "Let's keep going down, and if Octavian isn't there, then we can try the other way."

Down they went. Finally the tunnel leveled out and they faced an open chamber with rough walls, which had been cut from bedrock. At the far end of the chamber the passage continued. Xanthe was fairly certain they were underground. Her heart raced and her legs wavered as her mind was gripped by the image of the three of them in a little hole, covered by thousands of tons of rock. One small avalanche and they would be buried alive.

She felt Nina's hand on her shoulder, and she opened her eyes. Something was moving in the recesses of the chamber. "Octavian?" Xanthe murmured. But it was not Octavian. A cobra slithered into the pool of light cast by the torches, followed by another and another, and then three more. Six snakes in all, raised up like six curious question marks.

"It's the riddle," Xanthe gulped. "'Three beds for one king are made, guarded well by lion's shade. One below where serpents lie...' This must be the first bed. The first burial chamber for the king."

"Photinus must have put them here," Rowan whispered. "He's the one who made up the riddle. Which means," he said slowly, "Octavian must be back there, beyond the chamber. Where the passageway continues."

"Oh, my gosh!" Xanthe exclaimed. "I totally forgot, but when Xave and I went to the Owatannauk Library in the alternate universe, to find out where history had gotten off track, we read that Octavian had been killed by a snakebite. These must be the snakes!"

"So what do you think happened? He got bitten here, then whoever put him in the pyramid brought him back out and put him somewhere in Alexandria where Caesar could find him?"

"Something like that. Maybe they hoped his death would appear accidental. Except, according to that history book, the plan didn't really work. Caesar blamed Ptolemy anyway— probably after talking to Cleopatra—he killed him, and the rest is . . . well, alternate history."

Just then, they heard a low moan from the passageway.

"That's him!" cried Rowan. "We still have a chance to save him!"

"Whoa, we're blocked by six snakes!" Nina said. "And those are just the ones we can see!"

Xanthe thought for a moment, watching the snakes slide over one another. A tiny voice in her head said, *Oil. Remember the oil. Light it on fire. Make a wall of flame.*

"I know," she said suddenly. "We take the extra oil for the torches, pour it on the ground to make a barrier between us and the snakes, then light it on fire."

Rowan nodded. "Pyrotechnics. Great idea. Sounds like something Xavier would say."

"Yes," Xanthe said, a little surprised at herself. "It's totally what he would say."

"You guys!" Nina shrieked. "Look out!" The pile of snakes was sliding forward. Xanthe fumbled with the bag, removed the cannister of oil, and quickly splashed it around the serpents. She touched her torch to the puddles and flames roared up, engulfing four of them. One leaped through the fire at Nina, who screamed and charged up the passage from which they'd come.

Rowan ran through the chamber and ducked into the tunnel on the far side. As the last snake flipped around to follow him, Xanthe slammed her torch on its back. It whirled, and she whacked it again and again, as it writhed and twisted. Then it sprung at her.

Xanthe shrieked, trying to protect herself with the torch, but the ropy snake body was suddenly coiling around her waist. She imagined that at any moment she would feel the sharp piercing bite, the injection of poison into her bloodstream. Would she go numb? Fall into convulsions? Foam at the mouth? Have a heart attack? But she never felt the bite.

She opened her eyes. The diamond pupils glared back at her an inch from her face. The cobra had sunk its fangs deep into the wooden shaft of the torch. She dropped it, and peeled the snake from her body as it began whipping its head around, struggling to free itself from the burning stick.

"I've got Octavian!" shouted Rowan, emerging from the

tunnel. He dragged the listless boy, who stumbled groggily after him. "Run, Xanthe! Get out of here!"

"You need help!" Xanthe said, grabbing one of Octavian's arms so that he was slung between them. Together, she and Rowan pulled him up the passageway. She heard a clunk and glanced back. The cobra had freed himself from the torch and was weaving after them, his tail aflame.

Nina, racing back down the passageway, almost plowed into them. "We can't go that way! Snake! I hit him with my torch, but believe me, he's not dead!"

"We can't go back down, either!" Xanthe cried. "We're trapped!"

The voice in the back of her head yelled so loudly it rattled her teeth. *Up! Look up!*

She looked up. There, in the ceiling, a few feet away from them, was a small hole. "Up!" she yelled to the others. "There's a hole up there! Nina, I'll give you a boost!"

Xanthe cupped her hands. Nina stepped in, and Xanthe shot her into the hole. Then she and Rowan shoved Octavian through.

"I've got him," Nina said, "but he's heavy!"

Rowan turned to Xanthe. "Up you go," he said, cupping his hands. He boosted her up. She felt herself immediately wedged against Octavian.

"Pull him up, Nina!"

"I can't! It's too steep, and he's slipping out of my hands!"

"Hurry, you guys, the snake is right here!" Rowan yelled. Suddenly, Xanthe felt Rowan crammed behind her. She grabbed his tunic, helping him into the thin passage that was filled with the smoke of burning oil. Xanthe's eyes stung. She couldn't breathe.

"Oh, Rowan, the smoke..." She coughed.

He dropped the torch out of the hole. It glowed faintly, then suddenly, as if somebody flicked a switch, they were plunged into darkness.

Xanthe moaned. She couldn't move, she couldn't breathe, just like when she was stuck in the window seat. Only this time, there was no Xavier to call their father. This time there was no rescue...

Have faith in yourself, Xanthe, just calm down. You're strong. You can make it, assured the little voice in her head. *This is an escape tunnel made by the workers both for ventilation and so they'd have a way to get out after they plugged up the passage that leads to the entrance.*

This time the voice was unmistakable. It wasn't her conscience, as she had first thought. "Xavier!" Xanthe gasped. "Is that you?!"

Of course it's me.

"But how...how can I hear you? Where are you? Please tell me you're not dead."

I'm not dead, just uncomfortable. I'm stitched up like Frankenstein with a big bandage on my back, and the whole thing itches like crazy.

"Where are you?"

With Nana and alternate-universe Gertrude, at her station in the Owatannauk, listening to you guys.

"How did you find us?"

Gertrude did. She's incredible! Just a few minutes ago, you mentioned a pyramid and lion's shade and multiple tunnels and that's all she needed. She pulled up information on the Great Pyramid of Khufu, and figured out the only area in the pyramid large enough to hold an alleviator is the King's Chamber. You've got fifty minutes to get there.

"Who are you talking to?" Rowan said.

"Xavier! He says this is an escape passage that leads to the King's Chamber. Gertrude's sending an alleviator there. We've got less than an hour!"

"Oh...Okay..." Rowan sounded wary.

Xanthe knew she must sound crazy, but now that she knew Xavier was with her she felt pumped. Energized.

"Help! Octavian's slipping!" Nina cried.

"Go up, Nina," Xanthe commanded. "Move out of the way." Nina did. Xanthe slid over Octavian's limp body, grabbing his arms. Then, she and Rowan tugged and pushed him up the steep slope, as Nina led the way.

They moved cautiously in the pitch-black passageway. Whenever Xanthe's confidence flagged, Xavier's voice reached her from the vast beyond, cracking jokes, doing impersonations—anything to get her mind off of her claustrophobia. He also kept her talking; she told him about what they'd gone through after he left them.

"I know how you can hear me, but how can I hear you?" Xanthe asked at one point.

I'm not sure. When Gertrude brought me to her station, I couldn't see a thing. Then I heard you guys talking and moving around, and suddenly I could see you, at least in my head. I could picture the dust on your clothes, the scratches on your hands, that intense look you always have when you're in trouble...and all of a sudden, I could hear you, even though you weren't talking. And when you were talking, I could hear what you were saying, but also what you were thinking, like a second recording track.

"Wow, Xave. You really *can* read my mind."

I guess so. And you're reading mine. I'm not talking out loud, you know, and you don't have to, either. I'm sure Rowan and Nina are wondering if you've gone bananas, babbling to yourself like a lunatic.

Xanthe laughed, but she stopped talking aloud.

I have to admit, Xave, Xanthe thought, *I misjudged you. I thought you came on this trip just to irritate me. But if it weren't for your knowledge about Caesar, Octavian, and gladiators...we'd be nowhere.*

You're not out of the woods yet, sis.

Nor out of the tunnel.

No. He laughed.

But how did you know so much? You've never been interested in history before.

Yes I have. Xavier sighed. *And I told you I was. You just wouldn't listen. I like military history. But whenever I brought it up, you never took me seriously. You didn't want to hear it. You wanted me to fit in this neat little box of math and science. But I don't like being labeled. I like to try on new hats once in a while.*

That's when it hit her. She'd done something awful to her brother, trying to put limits on him, dictating who he was and what he could be, and ignoring how he saw himself. She was suffocating him, suffocating his soul. It was incredibly thoughtless. She started to cry.

"Xanthe? Are you okay?" Rowan asked.

"Yeah, I'm okay. I'm just...Don't worry about me. I'm

fine." She heaved a deep sigh. *I'm so sorry, Xave. I guess I was only thinking of myself. I didn't see you trying to expand yourself, I just saw you stealing focus away from me.* Xanthe had never considered herself to be a selfish person, but looking at herself now, she realized that maybe she was. Maybe *she* was the person who had trouble admitting when she was wrong.

I know. It's okay. At least now you're listening.

Because I have to.

Because you have to.

Xanthe's arms were beginning to tire. The going was extremely slow, and she'd lost track of time, which was easy to do when surrounded on all sides by rock. Again she was reminded of her claustrophobia and she shivered.

Don't think about that, Xanthe. Keep your mind on moving forward, not backward.

Xave?

What?

What happened to you in the alternate universe? You seemed freaked out.

Silence. And then: *I saw myself. My alternate-universe self.*

What? I thought if you meet another version of yourself you explode from matter meeting antimatter... or something like that.

I guess we didn't get close enough to each other. Anyway, I could hardly recognize myself. I looked sick; all pale and stooped over. But even worse, I looked hollow. Soulless. Like the walking dead. And right away I knew it was because something awful had happened to you, and that I was to blame. And it shook me up, Xanthe. I couldn't bear to see myself suffering and tortured like that. And I realized how much we need each other, whether we like it or not.

You know what, Xave? Something awful was happening to both of us,
in our own universe. But I think we stopped it.

I hope so.

Finally, Nina announced that she'd reached the end of the tunnel. Xanthe felt the edge of an opening, and she crawled out,
hauling Octavian up with Nina's help, as Rowan pushed from
behind. Xanthe was grateful to be out of the cramped space, but
they were still in darkness and had no clue where to go.

"What do we do now?" asked Nina in a small voice. "I
can't even see you guys."

Xave, we're stuck, Xanthe thought. *How much time do we have?*

Fifteen minutes.

Fifteen minutes!

Xanthe, see with your other senses. Try to tell me what the room is like,
and I can lead you from there.

Xanthe told the others about Xavier's suggestion, prompting worried whispers between the Popplewells, who clearly
doubted her sanity. But with no other suggestions, they
agreed to let her try. Xanthe released Octavian to Rowan's
grip, then reached out with her hands.

Exploring Gertrude's station in the security room had
given her some practice. Xanthe walked forward and felt cool
stone beneath her fingertips. This she described aloud, for the
benefit of the others.

"We're in a corridor," she said. "The walls are smooth. Polished, even." Her voice rang through the cavern, and by the
sound of it the ceiling was quite high. Her voice had sounded

dull in the narrow tunnel, but now it almost sounded as though she were in a cathedral. She turned and walked in the other direction, pacing only six feet before she met the other wall.

As she described all of this to Xavier her mind's eye formed a picture in her head. They were in a narrow but enormous gash in the pyramid. A crack in timelessness. It made her feel insignificant. A tiny speck in the universe.

"Xave says we're in something called the Grand Gallery. The alleviator is in the King's Chamber above us," Xanthe murmured. "Follow my voice, you guys." She heard scuffling and scraping, and then the heavy breathing of the others nearby. "Okay, someone hold on to my dress, I'm going forward."

As she took tentative steps, she sensed that the ground had leveled out, and by the sound of the echo she knew the walls had become more confining. Sure enough, when she reached upward she could feel the ceiling. They were no longer in the gash, but in another tunnel, this one wider than the rabbit hole they'd squeezed through from the first room. At the end of the hall, she found a narrow door, and had to duck to get through it. The others followed, and soon they were all in another room.

"Okay, Xave! We're here!"

Fantastic! Jump in the alleviator! I can't wait to see you!

"What alleviator? There's no alleviator here."

There was a pause. *Xanthe, Gertrude sent the alleviator ten minutes ago. It should be there by now.*

Xanthe's heart sank to her stomach. Something was wrong.

Describe the room for me, Xavier said urgently.

She did. Groping with her hands she discovered walls of smooth stone. They were in a square room, perhaps fifteen yards by fifteen yards. There was a crevice cut into one of the walls where perhaps a statue had once stood. She even described the tunnel that led them to the room.

Hang on a sec . . . There was silence for a few moments. Somehow Xanthe knew that Xavier had left Gertrude's station. She had never felt so alone than in those seventy seconds she spent waiting for him to return.

"Xanthe, what's going on?" Rowan asked. "If you're really talking to Xave, and I'm not saying you are, what do we do now?"

"Wait a minute," Xanthe said weakly. "I'm on hold." This prompted more worried whispers between the Popplewells.

Okay, I'm back, Xavier said. Xanthe exhaled, relieved. *I went to check the book I took out from the Owatannauk Library. Right now you seem to be in what they call the Queen's Chamber. You should've kept going up when you went straight. You only have about eight minutes to find the right place and get out. How's Octavian doing?*

He's awake, but barely.

Xanthe, you've got to lead everyone back out to the area where the ceiling was high.

Xave, I can't see a thing! And there are too many tunnels in here! What if I go the wrong way again? We don't have enough time for any more mistakes!

We sent a guide. Just listen.

Xanthe listened. At first all she heard was a great nothingness, the sound of atmosphere brushing her ears, interrupted every few moments by Octavian moaning. Then, she did hear something. A light tinkling. Her mind created a picture for her. It was a jingle bell.

Who did he send? she thought. *Santa Claus?*

"Wait a minute...I hear a bell!" Nina said. Rowan murmured that he did, too.

The sound got closer. And then, a light. A tiny circle of light pierced the darkness like the beacon of the lighthouse, except this light had two eyes gleaming above it.

"What is it?" gasped Rowan. "Please, lord, no more snakes!"

But Xanthe had already recognized those bright, golden eyes. She picked up the cinnamon-colored cat and held him close, stroking him under his collar where a penlight had been attached with a thin wire. *Thank you, Xave. I've seen the light. We're coming back.*

The tiny flashlight illuminated the animal enough to see that his collar was serving as a sort of utility belt. It held the light, the bell, a thin rope extending into the darkness, and an alleviator key, which Xanthe supposed was for Octavian. It occurred to her that the cat had been able to time travel all this time without a key. She wasn't sure what that meant, but Xavier broke into her thoughts.

I wondered that, too. Gertrude said the short answer is they don't know why animals don't need keys. Listen, we're running out of time. Meet me at the Temple of Isis.

Again, Xanthe felt the emptiness that told her Xavier had left Gertrude's post to make his way to the bank of alleviators in the hotel and back to the Temple of Isis. But now she felt invigorated, as though she had an important appointment to make. She tugged on the rope and realized it was a lifeline. After telling the others what she'd found, she grabbed the rope firmly, then followed it hand over hand with Rowan, Nina, and Octavian in tow, linked to her like a human chain. She was thankful that Octavian had enough of his wits about him not to resist but to keep moving.

Through the low-ceilinged tunnel they went, back to the Great Gallery. Even with the flashlight she could not see where the gash ended. The walls were indeed made of huge pieces of polished stone, fitted together so perfectly, it was no wonder that the pyramids lasted for thousands of years. Her tiny light, casting a small circle of warmth, made the place seem almost holy, and as they continued through the gallery, Xanthe started to sing an old church song, a Negro Spiritual that she'd heard her maternal grandmother sing.

> *Swing low, sweet chariot,*
> *coming for to carry me home.*
> *Swing low, sweet chariot,*
> *coming for to carry me home.*

Another voice joined in, with a tone as clear as crystal and so sweet it made Xanthe tremble. At first she thought it was Nina, but it wasn't. It was Rowan. Then Nina added her lyre.

Then came Xavier's voice from the outer cosmos, heard only by Xanthe, but still a strong, unmistakable baritone. Apparently he was still with her after all.

Up the incline went the little choir, finally reaching the King's Chamber, where their sweet chariot, the alleviator, hummed and sparkled.

With only a minute left to the golden hour, they entered the time machine. Rowan took the key from Xanthe and folded it into the palm of the dumbfounded Octavian, whose mouth hung open like a stunned fish.

Xanthe held the cinnamon-colored cat tightly and punched in the coordinates for the Temple of Isis in 48 B.C. They had an important delivery to make.

+ CHAPTER TWENTY-ONE +
TIME TRACKERS

W HEN THEY ARRIVED AT THE TEMPLE OF ISIS, Xavier was already there. Though normally Xanthe and Xavier were not the sort of siblings who showed affection for each other in public, due to the "uncool" factor, now they flew together in a hug, locked like two pieces of a puzzle, intertwined so that you could no longer tell where one ended and the other began.

"Xave, you're okay! Thank God, you're okay!"

"It was just a flesh wound . . . but *you*! You made it through the snakes! And in the dark! I don't know how you guys did it."

"With you. We did it with you. We'd never have gotten through it without your help." She held up the cat, who, oddly enough, had fallen asleep in her arms. "Well, you and little Spice here."

"Uh-oh, you've named him," warned Rowan. "Sounds to me like you're planning on keeping him."

"We'll see," said Xanthe.

"I'd like to," Xavier said. "I think he'd make an awesome pet."

"Really?" Xanthe said, genuinely surprised. "I didn't peg you as a cat person." Xavier took the sleeping cat from her arms, scratching him gently under the chin.

"Maybe you don't know me as well as you thought you did."

They delivered Octavian to Cleopatra's room. He was confused, weak, and dirty, but, other than a few scratches, he was unharmed. Xanthe started to describe their adventure to the queen, but Xavier soon took over, bending the truth to include a large dose of godlike magic and mysticism. Xanthe was proud of herself for not getting mad at him; whether or not he was grabbing attention was not the point, he had a gift for lying that she did not share. Sure enough, Cleopatra was eating it up. It was a much more entertaining story than Xanthe could ever tell.

When Xavier finished, Octavian started mumbling, as if on cue. "Snakes...I was surrounded by snakes...and a cat with a glowing ember at his neck...and then a bright room covered with tiny circles..."

"You must have your physicians look at him," Xanthe said. "Then take him to Caesar."

"All-powerful Isis..." Cleopatra said hesitantly. "I am more surprised than anyone to see you back so soon."

"We Gods do as we must," Xanthe said. "Our ways and reasons must sometimes remain a mystery to mortals."

"I understand, but what I really want to know is, what happened to my boat?"

Xanthe's eyes widened, horrified. She'd forgotten all about the barge. She cleared her throat a few times trying to think of an excuse when Xavier, who had been hovering nearby, stepped in. "Queen Cleopatra, the boat is safe, at the pyramids. We did not need it anymore. You may send a messenger to inform them that the time has come for their return."

"I don't understand..."

"Do you question our actions, Queen?" Xanthe said as haughtily as she could, despite her feelings of supreme idiocy.

"No...no, of course not."

"When the royal barge is back, I predict your slaves will have a renewed loyalty and love for you," Xavier said meaningfully.

Xanthe stifled a laugh, remembering that the barge had been turned into a party boat.

Cleopatra nodded, clearly baffled.

While they waited for the silver hour to arrive so that they could jump back to 58 B.C., they joined Cleopatra and Julius Caesar in feasting Octavian's return to health. Caesar had been fooled into believing that Cleopatra's physicians had kept Octavian sequestered for two days because of his illness, and Cleopatra had been able to keep his mind occupied with other matters.

In the back of her mind, Xanthe was still concerned about how difficult it might be to spring Aunt Agatha from prison in 58 B.C., but it was hard not to enjoy herself. In fact, everybody was in the mood to relax.

After dinner, Xavier finally got the opportunity to talk military history and strategy with Julius Caesar, and Xanthe was impressed that he was able to keep the conversation going for several hours. Rowan and Nina explored the hundreds of rooms, for it was the first time they'd had a chance to really see the interior of the palace. Cleopatra invited Xanthe on a moonlight horse ride, and then afterward they took a dip in the queen's pool. It was an evening that none of them would ever forget.

Early the next morning, before sunrise, they said their good-byes. Xanthe took the queen's hand in her own.

"Cleopatra, this is our last meeting," Xanthe said gently. "You will not see me again."

The queen's face fell. "No, dear Goddess, I need you! You are my friend, the only one I can trust."

"You have a new best friend," Xanthe said, glancing at Caesar. "I have brought you this far. Now follow your own good judgment, and his. You make a wonderful team."

"I only follow your example, Goddess. The example set by you and your brother. Perfect companions. We should all be as fortunate as you."

Xanthe smiled. *Yes,* she thought. *We should all be so lucky.* "You have our blessings," she said, and the foursome departed from the palace, leaving Caesar and Cleopatra behind to wonder about just what had happened in the last few days.

The children jogged to the temple with a minimum of conversation. Xanthe assumed that the others, like she, were praying that they would be successful in getting Aunt Agatha released. Before leaving the palace, she'd found the satchel exactly where she had stowed it, behind the Poseidon statue. It seemed like she'd put it down years ago, but there it was, with Xavier's vest still inside. And in the pocket, a small piece of papyrus with a poem written upon it. She hoped Theodictes, the head librarian, didn't give them a hard time.

On top of that, Xanthe wondered if their mission had even succeeded. When they returned to the future, would it be to the world that they recognized? Even though they had saved Octavian, it might not have been enough to bump them back on course. They might never know just how much damage they had done. More than ever, she understood that every action was important, and that being careless could be costly.

When they reached the temple, Xanthe was surprised to see three alleviators sparkling in front of the statue of Isis and said so.

"It makes sense," Rowan mused. "One of them is the one you and Xave took from our original universe, the second is the one that Xave took from the alternate universe, and the third is the one that Gertrude II sent to the pyramid from the alternate universe, and which we used to travel back here."

"That poses a bit of a problem," said Xanthe. "How do we know which one is the original one? I mean, we can't take an alleviator from an alternative universe back to our own universe, can we?"

"But look!" Nina said, pointing.

Before their eyes the alleviators on the far right and the far left

slowly faded away, leaving only the one in the middle. It took a
moment for it to sink in, but in the next second they were cheering and trading high-fives. They had done it. They had gotten
themselves back on track. Xanthe's happiness was bittersweet,
however, for she knew that in that same instant, Gertrude II and
Agatha II, Nana II and all her rabbits, had ceased to exist.

Once they were back to 58 B.C., they spared no time in getting
to the library, but it was closed.

"This is very bad," Rowan moaned. "How are we going to
find Theodictes? In less than an hour?"

"He never mentioned to me where he lived," Xavier said.
"I don't think he was too social. Some of the other scribes said
he didn't have a wife or kids, and that he never went out—
just married to the scrolls, I guess."

"Well he's pretty serious about protecting them, that's for
sure." Rowan plunked himself down on the stairs.

Xanthe racked her brain, when suddenly she remembered
something from her day of sightseeing. "Hey, you guys, the
scholars who use the library live in a dormitory in the
museum. I bet Theodictes has a room there! That way he'd be
close to the books. Come on, I'll show you where it is!"

Xanthe led them to the museum. The door was locked, but
a window had been left open in one of the lecture halls. The
children slipped inside and ran through the corridor to the
great hall with its high, painted ceiling and its impressive
colonnade. Xanthe led them down another corridor to the
sleeping quarters. There they were met by a line of doors.

"Okay, which one?" Nina said.

Xavier grinned. "All of them, of course."

"No, Xave, don't do it," Xanthe warned, but it didn't matter. Xavier wasn't listening to her anyway. He ran down the line of doors, pounding on each one.

"Hello! Come out! Room service!" he yelled. He went back down the line, then up again. Xanthe couldn't help herself and started giggling.

"Xavier and I used to do this whenever we stayed at hotels," Xanthe explained to Rowan and Nina, regaining her composure. "I outgrew it. I guess he didn't."

The stunt succeeded in filling the hallway with angry, bleary-eyed scholars, each demanding in his own language why he had been wrested from his slumber at such an ungodly hour. The angriest was Theodictes, whose room had been the last one, in the far corner. His eyes darkened when he saw the children, but before he could summon any guards, Xavier handed him the parchment containing the poem. The other scholars drifted back to their rooms, grumbling, as Theodictes examined the document thoroughly.

"Thank you for returning it," Theodictes sniffed. "For your honesty, I won't have you arrested. However, it goes without saying that you and Rowanus are fired. I don't ever want to see either of you anywhere near the library again."

"We understand," Rowan said. "But what has become of my aunt? You must release her from prison, I beg of you. She should not be made to suffer any longer."

Theodictes shrugged. "She was sold into slavery yesterday."

"Slavery?!" Xanthe gasped. They had been too late after all.

"That's right," continued Theodictes. "Went for quite a bit, I understand. Three different families bid on her to be a tutor for their children. She's a smart woman, and her skills were in high demand."

"Slavery!" groaned Nina. "Well, who won the bid? Where can we find her?"

"There's the tragedy. None of the families won. She went to a sinister-looking Roman merchant, a woman as tall as a tree, with eyes steely as a crow's, and breath tinged with a strange, bitter smell. I daresay your aunt will be put to work on some unpleasant task with that one. They left immediately after the auction."

Xanthe almost laughed but stopped herself. Gertrude had rescued Agatha after all.

The children left Alexandria of 58 B.C. and arrived at the Owatannauk Resort with the usual tossing about. When the alleviator door slid open, there stood Gertrude, arms crossed, brows furrowed, and lips curled in a horrendous scowl. Xanthe had never been so overjoyed to see such a nasty expression. And best of all, peeking out from behind her was Agatha, no longer in Greek clothing but back in her usual explosion of color.

"Oh, Aunt Gertrude! Aunt Agatha! It's you! It's really you!" Xanthe grabbed them both, though her arms couldn't nearly reach around them. "We were so worried about you!"

"I wasn't." Agatha laughed and smiled. "I knew Gertrude wouldn't let me down. This isn't the first scrape she's gotten me out of, and it most certainly won't be the last."

"You shouldn't have been in danger at all. I'm sorry. It's my fault—"

"No it wasn't, we were both to blame," Xavier jumped in.

"But I started it."

"I made it worse."

"But we had such an adventure!" Rowan piped up.

"Rowan was so brave!" added Nina.

"And Xave, too! We'd be dead if it weren't for Xave!"

"We thought we were goners!"

"That's enough!" Gertrude shouted over them, abruptly stopping the conversation. "The Board of Directors has assembled for an emergency meeting. Now follow me. There's not much time."

They all understood what she was saying. They were back home, but the party was over. They'd failed the test. This would be their last trip.

The Constellation Room was set up as it had been for the interviews, except there were four chairs facing the long table now. Seated was the Board of Directors: Mayor Silverstrini, Jenny O'Neill, Captain Morgan, and Hilda Bingham, along with Albert Einstein, Thomas Edison, Madame Curie, and H. G. Wells. Nana sat off to the side, but jumped up to greet the children as soon as they came through the door.

"Sit down, sit down," Mayor Silverstrini rasped above the renewed hubbub. "Time grows short."

Captain Morgan rose, banging a gavel. The children sat in the four chairs, subdued by his grave expression.

"The motion has been raised and seconded as to the vote concerning Rowan Popplewell, Nina Popplewell, Xanthe Alexander, and Xavier Alexander. We have all seen what they have done."

"Point of order." Albert Einstein raised his hand.

"Yes, Albert."

"In fact, we have *not* all seen what they have done. Gertrude was only able to account for their activities up to a point. Then they disappeared for quite a while. I would like to know what happened during that time."

"The motion has been put forth...Oh, you all heard what he said. I'll second it myself." Captain Morgan turned to the children. "Would any of you care to fill us in?" Xanthe exchanged worried glances with the others, then rose to her feet.

"I'd like to explain what happened, because I am mostly to blame. First, I let my curiosity get the best of me and I struck up a friendship with Cleopatra. I used the alleviators to track her development throughout her life, and it was fascinating! She was so..." Xanthe stopped herself. "It was the absolute wrong thing to do. Then, Xavier and I were careless and said something that changed the course of history. That's when we all disappeared. We were on a different branch of time." She turned to Gertrude. "I met another version of you, and you too, Aunt Agatha. You were very different, but also the same. And this town was different, too. But the worst difference was that Rowan and Nina had become hotel phantoms. Xave and I knew we had to set things right so we figured out where we got off track, and then the four of us tried to change it back to the way it was supposed to be, which we did. Now we're back, and I'm really very sorry. I don't think everyone should have to pay for my mistakes, though."

Captain Morgan looked at his watch. "All right then. Gertrude, are you satisfied with what you've heard?"

Gertrude nodded stiffly.

"Good. All in favor of granting them frequent-flier status raise your hands."

Xanthe looked down, biting her lip, holding back the tears. Well, so what. In the scheme of things she was just glad to be home, safe, and with her friends.

"It's unanimous then," she heard the captain say. The gavel fell with a loud crack that made them all jump. "Xanthe and Xavier Alexander, Rowan and Nina Popplewell, welcome to the Owatannauk Twilight Tourists Frequent-Flier Club. Congratulations, kids! You're in!"

Xanthe looked at Xavier, who had a crooked grin spreading across his face. Rowan looked stunned, as though he'd been struck by lightning. Only Nina frowned.

"But we broke all of those rules!" Nina pointed out. "We changed history! We got trapped in another dimension!"

"Nina, shut up!" the other three said together.

"That's all right." Thomas Edison chuckled. "She's quite right to be confused. Normally under those circumstances we would toss you out on your fannies and bar the gates. You're a bit reckless, you see. And young. Awfully young. Prone to foolish hijinks and irrational behavior."

"Now that's not fair, Thomas. They did far better than most adults under similar circumstances," countered Hilda.

"But then why...?" Nina began.

"Nina!" Rowan gave her a hard nudge. "Just be happy and leave it alone!"

"I can't!" Nina insisted. "I have to know!"

"You want to know why you've been rewarded instead of punished, even though you broke the rules?" Albert Einstein said, wiping his glasses and returning them to his nose. "Because this was not a test to see how well you could follow rules. This was a test to see how well you worked together as a team."

So Rowan was right, thought Xanthe. *Somehow he knew.*

"It's an interesting chemistry you have, the four of you together," Einstein continued. "You bring out each other's strengths, and cancel out each other's flaws. Nina, your curiosity and persistence are a gift, even more than your musical ability. Xanthe, your intellect and powers of analysis are unusually strong. Xavier, your confidence and charm serve you well in times of trouble, and the competitiveness between you and your sister has turned you both into master strategists. Rowan, your moral courage is an anchor for the others. You make a remarkable team. And that, dear children, is exactly what we were hoping for."

"Frankly, we were worried about you at first," Madame Curie said, turning to Xanthe. "You seemed to be quite irritable and secretive. Vindictive even. And then when you all disappeared, we knew what had happened, and we were horrified. We were afraid we'd been too eager, and sent you into harm's way. We thought we'd never see you again. But then when Agatha came back with Gertrude, she insisted we hold this meeting. Said she had a hunch. And you never want to question Agatha's hunches..."

The children traded looks. By now they were all quite familiar with Agatha's uncanny sixth sense.

"But she was right on the button," Madame Curie continued, "for here you are, as unbelievable as that may seem."

"Too eager for what?" Nina piped up.

"What's that, my dear?"

"You said you might have been 'too eager.' Too eager for what?"

"To find the right combination," Agatha answered. "For ages the Board has been searching for a youngster, or a group of youngsters, who could handle the rigors and the dangers of time travel. We have looked for a very long time indeed. Because of our relationship with your mother, we thought you and Rowan might be the ones. But then when Xanthe and Xavier joined you, we thought we recognized something special grow out of that relationship. Something bigger than the four of you alone. And so we put you to a test, hoping you would succeed and also hoping that if you did, you would lend your talents to helping us."

"We'd be happy to help you hunt down stuff for your curio shop," Rowan said. The others nodded, chiming in their agreement.

"I can't think of a better after-school job," Xanthe said. "That is, if I went to school."

"Well, that's very kind of you," Agatha said, "but I don't actually need the help. We have more stuff in that shop, and even more things in storage, than we could ever hope to sell."

"But what about all those clients..." Rowan started, but Agatha waved him off.

"I just said that to get you to agree to come up again," she said. "No, I'm not the one who needs the help."

"I am." Gertrude stepped forward, and because she was two feet taller than the tallest child, she knelt down in front of them. "I need the help. Every day I get a lead on somebody who is stuck in another time and can't get back. And as much as I hate to admit it, my abilities are limited by my appearance." She drew herself up to her full seven-foot-tall stature. "I've been told that I stand out."

"But what can we do?" Rowan said. "We're just kids."

"What can you do?" Hilda laughed. "Look at what you've already done! You've gone to another dimension and come back! Only a child would be able to do that!"

"Why?"

"Because it's impossible," Thomas Edison chuckled. "Anybody who thinks they can get back from another dimension has to be completely out of his mind, a fool, a hopeless dreamer..."

"Or a child," Einstein said quietly. "Someone who still has faith, who hasn't been ruined by doubts and defeatism. So many adults have given up, you know. They're the ones who don't smile much."

"Nobody's ever done it before?" Xanthe said in a small voice. Gertrude shook her head.

"We can talk more about it later," H. G. Wells said. "But some of us need to get back to our own time. Come, every-body! We've only got a few minutes at best!"

Einstein, Edison, Curie, and Wells gave the children their last congratulatory handshakes, and then hurried from the room. At the same time there came a swish and a loud clunk from the pneumatic tube dispenser. A cannister had fallen into the bucket.

Nana retrieved it and opened it excitedly. Out slid four certificates, which she handed to each of the children. They looked quite official, written in elegant calligraphy.

Congratulations on your election to the Frequent-Flier Club. After careful consideration, you have been awarded the level of Bronze. With this membership, you are granted unlimited access to the alleviators as well as special invitations to members-only events.

And it was signed in an almost illegible scrawl, Archibald C. Weber.

"Was *he* watching us, too?" Xavier asked.

"Yes, indeed," Gertrude said. "After all, the test was his idea."

"Oh! I almost forgot!" Xanthe pulled out the bag of hore-hound drops, given to her by Gertrude II, and handed them to Gertrude. "They're a gift, from your other self," Xanthe said.

Gertrude frowned and opened the bag. She removed one of the drops, sniffed it, then tentatively put it in her mouth. As she sucked on it a change came over her face, and for a single moment in time Gertrude and Gertrude II looked exactly the same. "It's a little sweeter, with a hint of mandarin orange," Gertrude said. "Very strange, very strange indeed..." She closed the bag with a little smile. "Thank you, Xanthe. I shall cherish these as long as they last. Which may not be too long. They are quite good." Gertrude drifted ahead, lost in her own thoughts.

As they walked through the lobby Xanthe caught up with Agatha and tugged on her sleeve. "Aunt Agatha? You know there was a point when Xavier and I were separated. He was at the Owatannauk in the alternate universe, and I was still in Alexandria. But I could hear him. It was like he could read my mind from way far away. Is that what you do?"

"Sort of," Agatha said. "It comes from knowing somebody so well that they're like a part of you. You can feel what they're feeling, hear what they're thinking, see what they're seeing, as though you were one and the same. It only happens to people who are already sensitive to each other; using the alleviators only intensifies it."

"I used to feel that Xave and I were one and the same. I hated it. I felt like I didn't have any room to breathe, or anything that was just mine."

"Well, empathy can have its drawbacks, there's no doubt about that. But it also brings great joy, and the satisfaction of knowing someone completely, and also being understood so well. Feel sorry for the people who can't, or won't, share themselves. They are the loneliest and poorest of souls."

Xanthe saw the truth of this. If having people care about you and know you inside and out was a kind of currency, then she was rich beyond measure. She broke into a sprint and caught up with the others. Xavier was telling Rowan and Nina about all the changes he had seen in the alternate universe. Xanthe had a lot to share as well. It would take both of them to explain the history of Agatha II and Gertrude II. She wasn't sure if she would tell them about how mean-spirited and unpleasant the alternate version of herself was. They already knew about her untimely death; that was bad enough. But this other thing, this rotten, self-centered personality, was a fate she felt she had only narrowly escaped.

If she had been a little meaner to Xavier, things would be different. If she had been kinder, things would also be different. People are just a collection of their experiences, what they say and do, every thoughtless oversight, every careless comment, every generous gesture, every smile, every tear—it all makes a difference. She knew this because when Gertrude had knelt to talk with them she caught a glimpse of something she had never noticed before. On the nape of Gertrude's neck, where her spinal column met her shoulder blades, was a dark H. It was a foreboding symbol seared into her very skin, avoided in an alternate universe, but a permanent mark in this one. It had faded only slightly in five hundred years, but it was part of her, as much as her eyes or voice.

Xanthe wondered if they would live up to Gertrude's

expectations. She wasn't exactly sure what they were getting into; it seemed an awesome responsibility. Still, her whole body tingled, anticipating all the wonders of the past that lay in their future.

She felt exhilarated. She reached over and smacked Xavier in the back of his bald head and raced off. He shouted and took chase, and it was like they were six years old again, screeching, howling, and laughing.

Rowan and Nina ran after them, down the steps of the Owatannauk, along the driveway, and out into the morning mist, free under the big, pale, pink-and-yellow sky.

Agatha called after them, asking if they wanted to ride in the truck. But they laughed and kept running. They would run until they reached the village, and then the ocean, where they would sink their feet in the rocky sand and feel the pinch of the brisk, salty ocean breeze as they watched the rising sun. They could breathe deep the possibilities that lay ahead. Nothing could contain them. They wanted space, and it was theirs.

A HISTORICAL NOTE TO THE READER

HOUR OF THE COBRA IS THE SECOND BOOK IN the Golden Hour series. Like the first, it is a work of fiction. Much of the book takes place in ancient Alexandria, and though I made every attempt to be historically, culturally, and geographically accurate, I did find it necessary to depart from the truth at times in order to tell the story.

First, the characters. I tried to convey the personalities of the historical characters as accurately as I could; however any time they interact with the children, you may assume that those conversations did not really take place. Cleopatra's precarious life as a child, her relationships with her siblings and her father, her ascension to the throne, and her political difficulties with Ptolemy XIII and his Regency Council are all true. I turned Ptolemy XIII, Cleopatra's brother, and Photinus, the leader of the Council, into the villains of this story. Both were certainly Cleopatra's enemies, but perhaps not as openly antagonistic as I have portrayed them.

Cleopatra's relationship with Julius Caesar is quite true; they had one of the most famous love affairs in history. Cleopatra really did sneak back into Alexandria, after having been banished by her brother, and roll out of a rug to surprise and entice Caesar. (Sometimes truth is stranger than fiction!)

My description of Octavian, the future Augustus Caesar, as a sickly teen is accurate. It is interesting that a man who eventually became one of the greatest leaders in world history was so frail as a teenager. Octavian, however, did not accompany Caesar to Alexandria in October of 48 B.C. And he was never kidnapped or held hostage in the Great Pyramid of Giza.

I also tinkered with the timing of certain events to better suit the story. When Cleopatra's sister Tryphaena disappeared and Berenice took power over Egypt, several months passed before Berenice announced her intentions to marry Archilaus instead of her brother. Also, when Caesar first arrived in Alexandria and was presented with the head of Pompey, several days passed before he met Cleopatra; they did not meet that night.

I had a lot of fun researching the pyramids. Thieves breaking in and stealing treasures was a great problem in ancient Egypt, and so Egyptian builders became expert at designing passageways that could be plugged with granite blocks, creating secret hidden rooms and decoy chambers. This explains the complicated interior of the Great Pyramid of Khufu.

During Cleopatra's time, however, there was no access to the various chambers; the path that led from the descending passage to the Great Gallery was plugged by a granite block. In fact, the only chamber that was even known at the time was the lower chamber. It was not until A.D. 820, when Arab Caliph Abdullah Al Manum decided to break into the Great Pyramid and search for Khufu's treasure, that the full interior of the structure became known to anyone other than the architects. Unable to find the reputed secret hinged door to the entrance, Abdullah Al Manum had his workmen dig into the side of the pyramid, and eventually they found the descending passageway. They burrowed around the granite block and discovered the two other chambers (they incorrectly dubbed the middle chamber the "Queen's Chamber," though it is unlikely that a queen was entombed there), and they also finally found the hinged door! The tomb had already been plundered and emptied of its riches, but the Caliph did not leave emptyhanded. His men stripped the pyramid of its fine white limestone casing and used it for buildings in Cairo.

In 1638, mathematician John Greaves discovered the narrow shaft that connected the Grand Gallery with the descending passageway (in my story it's the rabbit hole that the children use to escape the snakes). Both ends were tightly sealed, and a large amount of debris was at the bottom. It has been suggested that this shaft was the route the tomb robbers took to infiltrate the pyramid; however, the opening is so small it is unlikely they would've been able to remove much of the massive treasure. What happened to the treasure, how the robbers got in and out, as well as the location of Khufu's mummy remain mysteries to this day.

For the purposes of my story, I decided to have all the passageways in the Great Pyramid unblocked, though this was not the case in 48 B.C.

ACKNOWLEDGMENTS

Part of the fun of writing historical fiction is the research. I spend at least half a year researching the history, locales, and personalities which appear in each Golden Hour book. This may include travel, consulting a broad range of books, interviewing experts, and even surfing the Internet. It's a bit like a treasure hunt; I never know what gems I may unearth! The challenge comes in weaving the research into the story and choosing which facts to include and which to discard. For every true anecdote or detail contained in these pages, there were at least ten I discovered in my research that didn't make the cut.

Writing about ancient Alexandria posed its own peculiar challenge, for most of the area I wrote about is now under the sea or buried beneath the modern city that stands there today. Most of my research was through secondary sources. I relied most heavily on *A Travel Guide to Ancient Alexandria*, by Don Nardo; *Cleopatra: The Life and Death of a Pharoah*, by Edith Flamarion; and *Alexandria: Jewel of Egypt*, by Jean Yves Empereur, which gave me a solid base on which I could build my story. *Cleopatra's Palace: In Search of a Legend*, by Laura Foreman, documents the 1998 deep-sea expedition led by Franck Goddio, which explored the East Harbor of Alexandria and unearthed magnificent artifacts from Cleopatra's royal palace, which was lost after being submerged by tidal waves and earthquakes in A.D. 335.

I also consulted ancient literary sources for eyewitness accounts of ancient Alexandria. Strabo (64 B.C. — A.D. 23), a Greek historian, geographer, and philosopher, described Alexandria and the Great Pyramid of Khufu in detail in his *Geographia*. Plutarch (A.D. 45 — 125), a Greek biographer, wrote *Life of Caesar and Life of Antony*, which were written within a century of the deaths of those two men. Though somewhat biased against Cleopatra, the biographies provide a fascinating account of the relationships between the queen and these two Roman men.

I used several online sources for information on recent discoveries about Egypt and Cleopatra. The only buildings mentioned in *The Hour of the Cobra* that are still standing are the Sphinx and the Great Pyramid of Khufu. Unfortunately, I was unable to visit this pyramid, but thanks to a Web site sponsored by Nova, I was able to virtually walk through Khufu's tomb, seeing each of the chambers and passageways that I described in the book! In 1997, less than ten years before the publication of this book, the ancient Necropolis of Alexandria was found during the construction of a bridge. Articles in *Al-*

Ahram Weekly online gave me a very good idea of the layout and interior of this site. There are hundreds of Internet sites about Alexandria, Cleopatra, Julius Caesar, and the pyramids—some more reliable than others. One site that I found to be trustworthy is sponsored by Dr. Zahi Hawass, who is (at publication) the undersecretary of the state for the Giza Monuments. Dr. Hawass's articles provide an in-depth understanding of the history and culture of the region.

Finally, I would not have been able to write this book without the continuing support and encouragement of friends and family. Most worthy of mention is my best friend and husband, Patric Verrone. He is always there to remove distractions (my wonderfully active children), so that I can meet deadlines, and have the peace and space I need to create. Thanks, Pat!

ABOUT THE AUTHOR

Maiya Williams was born in Corvallis, Oregon, and grew up in New Haven, Connecticut, and Berkeley, California. She attended Harvard University, where she was an editor and vice president of the *Harvard Lampoon*. She is currently a writer and producer of television shows, and lives with her husband, three children, a Labrador retriever, a Schnorkie, two guinea pigs, two mice, and a variety of fish in Pacific Palisades, California. This is a sequel to her award-winning novel *The Golden Hour*, which *The New York Times* called "a trip well worth the time."

The text of this book is set in Kaatskill, designed in 1929 by Frederic W. Goudy. It was made specifically for use in an edition of *Rip Van Winkle* for the Limited Editions Club. The type has an added interest in the fact that it was designed, cut, and set in the immediate vicinity of Washington Irving's story—in the foothills of Rip's own Kaatskill mountains, at Marlborough-on-the-Hudson. Display and chapter titles are set in Dalliance Roman, designed in 2000 by Frank Heine for Emigre. The inspiration for Dalliance Script comes from early nineteenth-century hand-lettering specimens.

Enjoy this sneak peek at

THE HOUR OF THE OUTLAW

the sequel to *The Golden Hour*
and *The Hour of the Cobra*

XAVIER WOULD HAVE THOUGHT THAT BY NOW HE'D BE USED TO the faded carpeting and peeling wallpaper, the thick layer of dust on the furniture and the stale air, but in truth it still raised the hairs on the back of his neck. Even though it wasn't technically haunted—the phantoms that appeared when the hotel transformed at the golden and silver hours were not exactly dead people—it was still creepy.

"Where do you guys want to start?" Nina said, brushing a cobweb from her face. "The dining room is interesting . . ."

"Oh, let's go up the staircase!" Xanthe pleaded. "I've wanted to go up there since the first time I came to this place!"

"I bet these will come in handy," Xavier said, waving a large ring of keys he'd found behind the front desk. The sound of the jangling keys excited the group, so up they went. At the top of the stairs they found a long hallway lined with doors, each with a brass number on it. Crystal sconces, opaque with dust, lined the wall, along with paintings from different eras, some of them modern. A Ruisdael seascape hung next to a Georgia O'Keeffe desert flower. A da Vinci sketch of an angel hung next to a Cézanne still life. Xavier's eyes were drawn to a stained glass window at the end of the hallway depicting

Saint Francis of Assisi, his eyes closed and his arms crossed. A dove sat in each hand. Animals lay sleeping at his feet: lion, lamb, dog, bear, rabbit, peacock.

"I guess these are the hotel rooms," Rowan said.

"Not this one," Xavier said, unlocking the door to room number one with the master key. He was surprised to find a staircase that led up to a landing, then turned to the left and disappeared behind a wall. "Come on!"

He bounded up the stairs. The others followed. At the first landing he made the turn and saw that the staircase continued upward and turned again. He scrambled up the second staircase, made the turn, then stopped. Xanthe crashed into him, followed by Rowan and Nina.

"Xave, what's the problem?" Xanthe snipped.

"The staircase ends. It just goes right up to the ceiling." He ran his hands along the walls and ceiling, searching for a trap door. "There's nothing here. Go back down."

Back in the hallway, Xanthe examined the door to room number one carefully. "It's got to be another one of Archibald Weber's puzzles. That guy spent way too much time trying to confuse people."

The door to room number two opened up to a brick wall. The door to room number three revealed another slightly smaller door of dark, burnished wood. When Nina unlocked this one, it revealed a light wood door, intricately carved with images of Hindu gods. Behind this door was a metal screen door, then a door with beveled glass, a sliding door, an upside-down door, a miniature barn door, a swinging door, a submarine hatch, and finally a painting of a door, which of course would not open.

"That was a big waste of time," Nina sighed as they made their way back to the hallway.

"There have to be bedrooms somewhere," Xanthe said. "Let's keep going."

Rowan opened the next door. The brass number four had loosened over the years so that it hung at an angle. Behind this door stretched a narrow hallway, wide enough for only one person to pass through at a time. They walked tentatively through the passageway, which twisted this way and that, leading them to yet another door. When they opened this door they found themselves back in the hallway, coming out door number six.

"This is ridiculous," Rowan said. "We're not getting anywhere. Let's just go back downstairs."

They started down the hallway, but stopped. The staircase had disappeared. In its place was a wall decorated with a mural painting of the staircase. It was a very good painting, a little faded by time, but nevertheless not the real thing.

Xavier whistled, impressed. "Wow. This is a good one."

"A good what?" Nina asked.

"It's called a trompe l'oeil. That's French for 'trick the eye.' A painting that creates the optical illusion of three-dimensional space," Xavier said, recalling trivia he'd picked up from an art history book.

"Thanks, Professor," Xanthe said wryly. "But that still doesn't answer the question of what happened to the staircase."

"Xave, you were last in line, right?" asked Rowan suddenly. "Did you close the door to room four behind you when we went down the passageway?"

"No . . ."

"Well, it's closed now."

They all looked at the closed door. A smile broke out on Xavier's face.

"Brilliant! He's brilliant!"

"Who's brilliant?" Xanthe said.

"Archibald Weber is brilliant," Xavier answered smugly. "This is not the same hallway where we started."

"Except for the staircase it looks the same," Rowan said, scratching his head.

"Actually, it doesn't," Xavier retorted. "First of all, as you rightly pointed out, the door was shut, and I definitely left it open."

"Maybe somebody else shut it," Xanthe said. "We might not be the only people here."

"Maybe," Xavier said, "but take a look at the number on the door. The four is straight. The other one was crooked. I know you're not going to say that somebody fixed the number . . ."

"Hey! Look at the window!" Nina cried, pointing down the hall. "They're awake!"

It was true. St. Francis of Assisi's eyes were open and the animals were standing. Moreover, the saint's arms were outstretched and the two doves had taken flight.

"We are in a different hallway!" Nina laughed, clapping her hands. "This is awesome!"

"And guess what?" Xanthe said. "I think we found the bedrooms." She had taken the keys and unlocked the door to room number one. This time, instead of a staircase to the ceiling, they found a four-poster bed with a thick, purple coverlet. There was also a small desk, a sofa with a coffee table, and velvet curtains tied back with a blue and gold cord.

They explored the room, opening drawers and examining the decor. Nina discovered a closet, and Xavier found the bathroom, fitted with a claw-foot bathtub and an old-fashioned toilet, the kind with the box perched on a long pipe with a pull chain to flush, much like the one in Aunt Agatha and Aunt Gertrude's house. A third door had a brass lowercase letter b on it, and when opened, led to another bedroom, which was a mirror image of the first. When they went back out to the hallway from this room, Xavier noticed that the brass number on front of the door was also marked "1-b."

"I wonder why this is labeled 'one-b' instead of 'two,'?" he mused aloud, but Xanthe, Rowan, and Nina had already moved on to the rooms across the hall.

The room behind the door marked with a zero was actually a janitor's closet, containing a large industrial sink, brushes, mops, brooms, and old bottles of cleaning fluid. Room number two, however, was a bedroom very much like room number one and one-b, except the coverlet and curtains were a rich, forest green.

Room number three was like the first two, but when Rowan opened the door to room number four, he found another trompe l'oeil painting, a vista of the Swiss Alps.

"Looks like they're not all rooms," Xanthe mused. "We're back to the optical illusions."

Room number five turned out to be a suite with two separate bedrooms connected by a sitting room. The door to room number six was the passageway that they had come through from the other hallway. Room number seven was another trompe l'oeil, but of a charming English country garden. Room number eight was another suite, bigger than five, with three bedrooms instead of two. Doors to rooms nine, ten, eleven, and twelve opened up to paintings of a rain forest, a Japanese tea garden, a charging African rhino, and a Mayan pyramid. Room thirteen was another huge suite, this one with five attached bedrooms and two bathrooms. The ratio of real rooms to fake rooms was getting smaller, and when Xavier quickly opened the remaining doors in the hallway, he found they were all trompe l'oeils.

"For a hotel, they don't have very many real rooms," Rowan commented after Xavier opened that last door in the hallway, door number twenty-four, revealing a trompe l'oeil of the Parthenon in Greece.

"Well, if you think about it, the suites have several bedrooms within them," Xanthe pointed out, "so the total number of usable rooms is probably the same as if each hallway door led to a real room. Right, Xave? Xave?"

Xavier was lost in The Zone. He stared at the doors. There was a pattern here, he just knew it. Out of the corner of his eye he saw that Nina was standing quietly next to him, concentrating on the doors as well.

"It's so weird . . ." she murmured, twisting a strand of hair in her fingers. "One and one-b. And there's a door with a zero on it . . . I've never seen that before. This is definitely a puzzle . . . a number pattern . . ."

"You noticed it, too?" Xavier said, somewhat surprised.

"Studying music gives you a head for numbers and patterns," Nina said matter-of-factly. "Does anybody have a pen?"

Xanthe whipped a ballpoint pen from her pocket and handed it to Nina, who started scribbling something on the palm of her hand.

"These are the numbers on the rooms that are actually rooms," Nina said as she wrote. Xavier leaned over her shoulder and saw she was writing a number series: 0, 1, 1-b, 2, 3, 5, 8, 13. With the numbers written out it was as plain as day; he was surprised he hadn't seen it sooner.

"The Fibonacci sequence," he announced.

"Oh yeah! You're right!" Xanthe squealed.

"It has a name?" Nina said.

"You add the last number to the number that came before it to get the next number in the sequence," Xavier explained. "It's really cool, because it mathematically describes a spiral pattern that you find in nature: in flower petals, the shape of shells, animal breeding . . ."

"Archibald Weber loves spirals," Xanthe added gleefully. "They're built right into the architecture of the hotel . . . like that spiral staircase to the ceiling!"

"Yeah, except it doesn't work," Rowan said. They all turned to him. "I mean, the pattern breaks down after door thirteen. If you're right, the next door that should have a real room or a suite behind it should be door twenty-one. But it doesn't. It's one of those trompe l'oeils."

Rowan opened door twenty-one, revealing a painting of prison bars. They all fell silent, wondering what it could mean. Xanthe drummed her fingers on the sill below the stained glass window. Suddenly she gasped.

"You figured it out?" Nina said.

"No, we're in trouble!" Xanthe cried. "Aunt Gertrude's here! Her truck's parked outside!"

"Look at the sun!" Rowan added. "It's almost the golden hour! C'mon, we gotta get back through the passageway!"

They dashed through door number six, raced through the twisted hallway, scrambled into the first hallway, then flew down the flight of stairs. As Xavier bounded down, taking three or four stairs at a time, he felt the familiar tingle of the onset of the golden hour. Every molecule in his body seemed to vibrate with increasing intensity until he was entirely numb. Then an explosion of color rushed upon them like a tidal wave.

The next thing he knew he was sprawled at the bottom of the staircase, his face in the thick, maroon carpeting. As the high-buttoned boots and wide crinoline skirts of the hotel phantoms brushed by, he noticed a pair of black penny loafers slowly approaching and then stopping right in front of his face. They were huge, like two leather canoes, size twelves at least. Xavier's eyes scanned up the tall, dark-trousered legs to the wool poncho, finally lighting on the stern glare of Gertrude Pembroke.

"It's time for dinner," she said.

Keep reading! If you liked this book, check out these other titles.

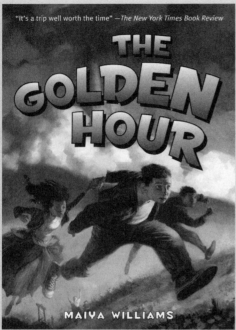

"It's a trip well worth the time" —*The New York Times Book Review*

The Golden Hour
By Maiya Williams
978-0-8109-9216-0 $5.95 paperback

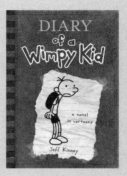

Diary of a Wimpy Kid
By Jeff Kinney
978-0-8109-9313-6 $12.95 hardcover

**Manga Shakespeare:
Romeo and Juliet**
By William Shakespeare
Adapted by Richard Appignanesi
Illustrated by Sonia Leong
978-0-8109-9325-9 $9.95 paperback

**Look for *The Hour of the Outlaw*,
the sequel to *The Hour of the Cobra*!**